Tea & Irish

TEA & IRISH

A thriller by
Geg

GSP

Tea & Irish
Geg

Published by Greyhound Self-Publishing, 2019

Printed and bound by Aspect Design
89 Newtown Road, Malvern, Worcs. WR14 1PD
United Kingdom
Tel: 01684 561567
E-mail: allan@aspect-design.net
Website: www.aspect-design.net

ISBN 978-1-909219-62-5

This offering is dedicated to 'G',
for she helped push back the darkness.
But then, sadly, with all of her secrets and things, vanished.

Contents

CHAPTER ONE
Holiday

The breezy uphill lane narrowed, but with high hedges it shielded them from the wind and rain, to a small degree at least. They didn't seem to care.

Their second day of holiday in Cornwall looked likely to be washed out, but they were in no humour to allow their spirits, high as they were, to be dampened.

A noise from up ahead and they huddled together, pushing into the hedge as a small red van came around the corner and now slowed as it passed them, going on down the narrow lane. They set off again.

"I didn't say that," she semi-gurgled as he poked her in the side and she laughed out loud.

"I beg to differ! You told them all that I was like Father Christmas . . ." He didn't finish, a tractor coming round the bend at speed.

She was in the middle of the road and turned. With only seconds to react she ran downhill, away from the approaching danger.

He was thrown back into the hedge, the huge rear wheel brushing past him as he saw the tractor bear down on his wife.

She turned back in that instant and fell out of his sight, under the huge machine.

The wheel passed him by but the trailer kept him tight into the hedge until it too passed, and now he ran after it, the machine slowing as the driver braked hard.

It came to a stop and Aaron caught up but couldn't get by. He heard shouting ahead yet couldn't make it out. He yelled at the top of his voice as he scrambled to either side of the trailer, again trying to get through. There was no way past! More yelling and he thought it was the driver.

"Ho!" He bellowed. "Is my wife alright?" He waited and then heard someone curse. A male voice.

"Get through the hedge and come down the field!"

"What?" he shouted. "What!" He asked again, with increasing volume.

"Come through the hedge, to your right!" The voice now yelled back. "Get through the hedge and come down the field!"

Aaron was distraught but his mind, slowly, now began to function. He looked to either side and then launched himself at the hedge to his right, pulling it apart, ripping away branches and thistles to create a small hole. It took him a little time and his hands were bloody; he was becoming breathless but managed to force his way through into a huge field that swept away as far as eye could see. He scrambled free of the thorns and fell. Getting up he ran downhill past the tractor. He could now see the shape of a man bending down at the front and, as he came level with him, began tearing at the hedge again, urgently trying to make a hole. The man saw him and he also ripped at the bramble, forcing a way for the frantic man to get through.

Aaron fell onto the road, quickly standing to look into the eyes of this man. He saw fear and doubt on his relatively young face, his head shaking as he spoke words that Aaron couldn't make out.

He stepped to the side but the man blocked his way, hands raised as he spoke urgently again, looking into Aaron's face, his mouth working slowly, seemingly trying to reason. Aaron couldn't understand and so stepped to the side but the man would not allow him past. He tried again but his path was, once again, blocked. With both hands he threw the man aside, stepping in towards the tractor, engine still trembling at tick over as he dropped to the floor.

He could see, at the back of the machine, under the massive tyre that was at least his own height, a coat. It was the same coloured coat Rose had worn.

He now saw the crushed body, head still under the huge rear

wheel, arms lying to the side. He saw his wife, his love, beneath the machine. He snatched a breath and then looked again, eyes adjusting to the lack of light. The shudder of the tractor was constant and he blinked. He shook his head and looked again. There was the coat, the familiar red coat, its lower edges seemingly darker somehow. A pool, crimson in colour, was creeping downhill, towards him as he now reached out to her, but he was held. He stretched forward again but still was held, and now he fell backwards, losing balance. He blinked once more as he sat on the road but could not move his eyes from the still image before him. He shook his head again and again, tears forming as he tried to break free from this spellbinding sight. He shuddered as his body went limp, eyes beginning to dilate.

The last thing he remembered was a hand on his arm, pulling him up and away.

CHAPTER TWO
Crown Court

"The accused awoke in the bar of the Lavender Screw My Lord."

"Lavender Screw?"

"Yes My Lord, a public house in the village of Oaksey, just over two miles from Latterminster where the Brindleys were staying, and less than half a mile from the location of the accident."

"Objection My Lord. It has not been ascertained that it was an accident at this time!"

"Sustained. Incident, I think, is more fitting Mr. Musgrave. Carry on."

"Thank you My Lord. Mr. Brindley was completely unaware of anything concerning the, er, incident, which took place at around twelve noon, until he awoke almost four hours later in the Lavender Screw."

"Very well." The judge scribbled a note. "You may continue Mr. Musgrave."

"Thank you My Lord."

The barristers acknowledged each other, returned to their desks and sat, the prosecuting lawyer cursorily glancing across the gallery.

The Crown Court was filled to bursting point. There were still queues around the block, all clamouring to get the best seat, any seat, both public and media alike, all of them anxiously waiting for the outcome of this case which had taken the country by storm.

The incident had initially been reported locally and considered to be, merely, a freak accident, until the tabloids had got hold of it, when it had been suggested it could have been more than an 'accident'. Questions were then asked and, seemingly, not answered substantially well enough for some journalists and so, with all the hype the papers had by this time created, the authorities were forced to open a police enquiry.

This had then created a nationwide sensation and, in turn, raised serious questions as to the reason one half of this couple had survived, and the other had not. The husband had then been arrested and questioned over several days and, with the frenzy that had been mounting, the authorities felt they had no other re-course but to prosecute, the magistrates court almost immediately deciding that the case was now too big for them to handle.

In Crown Court, the frenzy was peaking as the case approached its end.

Mr. Musgrave rose to his feet, papers in hand.

CHAPTER THREE
Witness

"Your name is?"

"Luke Anthony Wright."

"And you were the driver of the tractor at the time Mrs. Brindley was killed?"

"Yes I was."

"Can you tell us what happened that day?"

"Yeah. I'd picked up the trailer as normal and was on the way down the station and as I turned the corner there they was. I braked but it was too late as I'd already 'it 'er 'cos she was standin' in the middle of the road."

"Was that a regular trip, down to the station?"

"Couple of times a day, in the season."

"Quite. You said you braked?"

He nodded.

"You have to answer Mr. Wright."

"Oh, yeah."

"Why, in your opinion, was it too late, for the braking element of your story?"

"I'd 'it 'er!"

"Yes, but how did you hit her if indeed you had braked?"

He looked non-plussed and shook his head. The barrister continued.

"If you braked when you saw her then why didn't you stop instead of ploughing into her?"

"Cos it was quick! I only just rounded the bend and there they was. Oh, I braked alright but it was too late."

The barrister looked at him and was about to speak as he went on.

"The weight just pushed me on. You can't stop these things on a sixpence you know."

"Very well. Did you see her make any attempt to avoid the tractor?"

"Yeah. Well, she ran, for a second or so but then turned, and that was when she got 'it."

"Did Mr. Brindley attempt to aid her in any way?"

"'E was pushed back into the 'edge."

"How did he get pushed back into the hedge?"

"Well, 'e reached across at 'er and, it seemed to me anyways, lost 'is balance or pushed 'er, and that seemed to sort of push 'im into the 'edge."

Aaron stood.

"That is not true. I did not push Rose. If anything I would have tried to help her. I loved her for God's sake."

The judge intervened and motioned for him to sit. He did so and the gallery eventually quieted. After a short while the barrister went on.

"Why do you say he pushed her?"

"It's what I saw; 'is arms reachin' out as she was pushed and 'im fallin' back."

Aaron looked at him, eyes wide and head shaking.

"You saw no attempt by Mr. Brindley to aid Mrs. Brindley? Grab her or try to pull her to safety?"

"'E reached out for 'er but it seemed 'e pushed 'er, none o' that other stuff."

Aaron dropped his head, murmuring something which could not be heard.

"And after the incident, when you managed to bring the machine to a stop, what happened next?"

"I jumped down by the front and got down on my belly. I was goin' to scramble beneath and pull 'er out, or try and 'elp 'er get free if she'd been caught but there was nothin' to do."

"Nothing to do? Would you explain just what that means Mr. Wright?"

"Well, it was too late. The lady had fallen in front of the rear wheel of the tractor and was underneath it as I looked."

"Was she still breathing?"

"What?"

"Was she still breathing Mr. Wright?"

"'Ow the 'ell could she be breathin', 'er 'ead were crushed, the 'ole body were crushed!"

It took several minutes before the noise from the gallery subsided.

"Mr. Xantilesny, you became acquainted with Mr. Brindley in the bar at the Wyndsor Arms in Latterminster, is that correct?"

"Yes sir, 'im and his lady wife, about a month ago now."

"Thank you. And this was the Monday night, being the fourteenth day of September?"

"It was sir."

"Would you tell the court exactly how you came to know the accused and his late wife?"

"Oh, well. They come in, see. 'E was laughin' a lot and she were too, but a bit muted like, as if they'd 'ad an argument."

"We had not had an argument!" Aaron was on his feet, annoyed.

"Thank you Mr. Brindley. We all have our opinions and so Mr. Xantilesny has the right to voice his, now please sit down."

"That's not an opinion, it's a lie!"

The judge once more intervened and Aaron slowly sat down, but it was obvious he was displeased.

"Now Mr. Xantilesny, you were saying that it seemed Mr. and Mrs. Brindley had been arguing?" The man nodded and looked a little nervously across at Aaron who stared at the ground.

"Voice your answer if you please Mr. Xantilesny."

"Oh, sorry. Er, yes sir."

"In your opinion, why would you say Mr. and Mrs. Brindley had had an argument?"

"Well, it weren't no lie but I suppose I could've been mistook."

"Please Mr. Xantilesny, give us your opinion on this; we would love to hear the reason you considered that this couple, whom you had never seen before this particular day, had been arguing."

"It were only that after about a minute I leaned across and said a funny to 'er, while 'er 'usband were at the bar orderin', and she laughs out loud, spontaneous like."

"And why did this lead to your thoughts concerning a prior argument?"

"She laughed with gusto a bit too quick, and a bit too loud. It weren't that good a funny and she seemed to want to laugh, as if it would blow away any . . . well . . ."

"Any?"

The court fell silent as the barrister eyed the man.

"Well, any unpleasantness what had happened before they come in the pub, it seemed to me anyways."

"Unpleasantness."

"Well, that's what I thought."

"Very well. Now, as to the rest of the evening, could you give us a brief summary?"

"Oh yes. They was chatty, first off between themselves and there was lots of laughin' and such. Rose was . . . Oh, sorry I didn't mean to say 'er name. I am sorry . . ."

"It's quite alright Mr. Xantilesny, I think we all understand. Your sensitivity is appreciated."

He looked across at Aaron. After a slow moment he nodded his agreement and, once again, bowed his head.

"Please carry on."

"They was in each other's face a lot in the firsts but later, and after a few sherbets, we starts to get to know 'em."

"Mr. Xantilesny, whilst we all applaud your colourful use of language it would be appreciated if you could explain. Firsts?"

"Firsts, yeah. Well, in the beginnin', at the start."

"Very good. Sherbets?"

"Bevvies. You know, a couple of beers that loosens 'em up."

"Thank you. Please continue."

"Well, the lady was a fun un, and she keeps makin' jibes at 'im, loud enough for us all to 'ear mind, and 'e makes out 'e's upset which 'e's not cos 'e eventually just laughs which makes 'er do it all the more and in no time we was all joinin' in, you know? We was makin' tales up about our wives like what she was makin' about 'im and it made a right good night 'cos it didn't stop, not until they'd 'ad enough and went on back to their place. Best night in a good while, I'll say."

"So they seemed to be getting on; at least by the time they left the pub that is?"

"Oh yes. They was laughin' a lot throughout their time at The Wyndsor. We 'elped 'em pick their sightseein' trips an' all. They was appreciative o' that."

"Quite. Was there anything else in their demeanour, the way they were with each other that stood out to you?"

"They was proper in love, that was clear; well, 'e was anyways."

"He was? Surely you mean both, that both of them were in love?"

"It was clear 'e loved 'er, but she weren't quite as enamoured."

"Michal?" Aaron now looked up. "Why do you say such a thing?"

"She didn't look at you the way you looked at 'er my friend, she did not."

"Was there an antipathy between them?"

He just looked at him blankly.

"Forgive me. I'm asking if there was an air of disagreement; a feeling that the love shared was, possibly, not quite even?"

"'E loved 'er, of that there is no doubt. She loved 'im you could see, but not nearly as much."

"This is rubbish!"

"Why did she give young Darren the eye then? Not just once neither?"

"Darren?"

"The barman, waiter an' all."

"Elucidate please Mr. Xantilesny."

He looked at the barrister and shook his head, frowning.

"You mentioned the barman, the waiter? Please tell us about him."

"Oh, yeah. Young lad, about twenty-five, just started, and she looked at 'im almost as much as she looked at Aaron."

The murmurs began afresh in the gallery.

CHAPTER FOUR
Wyndsor Arms

"And your name is?"

"Darren Standish."

"Occupation?"

"Barman and waiter at the Wyndsor Arms."

"And this is the Wyndsor Arms public house in Latterminster, is that correct?"

"Yeah. On the main drag."

"Quite. And how long have you been barman and waiter at the Wyndsor Arms Mr. Standish?"

"On and off for the last six months."

"We have been reliably informed that you were new to the post."

"Just started again, since I came back from Uni. Mitch always re-hires me when I get back."

"I see. Mitch?"

"Yeah. He's the landlord, my Dad's brother."

"Thank you. Now, on the night in question, the fourteenth of September this year, you were working in the Wyndsor Arms, is that correct?"

"Yes it is."

"And am I right in thinking that you served a couple from outside of the village, the gentleman of which is sitting over there?" He pointed to Aaron.

"I did."

"And how did you find them?"

"They were OK. They tipped well, I know that."

"But, apart from the tip, how were they with you?"

"They were alright. He came to the bar and I served him their drinks and he asked for a menu and I went to the table and took the order."

"What about Mrs. Brindley, how did you find her?"

"For god's sake! Can't you leave my wife alone?"

Aaron had tears in his eyes and it was obvious he was trying to stem a very deep emotion.

"I apologise Mr. Brindley for mention of your wife, and I feel sure this must be causing you some quite serious distress. I do not, however, apologise for the line of questioning as I feel sure it will shed further light on the case in question and so must proceed."

Aaron did not raise his head, but his body tremored a little in the silence of the court. The barrister looked to the Judge who motioned for him to continue.

"So, Mr. Standish, what can you tell us about Mrs. Brindley?"

"Er, well." He looked across at Aaron and made some sort of grimace.

"You are on oath Mr. Standish and, while you might feel uninclined to speak, speak you must, and with clarity or else what you obviously consider to be somewhat of an ordeal will have to be prolonged."

The young man nodded and took a breath.

"She was nice, laughing and joking with Michal, Mitch and a few of the regulars. I just said that her scarf was very Pre-Raphaelite and she came back with, 'Burne-Jones or Holman Hunt?' I replied, quick as a flash; 'I was thinking more like Millais' and she came back again and said, 'I think Dante Gabriel would argue with that'."

He now laughed out loud, seemingly pleased with what he'd said, but quickly suppressed it as he wiped the smile from his face and looked around the silent court.

"You were quite impressed she knew about the Pre-Raphaelite Brotherhood?"

"Well, yes. No-one around our place has a clue about art and so, when she went on about John Ruskin, Turner and the like I just felt I'd met some sort of soul-mate."

"Soul-mate?"

"Yeah. It's only at college I get to talk the Arts, not when I'm home."

"Did you like her Mr. Standish?"

"Everyone did."

"I think you know what I'm asking Mr. Standish. Did you *like* her?"

"Well, yeah." He shot a glance at Aaron whose head was still lowered. "She was a looker; who wouldn't have liked her."

Aaron looked up, to stare straight into the young man's eyes.

"Hell! If you have a good looking woman on your arm you're gonna get looked at, everyone knows that!"

"So, you liked her?"

"Okay, I liked her; so what?"

"Did you have any idea what age Mrs. Brindley was?"

"Hell, age doesn't matter, not these days. You seen Sandra Bullock?"

"She was more than twice your age Mr. Standish."

"If you have a certain look then you have it, that's all."

"So, she had a 'look' then."

"Yeah."

"And is that why you 'gave her the eye' then, is it?"

"I didn't give her the eye!"

"We have testimony to the contrary Mr. Standish."

"I didn't! She gave me the eye; I didn't do it back."

"So, she gave you the eye but you didn't reciprocate?"

"She was married; I don't do that stuff."

"Your name please."

"Mitchell Adams."

"Thank you Mr. Adams. What is your occupation?"

"Landlord of the Wyndsor Arms."

"And you employ Mr. Standish when he comes back from university, is that correct?"

"Yes, we always give him a job; good lad he is, Darren."

"On the night in question did you observe anything untoward, or out of the ordinary, concerning the couple, Mr. and Mrs. Brindley?"

"When I came down they were eating, but they seemed a fairly convivial sort. As the night drew on I could see that she was . . . her, Mrs. Er . . ."

"Brindley."

"Yes. Mrs. Brindley had taken a shine to young Daz; but they do, the women, though not quite the age . . ."

His voice trailed off.

"I am taking it that the term 'Daz' is the abbreviated version of Mr Standish's first name, Darren?"

"Sorry. Yes, Darren"

"It is more the younger element that take a 'shine' to Mr. Standish, Mr. Adams; is that what you were meaning to say?"

"Yes. The young girls mostly, but older women do too, sometimes."

"And how did that 'shine' manifest itself Mr. Adams?"

"They had a rapport those two. Whenever Darren took something over, food, drinks, sauces, whatever, there was some sort of badinage that resulted in the lady, and the gent at times, bursting into laughter, and young Darren as well. Eventually, because of the fun being generated, it overflowed and, shortly, the whole of the pub, locals and all, were joining in. A good night it was."

"And did Mr. Standish join in as well?"

"He was at the heart of it he was. He took over at the bar when he'd finished serving food which let me have a sit down, and there were quips from her and him flying thick and fast all evening."

"And did he give her the eye at all Mr. Adams?"

"I think it was more the other way if you ask me."

"So, it was Mrs Brindley that looked at the young man and not the other way round?"

"That's the way it seemed to me."

CHAPTER FIVE
The Lavender Screw

"So, you are the manager of the Lavender Screw Mr. Tyndale?"

"I am."

"And when did Mr. and Mrs. Brindley come into your establishment?"

"It was the fifteenth of September, the Tuesday night."

"Can you tell us what you remember of that evening?"

"Yes Sir. Well, it were a bit nippy and we had the fire on like normal this time of year, and these two, this couple . . ." he pointed to Aaron and seemed a little lost for words.

"Thank you Mr. Tyndale, we appreciate the sensitivity you are showing, and I am sure that Mr. Brindley does also."

Aaron's head, though still lowered, nodded slightly.

"Please continue Mr. Tyndale, in your own time."

He cleared his throat and began, then coughed again as he now turned to face the distraught husband.

"Sorry for your loss young man, truly sorry."

Aaron looked up and saw the tender look on his face as fresh tears arose.

"Thank you Mike," was all he said.

Mike nodded, cleared his throat once more and looked up at the barrister.

"They came in, like a breath of fresh air they were, all smiling and chatty and such. I asked if they was eating and she, er, Rose." He stopped and looked again at Aaron.

"It's really alright Mike," Aaron said, raising his head to smile a little at the uncertain publican.

"Alright," he smiled back. "I asked if they was eating and Rose said, 'Yes, we are, providing I can chuck a log or two on the fire'. I told her that, as it was wet out, she could chuck her husband on if she had a mind and she came back, quick as you like, 'No, it would go out because he's been wet for years!' She had the place in uproar in minutes."

"How did Mr. Brindley take the slur?"

"All in good part. In fact, he laughed louder than most, and it was like that all the night."

"Was there any altercation between the couple at all?"

"Not as I saw, and I was tending all night."

"Tending?"

"Tending bar."

"They drank quite a lot that night, isn't that right Mr. Tyndale?"

"By their standards I suppose, but not by most."

"How much did they drink, by your estimation Mr. Tyndale?"

"It was, let me see. A couple of pints, two glasses of Sauternes and a bottle of white with the meal and two, or was it four brandies after? Yes, four."

"Too much for either to drive it seems?"

"Yes. That was when he asked for a taxi and I called young Barry for them. He came and took them back home."

"My name is Barry and I drove the couple 'ome after they was drunk at The Lavender."

"Thank you Barry. So, you believe that Mr. and Mrs. Brindley were drunk do you?"

"Oh yeah."

"Why?"

"Well, they 'ad brandy as well as wine, they 'ad to be drunk."

"Did they do anything to indicate that they were drunk?"

"Oh, yeah. They giggled and laughed a lot, then argued and shouted."

"They argued?"

"They did. But then they shouted an' all."

"And just what did they argue and shout about?"

"Oh, the price of the meal; 'avin' to leave the car at The Lavender. And then 'e started shoutin' at 'er for losin' the keys to their place."

"It was a joke. We were joking about all that; we always did!"

"Thank you Mr. Brindley. You will get your chance to answer all accusations at a later date." The judge motioned for the barrister to continue.

"Did you hear anything else Barry?"

"Oh yeah. When we got 'em 'ome 'e was gettin' even more upset, so much so 'e got out the car and stormed off."

"And why was that?"

"'Is missus just laughed and said to take no notice. She paid me and then got out when 'e started at 'er again."

"Could you make out just what was being said?"

"It weren't bein' said, it were shouted!"

"What was shouted?"

"Swear words, and bitch. And then 'e chased 'er into the drive. I was goin' to jump out just to see that she was alright but she came back to the road, called and waved bye bye to me and so I thought they must be alright and so off I went, 'ome."

CHAPTER SIX
Sister

A young woman took to the witness stand and there was an audible gasp as she looked up.

"And so, you are?"

"I am Sonia Langford, sister of Rose Langford, the woman that bastard murdered!"

There was pandemonium in the gallery. The girl looked directly at Aaron and he held her gaze. There seemed to be little love lost. Noise abounded from the public area and accusations flew across the court as the judge struggled to be heard.

It took five minutes for the court to be cleared.

The woman was cautioned and informed that if she did not behave in a proper manner she risked being charged with contempt of court.

"And so, once again, your name please?"

There remained only a fragment of journalists and artists in the gallery, all of which scribbled furiously.

The young woman had not taken her eyes off Aaron, who had looked down ever since the court had been cleared.

"My name is Sonia Langford," she stated.

"And your association with the deceased?"

"Rose was my sister, my younger sister."

"Was not your relationship a little closer than merely that of sister?"

"We were close, very close before she married him."

Her eyes had never left Aaron. The court saw him shake his head a little.

"Yes, you were very close. Could you explain to the court how close?

To be exact, the biological relationship between yourself and your younger sister Rose?"

"Rose and I are identical twins," she said. "Sorry. We were identical twins, until she was murdered!"

"Miss Langford, kindly refrain from unfounded accusations at this time, if you please. This is your final warning."

The judge instructed that her comment be struck from the record.

"Can you tell us please, Miss Langford?" The barrister paused, looking at his notes.

"Ms."

"I beg your pardon?"

"My title is Ms., not Miss," she corrected him.

"Quite. My thanks. If you could, please Ms. Langford, tell us of your relationship with your twin sister Rose and Mr. Brindley from the time they were married?"

"It was quite good at the start. I was their only bridesmaid, Rose wanted that." She looked annoyed, but her eyes never left Aaron. "She was happy and so I went along at first, just pleased that she had found Mr. Right; well, thought she had. It didn't take long, it didn't last."

"And why do you say, 'it didn't last' Miss Langford? Sorry, Ms. Langford."

"Because he didn't treat her right."

"Could you give us some insight into the reasons you believed Mr. Brindley was treating your sister in a less than acceptable fashion?"

"He bullied her, wouldn't let her see her family when she wanted, kept her short of money, lied to her. How long have you got?"

Aaron kept his head lowered but the phrase, 'Oh God', was easily heard by all.

"You can play the grieving husband all you like; you won't get away with it."

"Ms. Langford! You really must not address the accused. Please direct all of your answers to me."

She glared at Aaron but then turned to the barrister.

"I am sorry," she said in soft voice. "I find it difficult to keep my emotions in check. It is too soon since . . ."

It was obvious she was close to tears.

The barrister acknowledged this. The judge indicated to the clerk of the court, then spoke.

"Do you need a moment," he asked.

She took the offered handkerchief and now dabbed her eyes, shaking her head.

"Thank you," she said. "I'm all right now."

"Ms. Langford," the Barrister addressed her in soft tones. "It is obvious that you had a strong relationship with your sister and, therefore, we appreciate all of your feelings and incredible strength in this." He paused awhile. "We do, however, need to creep closer towards the truths of this case and so need to ask certain things that would require your ability to detach yourself from the emotions which are rightfully yours. The question, therefore, is this. Do you feel that this is within your remit at this moment, or would you prefer to take a short break?"

"I can carry on Sir."

"Thank you Ms. Langford."

He asked her about the relationship between her sister and Aaron.

She was not backward in her response!

She explained that, in the beginning, everything seemed to be wonderful; that Rose was madly in love and that he, Aaron, was a good husband and they were both extremely happy. But then things began to change. She and Rose would talk on the phone at length and her sister would say things that made no sense at all, and which made Sonia uncomfortable.

"That was when I began to follow her."

"So, you followed her did you?" Sonia nodded. "Why?"

"She wasn't happy. There were things she was saying that made me realise there was more going on than she was actually saying."

"And you knew this because Rose told you?"

"No!" She seemed irate. "There were signs. She said things. I just knew. We were close."

"Yes Ms Langford, but we need to know what it was that you 'knew', and also how you knew!"

"I just knew, alright!"

"No, it is not 'alright'! He took a moment then pointed to the desk in front of him. "This coffee cup is almost empty. I do not ask you to believe that for I can prove it by holding it up for your inspection. I need you to hold up your 'coffee cup' for inspection so that I, we, can also believe; so that we can understand why you would say such a thing. Can you do that?"

She seemed a little put out.

There was a long moment and the barrister just stood there, arms folded. Eventually she spoke.

"I might not be able to bring to life feelings and thoughts my sister and I shared, or prove that we shared them, but that does not alter the fact that they existed. We loved each other, grew up together and knew each other very well. She knew, before I did, that my heart had a murmur. Mother was told but she would not believe, and it was just over a year later that the doctors discovered it. Because of my condition Rose always looked out for me. She kicked me once, in the presence of the other girls at school, one of which that hated me and had stated that she and her gang were going to beat me up. My friends couldn't believe Rose kicked me, but it was that presence of mind that saved me from a beating by that girl, because she now felt I had had my come-uppance from my own sister, and so she and her gang all left me alone. It was that sort of thing that set us apart from all others. We were close."

"Thank you for being so frank and informative. But if we could now come back to the question in hand, being your reasons for doubting Mr. Brindley's role in this very sad scenario?"

Sonia stood tall and faced the barrister as she wiped a remaining tear from her eye. She nodded.

He held her gaze for a moment then dropped his head, looking at notes.

"What can you tell us," he said, eyes still lowered, "about the man your sister married and, apparently, loved."

CHAPTER SEVEN
Accused

After the testimony of Rose's sister there had been a short break, after which the court had resumed and the public gallery opened once again.

Aaron Brindley had sat in the dock and listened while evidence had been given over the last week, but now stood forward to the witness stand.

The whole court sat silent, eyes fixed on the accused.

The prosecuting barrister stood.

"Mr. Brindley, would you kindly give us your account of events leading up to your wife's death."

The focus of the court was now on the man who stood, dishevelled and unkempt. He seemed not to notice them as he took a deep breath, his look one of despair and utter dejection. He took a moment, then spoke.

"We had a light breakfast and decided to walk the two or so miles to the place we had left the car the night before."

"You had left your car Mr. Brindley? Where?"

"We had eaten at the Lavender Screw and decided to leave our car there that night and get a taxi back to our holiday home."

"With a view to collecting your vehicle the following day?" He nodded. "You must answer Mr. Brindley."

"Yes, we went to collect the car."

"Please continue."

"We set off, still laughing."

"Laughing Mr. Brindley. What was so funny?"

"We were laughing about the antics at the pub the night before."

"Antics Mr. Brindley? Could you explain?"

"We had been chatting with staff, and people who were dining there. My wife likes to chat and she makes friends quite easily and so we were laughing about the things that had been said."

"Such as?"

"My wife likes to have fun and she says things that provoke a lot of fun, mostly about me and that might seem a little unkind on the surface but yet are merely jibes that sometimes lead to . . . which generally do lead to laughter, at my expense of course."

"Laughter at your expense?" Aaron nodded. "Did that anger you at all?"

"Oh no! Rose always said things that made me seem to look bad. It was her way and meant nothing at all, except that it made everyone laugh."

"Including you?"

"Especially me."

"I see. Carry on."

"We had wrapped up due to the wet weather and walked quite briskly into the village in order to keep warm and then turned left, uphill. We were still laughing and probably not taking enough notice of the dangers that such a narrow road presented for, when a van, a small red van came around the corner, we had been in the middle of the road and he had to slow down as we quickly stepped to the side and lent into the hedge to allow him past. He went on by and we stepped into the road once again, still laughing at something Rose had said the night before. It was then that the tractor appeared."

"How did you not hear the tractor before it appeared?"

"The van had a bad exhaust."

"The van had gone Mr. Brindley. Why did you not hear the tractor?"

"It had only just gone and the exhaust was loud. I think it was that noise, from the exhaust, which covered the noise from the engine of the tractor."

"Tractors are quite noisy machines Mr. Brindley. How is it you did not hear a noisy agricultural machine that was only a matter of yards away from you, maybe ten at the most?"

"We were laughing with one another and . . . The van had just gone past and its engine noise was still quite loud and so . . . I think all of that covered the noise of the tractor."

"So, you did not hear a six cylinder, six litres plus engined tractor, pulling a fully laden trailer as it turned the bend and bore down on you!" He waited awhile, looking at Aaron, waiting for a reaction. He did not get one and so continued. "What did you do Mr. Brindley, when you eventually realised that there was a massive vehicle rapidly approaching you and your wife?"

"It all happened so fast, I didn't have time to think."

"Quite." The Barrister took a moment to look Aaron in the eye. He didn't flinch. "A gut reaction then Mr. Brindley; what did your gut reaction inspire you to do?"

"I'm not sure. It was quick . . ."

"Did you just stand there?"

"I didn't stand . . . I . . ."

"Did you shout a warning Mr. Brindley?"

"I can't . . ." He shook his head. The barrister waited but nothing more seemed to be forthcoming.

"Did you shout a warning Mr. Brindley?" He asked again.

Aaron tried to speak but seemed unable.

"Did you shout any kind of warning Mr. Brindley? Did you attempt to bring your wife to the side with you? Did you grab her? Pull her maybe? Push her? Scream at her? Did you say a prayer Mr. Brindley? Maybe do a tap dance?"

"Objection!"

"I withdraw the last two suggestions My lord. But please answer the question Mr. Brindley. What, if anything, did you do in that instant?"

"I really don't know what I did, it all happened so fast."

"Did you only think of yourself and push back into the hedge to leave your wife to her fate?"

"No, I . . ."

"Did you shout a warning to her and then push yourself back into the hedge as the tractor rushed past?"

"I think I might . . ." He fell silent.

"Well, one thing we do know for certain is that you did throw yourself into the hedge, no matter what action you took prior to the machine hurtling past you and taking your wife with it!"

Aaron just looked at the barrister and shook his head, mouth working yet nothing emerging.

"I see Mr. Brindley. No answer, no explanation and no tears it would seem, concerning the fate of a person you claim to have loved and whom you did not try to help."

"I miss . . ."

"Did you push her Mr. Brindley?"

"What?"

"Well. As you did not shout a warning, pull her to you, do anything else that might have aided her in her darkest moment, did you push her?"

"Why would I do that?"

"Why indeed!"

He paused and waited. Aaron seemed lost.

"But did you Mr. Brindley?"

"No!"

"It has been suggested that you did!"

He did not answer, merely looking at the barrister with eyes wide and a barely discernible shake of the head.

"We have the sworn statement from the driver of the tractor that as he turned the bend he saw a couple in the road, the female being closer to the centre with the male next to the hedge and, as he drew closer, and in that instant, the male pushed the female, with the direct result that he was thrown into the hedge and she was propelled directly into the tractor's path!"

"That is not . . . How could he say such a . . . I could never have done such a thing; I loved her more than my own . . ."

"If that is not the state of affairs, then why did you survive and your wife did not?"

"I cannot remember. I only see her beneath . . . I don't know how it happened, it all came and went so quickly. I would take it all back if I could."

"Take it all back Mr. Brindley? Take what all back. You didn't do anything to take back, did you?"

"No. I meant that she was dead . . . is dead, and I wish it were me. That's what I want to take back."

"But she is dead Mr. Brindley and, despite your wishes, you are not. And what we need to ascertain is why she is dead, and not you!"

He looked at the barrister, head shaking, trying to take in his words. He seemed to shudder a little and grabbed the rail in front of him for support as he dropped his head.

The barrister put down the piece of paper he had been holding and sorted through more on his desk. He looked through three or four, eventually picking one. He adjusted his glasses as he looked at it for a few seconds and then addressed Aaron.

"What provision had been made in the event of one or both of your deaths?"

Aaron looked up, shook his head and, just as the barrister was about to reiterate, spoke.

"There hadn't. We both believed that if one lost the other we didn't want to capitalise on that."

"But surely, if one of you died then the other would be made financially secure. I would have thought that an intelligent couple would want the best for their partner if the worst happened?"

"We discussed it several times over our relatively short time together, and we both agreed we did not want to be 'secure' as you call it. Our love was unique and no amount of money could replace it, which is why we didn't take out any insurance policies."

"So, you had discussed the idea of insurance?"

"Yes we had."

"And you had come to an agreement, both of you?"

"Yes we had. We did not want any insurance money in the event one of us passed away."

"Both of you had agreed that?"

"Yes, we both agreed, I have just said."

"Then why did you have your wife insured Mr. Brindley?"

"I didn't."

"Oh but you did! You had her insured just over two months ago, and for a significant amount."

"I've told you, we discussed it numerous times and rejected the idea, both of us, out of hand!"

"And yet I have in my possession a document, an insurance document that states, Rose Elaine Brindley is insured against death by any circumstance for the amount of two hundred thousand pounds!"

There was a stir in the crowd watching. Lots of mumblings and chatter between people in the gallery could now be heard. The judge had them quietened.

Aaron looked dumbly at him as the barrister gave it to the clerk to give to him.

"How can this be," he said, taking the document. "We both agreed we wouldn't do this."

"And yet there it is, plain for all to see." Aaron handed it back after looking cursorily at it.

"I can't explain. I have no knowledge of this document." He looked across at the barrister, a deep furrowed frown on his face. He looked around at several people in the court as if they might explain, then shook his head. "May I see it again?" He asked.

It was handed back to him and the court now fell completely silent as he perused the document for several minutes.

"Do you see your signature on the final page Mr. Brindley?"

"I do."

"And so, what do you have to say?"

"It looks like my signature . . ."

"We also have verbal confirmation, recorded by the insurance company for training purposes."

"I can only tell you that I never gave any verbal agreement to a policy such as this, and that I have never seen this document, or any other such-like document in my life before."

"And yet you look to be inheriting a vast sum of money Mr. Brindley, because of a document you say you didn't sign, and that you claim to have never seen in your life before."

Aaron looked up at him, document in hand and simply shook his head.

A murmur ran through the crowd as a lot of them rose and made for the exit, pads and pencil's rapidly being replaced by mobile phones that were coming to life.

CHAPTER EIGHT
Judgement

The barrister had continued for only a short while after the press had left, and counsel for defence made only a brief cross examination, simply to affirm from Aaron that he had not taken out the insurance policy on his wife.

The judge had then ordered the jury to retire and called a halt in proceedings for lunch.

It was just two hours later that saw the court re-convened, and the public gallery full once again. There was a buzz in the air, apprehension rife.

The judge entered and took his seat. He slowly surveyed the court, and then spoke to the clerk who quickly crossed the court, took a note from the foreman and returned to the judge, giving him the note. He slowly opened it, glanced at it for a few seconds and handed it back to the clerk who returned it to the foreman. The judge leant back in his chair and made a gesture.

The foreman rose.

"We find the defendant not guilty."

A stunned silence reigned, but only for a short time.

Pandemonium.

The whole court virtually erupted, men and women shouting, and abuses aimed straight at the accused man.

The judge ordered quiet and, eventually, after a long period of serious unrest, calm resumed. He waited until even the murmurs quietened down.

Once order had been regained the judge re-iterated the verdict.

He then told the accused he was a free man, and announced that the case was now formally closed. The court was ordered to rise and the judge left the courtroom.

Pandemonium again.

Aaron stood in the courtroom in a haze as, all around, people were shouting and screaming. Papers were passed to him and he took them, almost absently. His counsel spoke in his ear and Aaron nodded, then shook the outstretched hand, the man now walking away, with the vast amount of legal papers that had littered the desk under his arm.

Aaron had heard the verdict but now, still standing, the whole room and all in it seemed to be unreal. He looked at the papers he held and read words he did not understand. He looked up amid the noise. No-one now approached him, though many were staring, both in court and in the gallery.

He thanked his barrister's team, shook a few of the hands that were offered, though few were, turned and left the court.

He made his way downstairs and walked towards the double doors that led out to the main street. The police officer opened one of the doors and he exited and was immediately confronted by a dozen or more people, all clamouring for his attention it seemed. He began to be jostled as questions flew at him from all angles.

"Did you do it Mr. Brindley?"

"Why did you want her killed?"

"How will you spend the blood money you gained from your wife's death?"

He tried to evade them but each turn simply put more questions in his face. He turned again and attempted to move away but could only manage a few steps due to the throng of people surrounding him.

"I have nothing to say," he blurted out as yet another microphone was thrust into his face. "I do not want to make a statement at this time!"

"Why did you do it?"

"I didn't do it! The jury found me not guilty."

"We all know it was you who engineered it!"

"You might have fooled the jury but you don't fool us!"

"Let me out. Just leave me alone!"

"You might run but you'll never escape. The truth will be found out!"

"Get out of my way!" he yelled and began pushing forward as two policemen appeared, taking station each side of him and then began forcing a path, enabling him to make his way through the crowd.

"How the hell could I have had her killed? I wasn't driving the bloody tractor!"

"No, but they say you could have managed it, just because you survived and Rose didn't."

"Is that what you think, and Maggie?"

The young man looked away but Aaron stood up and grabbed him by the shoulder.

"Please don't Dad." He said, not looking him in the eye.

"I'm not going to hit you!"

"I know," he said.

"Why isn't she here?" he said. "Why isn't she here, does she really think I did it?"

"It's because of the money Dad," he said. "All Maggie's friends knew Rose very well, and they all loved her. She treated them like adults, all of them, unlike the rest of the teachers. They knew that you two argued, and that didn't go down well. They also knew that neither of you had taken out insurance, it was part of a lecture Rose gave; she used you and her as an example. And then you inherit two hundred thousand pounds because of her death!"

"How did they come to know, to think, we argued? Who the hell told them that then? We didn't argue, not much anyway."

"Maggie's still a kid. She listens to her friends and they all loved Rose. All they see is the fact that her husband, who argued with her all the time as far as they were concerned, inherited a lot of money because she died. With all the media attention, the hype around the insurance money, the fact that you drink yourself into oblivion each day now, as well as the court case that damned you to all intents and purposes; how can you blame a nineteen-year-old child for thinking the worst?"

"I gave it all away."

"Gave all what away?"

"The money, I gave it all away!"

"You did?"

"Yes."

"No-one's ever seen that Dad. All they see is the bastards on the telly saying every bad thing they can think of about you."

"The court cleared me of all wrongdoing!"

"Come on Dad! It might have cleared you but the people still think that you did it, and the hype on the TV just enforces that."

"And is that what you think Ben?"

"Of course not, I know you. I also know Rose, and I know the relationship you and Rose had. I know it was nothing like they say. I also know that, no matter how loud you shout, those people out there, the paparazzi, the media, they won't hear because there's no story in what you say; there is not a story in the truth. Maggie is similar. She hears all the rubbish people say, as do all her friends, and they fall into line, shouting loud and saying not a word of truth. It doesn't matter about truth when there's a good story to tell, and the insurance policy together with Sonia's testimony just finished it off."

"Oh god, Sonia!"

"The things she said dad, they just put the lid on it, as far as the media are concerned that is."

"I know, even though it was just hearsay from the 'twin sister'."

"It didn't matter to them, it was sensational."

"What! All that crap about, 'We were in touch on a plane higher than anyone else because we were identical twins, I knew what Rose knew, and she knew what I knew'? Rubbish, all of it."

"It was the identical twin bit, and the fact that Sonia said they had a 'supernatural link' that nailed it."

"But it was rubbish, they didn't have a 'link', any sort of link. Rose wasn't even that fond of her."

"It seemed like Sonia hated you Dad, why would she hate you like that?"

"Oh, she just didn't like me taking her little sister away."

"Well, whatever it was, she was convincing and that's why the media are camping outside."

"Who believes in all that sixth sense rubbish between twins anyway?"

"They do, the media, because they want to, because it's sensational and it sells newspapers."

"I could bloody well kill Sonia!"

"It seems she'd like to kill you; she's certainly done as much as she can to destroy you anyway."

"Why can't she just leave me alone."

"She must really have hated you marrying her sister."

"She did."

"I don't understand why."

Aaron looked at the young man, then dropped his gaze.

"Because we had an affair before Rose and I got together."

"What?"

"About a year before Rose and me got married. It was just a drunken fling, meant nothing."

"Hell. It must have meant something to Sonia. She's virtually crucified you."

"She had debts you know, Rose, far more than I ever knew about. They only emerged after her death."

"What?"

"They turned up before I was even arrested."

"Who did?"

"They almost smashed the door in."

"Lots of people come out of the woodwork Dad, when you get a windfall, win the lottery or whatever. There are always people that want a hand out."

"No, it wasn't that sort of person. These came two days after she died. They were more like gangsters and they said she owed tens of thousands of pounds. It was before the court case and so I didn't even know about the insurance policy. These people didn't even know about that."

"Did you pay them?"

"I argued at first but then they showed me iou stubs and betting slips with her name on."

"They could have made those up Dad."

"Of course they could, but they didn't strike me as the kind of men that would have bothered to do something as normal as that. They didn't come to argue with me. They came to get the money my wife owed and, according to them, as she had died, the debt became that of her surviving partner."

"How much?"

"It was just over a hundred thousand pounds!"

"God!"

"I know. I had to borrow most of it, but it was worth it to get them to leave and not come back."

"How do you know they won't come back?"

"They told me the amount she owed, and took just that."

"They didn't know about the insurance money at all then?"

"It seems not. When the insurance company told me the money had been paid into my account I checked it the following day, just to see if it really was true. I didn't believe it even then but, if it was true, I was going to use it to pay back the numerous loans I'd had from friends, and so I expected two hundred thousand pounds to be there. There was less than fifty thousand!"

"What? But how come?"

"Apparently, and without my knowledge, a loan had been taken out for a hundred and fifty thousand pounds, and when the insurance money was paid in, the bulk of it was automatically taken to pay off the remainder of the bill as it was seriously overdue."

"Are you telling me that Rose took out a loan without your knowledge?"

"I spoke with the bank manager and asked to see the initial documents. It seems that she forged my signature, took out the loan, and the day it was paid in it was re-directed in to another account. From there it seemed to have disappeared."

"And you're absolutely certain about this?" He just nodded.

"But there's still more than this Ben."

"More?" Aaron simply looked at him. "I must admit I am finding this difficult to take in, knowing Rose as I did."

"The savings, which had been kept in a high interest bond ever since your mother passed away, had also been taken out without my knowledge."

"She took Mum's money? But you put that in to the bond for Maggie and me. How could she have done that, and why didn't you bring this up at the court case, it would have helped you?"

"Because, like the insurance money, I didn't have a clue until afterwards. It seems that Rose had put all these operations into action a good few months before we went on holiday. The bond, like the loan she took out, had been put into another account, and then disappeared."

"Have you told all of this to the police?"

"I think the media would have a ball if I did. I can see the headlines right now 'murderer defames beautiful wife'. I would never get the money back anyway, but it would definitely prolong the media's interest in me."

"I'm so sorry Dad. I had no idea."

"Neither did I Ben, neither did I."

"Have you any idea why she might do such a thing?"

"None whatsoever. I simply loved her and thought she loved me." He looked away and grabbed the bottle. "If you could manage to speak to Maggie at all, I would love for her to not feel quite so bad about me. I doubt she will though, given the media coverage and all. Hell, she never took to me during the so-called marriage to your mum anyway, even less after she died, so I'm not holding my breath. But, if you could suggest one or two little things that she might just mull over then, who knows, there is a chance she could stumble across a truism or two."

"I will Dad, but in the meantime maybe you could pull back a little on the alcohol?"

"I will try Ben, but at this moment I have very little left, and I'm not talking about money!"

Ben looked at his step-father and nodded. It seemed like he understood.

CHAPTER NINE
Aaron's Place

A knock at the back door woke him for about the seventh time and he scrambled to his feet, trying to throw the alcoholic induced dizziness aside as he went into the kitchen.

"Who is it," he yelled through the closed, curtained door.

"My name is Alki. I'm here to cast a little light on some of the problems you've been facing?"

"I don't need any help. I've done with all the help the likes of you can provide!"

He went back to his living room and would have sat down again had not the door been knocked, more loudly this time.

"Bastards!" he muttered, and got up again, heading back into the kitchen. "Go away! Just go away and leave me alone!"

"Mr. Brindley, I have some news for you, some evidence that I think will have an impact in your life, which will provide healing for some of your hurt."

"Oh god. I don't need religion, I have enough with the paparazzi!"

"Not religion, just facts concerning you, Rose and some of the people who claimed to be friends in your trial!"

"So, who are you and what can you tell me?"

He stood in the kitchen of his home and confronted her. The little lady shuffled on her feet, standing just inside the rear door and smiled up at him.

"I can tell you this," she said. "The hype that surrounds you is a veneer created to blind those that could aid you, and who could bring some understanding to the charades you have had to face and come to terms with."

"How so?" He was unconvinced.

"There are things in the court case which concern you and your wife and her subsequent death that are similar to those of another. The case I refer to happens to be that which my late husband and I were a part of. Both of these cases are the reason for my being here right now."

"How did you get through the ring of rubbish that has sat outside my door ever since the court case?"

"The paparazzi were called away, well, most of them anyway. There seemed to be another story that had to be covered and so I took the opportunity to call when the bulk of them at least weren't here, which is why I used the back door to make sure I wasn't seen."

He laughed and beckoned for her to follow him into the living room. He took a bottle and poured, indicating for her to sit. He quaffed the liquor and poured again. He placed another glass on a coaster; half-filled it and handed it to her. As he sat he raised his glass and then downed the lot. She sniffed at hers, sipped it and placed it back on the coaster.

"We have lots to talk about," she said. He looked at her through semi-closed eyes, unsure.

She was elderly. He put her at about mid-sixties and smiled as he knew he would never suggest it, just in case she was younger. He doubted it. Her clothes were quality and complemented her shape which was slight, though she was average height, around five feet six. She had a porcelain-like face with high cheek bones, and eyes that resembled crystalline marble. He concluded that, as a young woman, she would have been of the 'drop dead gorgeous' variety.

He began to throw questions at her and she answered them, mostly to his satisfaction. She then put forward her own questions concerning his trial and various other things. He tried to answer but seemed unable to string even a sentence together. She pointed out that there were lots of suchlike questions upon which she might be able to shed some light. He seemed to concur, but through unseeing eyes. She sat back, looking at him and considered, as he had been imbibing lots of alcohol since she had been invited in, together with her consideration that he probably had been drinking heavily throughout the day as well, whether he would able to comprehend what she said? She thought not and so she waited and watched as he, eventually, fell into an unquiet sleep. She tried a few times to gently awaken him but then gave up and put a blanket over him instead and let him sleep.

He slept through the night and into the morning.

She awoke before he did and began her daily routine of light stretching, reaching forward, clenching muscles and standing, sitting then standing again. She repeated her routine several times then sat back, a little out of breath. He was still asleep and she watched him breath for a while.

She cleaned the area before her and then ventured quietly into the kitchen and turned the light on, which revealed the extent of the depths to which this man had sunk.

There were bottles in abundance, and plates that had mould the size of small animals growing on them.

She opened the hot tap to its extremity and dug in.

She was into her third kitchen sink load when she heard movement behind her.

"Who the hell are you?!"

She turned from the sink to look into those bleary eyes. She went to speak after a brief moment but he stopped her.

"Oh. Of course, forgive me," he said and turned around in the doorway. "I remember now." He gingerly made his way back into the living room to sit. She followed him in and watched as he reached for the bottle he had dropped the night before.

"I could do some tea, or coffee for you if you prefer?" She now came to him and sat opposite. He looked up at her, a sight that reached into the lady's heart. He shook his head and raised the bottle with shaking hands. "Can you remember what we discussed last evening?" she asked. He thought for a moment, bottle in mid-air.

"I only know you've not accused me of all the lies the others have," he said, and put the bottle to his lips.

"I told you several things last night, about me, about you; more importantly about Rose. I can tell you them again Mr. Brindley but I doubt they will have meaning for you if you can't, first of all, remember them and, second, when they have sunk in and you begin to see the significance of what I am saying, do something about them."

He lowered the bottle and looked at her through red eyes which now began to water.

"You have no need to fear me Mrs . . .?"

"Alki. Just call me Alki. And I do not fear you Mr. Brindley. In fact, I know you better than most."

"You don't fear . . . Hang on. What's your name?"

"Alki."

"Alcy!" He looked hard at her and nearly dropped the bottle. "Alcy?" She nodded as he laughed out loud. "I don't believe this!" He looked to the heavens and shook his head. "Is this a joke?" he almost shouted. He looked back at her and now put down the bottle. "My god!" He stood tentatively and looked up again. "You take the only woman I've ever loved, in the most horrible manner I could ever conceive. You then make it so that I'm accused of her death, and that I had planned it all as well. They call me a murderer! And then, you have the scum of the earth hound me for weeks after I get off by the skin of my teeth and, to top it all, you send a woman to me who calls herself Alcy? which is precisely what I have become!" He looked back at her and she could see the pain in his now watering eyes. "Jeez! Who said you didn't have a sense of humour!" He sat and reached for the bottle but knocked it over and scrambled for it as it rolled away from him. He lost the contest and cursed as he sat back, out of breath.

She picked up the bottle and slowly looked up to see him, sitting in the chair, a broken man who didn't cry, and yet tears now began to fall with no sound, seemingly without any emotion.

She allowed the time to slowly course its way without comment. She knew he needed the moment to pass at the pace necessary for him, and him alone. It took an age and yet she just sat and waited, on his timescale now.

The tears began to dry and he, with effort, sat forward. His eyes didn't seem to focus and it was a short time before they turned to her, sitting peacefully. She didn't smile, neither did he, and after a short while she held out the bottle to him.

"I don't fear you," she said; "but I do fear this, yet for you not me." She still held it out to him. "But, if it helps with the pain you feel at this moment then you must do what you consider best."

He looked at her for a long moment, and then took the bottle.

She sat back in the chair, never taking her eyes off him.

"What is with the name then?" he said. "I don't mind if it's a joke, even if it is aimed straight at me."

"I was christened Ilka but my Father, whom I lived with since a child, had a sense of humour and so, as far back as I can remember, he called me Alki."

"Why?"

"Well. He had a problem and this was his way of throwing it in everyone's face. In effect, saying 'I don't care what you think. This is how it is so get used to it!'" Her face softened a little as he looked at her with a slight frown. "He loved me all his life and so I refused to give up his pet name for me, an homage if you like."

He blinked, the frown slipped away and he almost smiled.

"That's good enough for me," he said, raised the bottle and drank.

He grimaced as he swallowed the dregs and stood.

"I'm a Darjeeling man," he said. "What about you? Real tea mind, no tea bags, or pyramid stupidity in this house."

"Darjeeling's fine," she said.

He went into the kitchen, dropping the empty with the rest as he put the kettle on.

An hour later saw the sweat pouring out of him as he drank his fifth cup of Darjeeling.

"You said that you knew me better than most. How is that? I don't think I've ever met you before today, or yesterday should I say, even though I can't remember a thing about it."

"You said you did."

"I lied." She looked at him. "It's what drunks do. We say the things people want to hear; It deflects further questions we want to avoid."

"Alright, but no more lies. We have to be honest with one another if we are to work together."

"Fair enough. So, how do you know me?"

"I followed the court case from the beginning. I scrutinized the evidence against you and also the details provided from some of the so called witnesses. I also made my own enquiries and, after some time during which I managed to piece it all together, I came to the understanding that you had not manufactured your wife's death." He simply held her eyes with his, saying nothing. "I am also positive that it was not an accident. And not just that Mr. Brindley. I would even go so far as to say that I believe what has happened to you, and your late wife, was nothing less than a contrivance!" He shook his head. She went on. "Oh yes Mr. Brindley. I am convinced that you have been the victim of a scam, the likes of which even I have never seen before!"

He stood and walked to the curtained window, parted them slightly to look out, closed them again and turned back to her. Speaking soft and very slowly he said.

"Can you possibly be telling me that Rose wasn't killed by accident? Because if you are saying that then . . ." He seemed to be trying to put things in order in his head. "If that is the case then how could they . . . Who would do that . . . Why would they . . ."

She saw him scrambling for the words, and could see he was struggling to put things into some kind of order, attempting to understand. She spoke.

"I know it seems incredible to you at this time. I know that you have far more questions than answers and incredulity weighs heavily on your mind, but I do not say these things on a whim. I have deliberated on them over the long time of the trial and every day since then and so I would ask you to suspend your disbelief, of which there must be an abundance, and trust me, a woman you have never met before, and a person you have no reason to believe. But believe me when I say that I am someone who has come into your life for a very special reason. Trust me for a short time Aaron, and allow me to provide all the answers you seek. If I don't provide then simply put me out of your life and crawl back into the bottle. But, if I do open your eyes, make any sort of sense to you, give you cause to question things that were put before you in your trial, then come with me and look further. If you let me show you more than you know and more than you've been shown, I know that you will be shocked but at least, then, you will know the truth!"

There was a heavy knock at the front door, but he ignored it and sat down instead.

"Aren't you going to answer that?" she asked.

"It's only journalists. They try at least five times a day. It'll go on for another few times yet, before they give up." He picked up a mobile phone, cheap and outdated but new, checked it and put it back. "Everyone I want to speak to has this number, and they know to phone before coming here." The knocking began again, harder. He turned away and fixed her with his eyes. "You have a way with words Alki, but you have yet to show me anything concrete. I need something to hold onto, almost as much as I need a drink right now! I can forego the drink but you need to start giving me something I haven't seen, something that adds weight to your words." The knocking stopped.

"I can and will, right now."

He smiled and raised an eyebrow.

"Very well, amaze me," he said.

"Why did you insure your wife against death of any kind?"

"I didn't!"

"Two hundred thousand pounds you gained and yet you say you didn't instigate it?"

"I did not want to gain anything from her death."

"Where did it come from then?"

"I don't know. Maybe she put it into operation, in my behalf."

"Seems logical. How come it had your signature?"

"It can't have had."

"It passed inspection in court. It had your signature."

He seemed a little put out at this.

"I don't know how that happened. I didn't sign the damn thing!"

"So there we have it, a case in point. You benefited from your wife's death and you have no idea how it came about."

He nodded in agreement but could not speak. She spoke instead.

"I know. You cannot explain it and yet, there it is, damning evidence against you."

"But I just don't understand."

"I do. A similar thing happened to me when my husband was killed!"

"What?"

He looked up at her, in seeming shock.

She now produced documents from her briefcase and placed them in front of him.

"These prove that I was to benefit from my husband's death. The documents are clearly from a different source but they are not dissimilar to those that seem to have been drawn up prior to the death of your wife."

He picked them up, slowly, and began to peruse them.

It took him ten minutes to speak again.

"They accused me of insuring Rose for my benefit, to see her dead and I did no such thing. You show me similar . . ."

The man crumpled.

He wept silently.

She sat opposite and waited for a while, then reached forward to lay her hand on his arm and allowed him his time of grief in realisation of a truth, possibly the hardest, most destructive truth of his life.

"You've been through this?" he asked her. She nodded and he looked deep into her eyes. "Well, you look sane, so that bodes well for me!"

"The pain still abides, but it is managed." She could see that he was still struggling to come to terms with this knowledge, and he was losing the battle. She now got up and went into the kitchen. She came back with a glass almost full of whiskey. She gave it to him.

He drank half of it.

"Thank you," was all he said.

"When it's time, it's time. This is the time for the jolt that alcohol provides; but only a sufficiency, for to imbibe more than is needed would only lead to folly."

"Agreed!" He now sipped the neat liquor. "But you need to educate me, for I am sorely remiss in my understanding of these things."

She nodded and began to do his bidding.

CHAPTER TEN
A Friend

Alki had warmed to him and also seemed to understand his position. His love of his wife was obvious and she likened it to her love of her own husband. With this in mind she now began to explain her own story.

She had been married for about two years, and also considered that it had been a happy relationship. She had inherited an amount of money from her father, almost four million pounds, and she and her husband had lived happily off the interest that it provided. She told him that they had had a full, enjoyable community existence in their little village, taking part in jamboree's, village fetes, the yearly nativity and frequent plays.

Life had seemed wonderful but, since her husband's demise though, she had been subjected to abuse from people who had been friends, but who now considered far less of her due to her inheriting money from an insurance policy paid out on his death. It was shortly after this she found out that most of the four million pounds passed on to her from her father had been systematically drained from her bank account.

"Were you accused of murder as I have been?" Aaron asked.

"No. And I was lucky enough to avoid the media coverage as the insurance policy only came to light long after my Husband's death. The people in the village found out though, and that was when they made it quite clear I was not welcome. I found out at that time who were my true friends, and there weren't many."

"Whatever happened to the inheritance from your father?"

"I didn't ever find out, but I studied the bank records and saw that

Reg had, over the short time we had been together, taken out most of the funds. He had also had loans paid into current accounts for our day to day living, so that it did not become apparent that the investment money had gone until such time as I had to take on the finances after his death, and it was then that I saw just what had taken place. There was less than a hundred thousand pounds left, and then there were the loans I had to pay back as well. The house had had most of the equity released also and so I had to move into a rented property."

"How did you come to link what had happened to you with what happened to me Alki?"

She looked at him for a short while, smiled and dropped her head.

"Do you think there is something not completely explained Aaron, about your situation or the situation as it was when Rose was alive? Or, perhaps, the way things turned out to be after her death? Do you think there are things unexplained that you might like to have explained to you, wherever they might lead?"

He looked at her a little concerned and shook his head.

"I don't know." He checked his glass but it was empty.

"I have told you of a similar insurance mystery to your own. You have given most of the money you gained from the insurance away, and I had to use most of mine to pay off loans and debts my husband left me with. You also found out that Rose had stripped you of most of your assets, leaving you with only the insurance money. Almost exactly the same had happened to me. Apart from that there is very little I have told you to lead you from the understanding that your wife, like my husband, died of the most terrible accident."

"Correct" was all he said.

"I have told you of my background, and a few of the similarities of both our cases. But there are a lot more similarities, and they will show a far different picture than the one that has been painted for you since this jamboree began. There is a lot more to show you, though not here, if you are of a mind to look into the discrepancies, the inconsistencies and the doubts they might generate. But we need to move from this place."

"Why do we need to do that?"

"Because we are seriously hampered here. If we began looking locally for things, we would be seen and the media would take an interest. We need to be somewhere away from here to carry on our investigations, unnoticed."

"Why should I trust you?"

"Why should you not? Look at me, twenty years your senior. What have I to gain from you, a penniless drunk? No slur intended young man but, come on!"

He laughed.

"I have information and, maybe, more answers than you have considered possible, if you have the stomach for it?"

"Well, I have little else left, and I'm not just talking about the stomach, so what the hell. The step kids hate me, all Roses friends hate me, and mine too. I may as well follow you; two alcys together!"

"Yes, well. Whatever." She too smiled. "We need to move from here, and fast. If they see me, we would lose all advantage."

"So what do we do?"

"We go home, and lie low awhile."

"Okay. Where is 'home' then?"

"A place somewhat familiar to you but trust me, it will be safe. Right now, though, we need a diversion."

"Diversion? How do we go about that then?"

"I have a plan already sorted out, if you are of a mind to listen?"

"Fairly sure of yourself aren't you, coming here to talk to me with a plan already sorted out to get us both out of here."

"I'm a good judge of character Aaron. But, if it's any consolation, I also have a plan B, if you decided not to come."

He laughed.

"Then enlighten me, do."

"Have you got a friend, someone that cares?"

He nodded.

"Do they live nearby, and can you truly trust them?" He nodded again. "Good. When I've explained the plan, and if you agree with it,

I want you to call this friend and ask him to come round straightaway and tell him you are feeling low."

"Her."

"Sorry?"

"My friend is a woman."

"But can you trust her?"

"Oh yes, I can trust Megan. We've been friends since primary school."

"Great. Then this is what we need to do!"

All of the paparazzi vehicles were parked on curbs and grass verges, the actual highway being clear so that access to Aaron's house was viable, this having been insisted upon by the police. And so, when the garage doors attached to his property were thrown open and a classic BMW emerged, shooting forward into the road, being driven by a scarf-clad driver wearing the darkest sunglasses, it threw all the paparazzi into chaos.

The garage doors quickly closed as the vehicle sped through the startled journalists and hurtled down the road at increasing speed.

It was less than a minute later, just when all the media, with their special lenses and tripods and other such paraphernalia, were grabbing gear and running for their cars, that a drunken, whiskey bottle wielding, guilty (though not convicted) shabbily dressed man came bursting through the front door of his cottage, shouting oaths of disgust and outrage, that he should be subjected to such indignities as their presence represented, which diverted their attention back to the man they had come here to photograph.

They now swarmed towards the door.

Instantly it slammed shut!

It was around five minutes later that Megan turned up and made her way through the massed media, refusing to answer all questions, half-hearted though they were as she was a regular and they knew she didn't answer questions.

She knocked the door and then, it seemed, also unlocked it and let herself in.

Shortly after, music was heard coming from the house, being played loud.

Almost fifteen minutes later Megan appeared at the door and stepped out, turned and, it appeared, locked the front door. She made her way to the gate, stopped and held her hand up, causing all of the half-hearted questions to cease.

"Aaron is not feeling well and, as you know, has turned to drink a little in the last few days. I have made sure he is not unduly at risk and asked him to eat some food and go to bed. He has assured me that he will do this and so, ladies and gentlemen, I am here to ask that you leave him alone."

There were grunts of disgust and alarm and a hail of questions, backed up by about ten microphones being thrust into her face, as almost all the journalists came and congregated at the gate to the beleaguered house.

She held up her hands and waited for the noise to wain as she began to answer.

The curtain fell back the half inch it had been moved, once more fully covering the window.

Aaron, with dark coat and muffler, Trilby hat with walking boots strapped firmly on and packed disraeli bag in hand, now quietly slipped into the kitchen and through the back door, out into the cold night, silently locking the mortise lock. He stopped and waited, looking for movement beyond his back fence and gate. He could hear a babble going on at the front of the house, and ten seconds later he was on the path and into the back field where he hugged the bramble hedge, bobbing down as he quickly slunk away from his home.

"And so if you could, please, just for this one night, afford him the courtesy of not knocking his door and allow him the rest he needs without disturbance!"

Murmurs of assent greeted her and she thanked them, now coming through the gate and getting into her car to head back the way she had come.

It was about ten minutes later that the music stopped and the light in the living room went out, together.

At about that time, Aaron reached the car that Alki had parked more than a day ago. It stood by itself, at the back of the car park of the only pub in the small village. He marvelled at its condition and unlocked the old Morris Oxford. He started the engine and found the hidden sat nav. He turned it on and sure enough it was set up with his pre-determined destination and so, after a couple of minutes to familiarise himself with the controls of this archaic vehicle, and having to bob down over the passenger's seat as two locals, both who knew him well, passed close by the car, he set off. After stalling the vehicle twice, he managed to get it through the gates and onto the road out of the village. He had decided to keep the trilby on, and it seemed to do its job for three or four times he passed people he knew and who could possibly have recognised him, but for the shadow of the trilby's rim.

He kept it in second gear and only changed up after reaching the national speed limit sign at the edge of the village proper.

It was Hank, one of Aaron's friends from the pub and well known for his dislike of strangers, who had taken down the number of the car whose engine had been over-revving whilst driving slowly through the village, deeming the person behind the wheel, who had deliberately kept his face in shadow, to be 'up to no good!

CHAPTER ELEVEN
Journey

Alki had driven the BMW away at speed, expecting at least a couple of the paparazzi to follow and she was prepared for that, but no-one did and so, although surprised, she now drove a little slower and with a tad more care.

It was just under an hour later that she parked up, out of sight at the back of the British Rail car park and sat, waiting.

Shortly after, she got the call she had been waiting for.

"Well done," she said. "Now stick to the plan and I'll see you shortly."

She hung up, picked up her bag, locked the vehicle and went in to the train station. She bought a ticket for the next stop, crossed the bridge and waited. It was on time and she boarded, standing for the short journey. She left the train and walked up the exit slipway, handed over her ticket and sauntered into the car park. She didn't have to search for too long, and quickly got into the old Morris Oxford.

She exited the car park, turned left; turning immediate left again into a petrol station and filled the tank. She pulled out of the petrol station and turned the corner, going into a pub car park where she locked the vehicle and went into the lounge bar.

"Am I glad to see you," was all Aaron could say.

"I am so glad to see you followed the instructions to the letter," Alki said. "We can't be too careful at this stage."

"I don't see why we need to be so cloak and dagger. I thought getting away from the house was the main thing; all this, dropping the car off at the station, going to the pub and phoning from there, waiting thirty-five minutes before phoning again if I need to? It seems just a bit too Sherlock Holmes if you ask me."

She nodded in seeming agreement.

"I agree, but when you take into consideration all that has befallen you since your trip to Cornwall, to take a few well thought out diversionary tactics that don't cost anything and might well shake off any pursuit we are not aware of, could be well worth the effort."

"Alright, if you say so."

"I do."

"Okay boss." He took on a mock subservient attitude. "Should we have a drink here, checking to make sure it isn't poisoned, or should we head off, hoping that Moriarty isn't hot on our trail?"

"Well." She now smiled, and beckoned for him to come closer. "I think that," she spoke in a whisper, furtively looking around the room. "You should walk up to the bar, Watson, get me a soda and lime, heavy on the ice and lemon, get yourself a shot of Irish, and order us some food."

He looked at her with a wry smile.

"Soda and lime, Sherlock?" he said.

"Yep."

"Lightweight." He got up, shaking his head, but still smiling.

"I'll have a salad," she called after him.

"Salad it is."

She smiled. 'He seems to be a little happier now,' she thought. 'I just hope he has the strength to maintain that happiness when he begins to realise what the truth really is!'

They ate and were underway before ten pm.

Alki drove, asking many questions while she did so, Aaron pulling heavily on his memory to provide answers for his new mentor. This continued for many a mile and all sorts of subjects were drawn into the conversation, Aaron answering as best he could.

They drove into the night, talking and chatting, and it was about eleven thirty when Aaron fell asleep and Alki reduced her speed on the A road she had elected to take instead of the motorway. She glanced at him from time to time and often shook her head, her eyes sometimes filling with tears which were quickly dispelled.

Her thoughts were of his situation and how she might be able to help him. She wondered if she were giving him false hope, and prayed it wasn't that. Images floated through her mind and she realised her age when she felt herself falling into sleep. The danger grabbed at her mind and dragged her back into wakefulness. She quickly found a lay-by and pulled in, giving in to the fact that she needed to sleep. Three hours later she awoke and set off once more.

It was around five in the morning when she pulled into a huge truck stop and parked amid the rigs.

"Aaron?" she gently nudged him.

They had steaming mugs of tea and bacon sandwiches with lots of brown sauce and burnt onions.

They both felt refreshed as they got back into the car together.

"So sorry for falling asleep," he said.

"Alcohol weakens you and so you had little chance. It's fine."

"Aren't you tired Alki?"

"Oh hell yes," she said.

"I'll drive if you want."

"It's okay, "she said. "I stopped and had a few hours. Anyway, we're less than an hour away now."

She started the car and swung out of the car park.

"You do know that you haven't yet told me where we are going."

She slowed the car and took time to look him in the eye. She sped up again before she spoke.

"You know that there will be lots of revelations in this journey that you have embarked upon with me?"

"Of that I am sure." He seemed to be smiling at the prospect.

"The first of those is not far off. Do you recognise where you are now?"

He looked out at the approaching dawn, at the scenery passing by. He shook his head.

"No. Never been this way before."

"We are approaching from a different direction than you would have done, but I need you to look out and get a feel for the place we are in now, to get a feel for where you are in the country?"

"Well, we have been heading south, mostly, but now we're heading in a fairly westerly direction if the dawn is anything to go by."

"Very perceptive Aaron."

"Not difficult Alki."

She smiled, as did he.

"The place I'm taking you to is my home, but its location is the reason that will give you cause to wonder, for it is a place you know!"

"How so?"

"That will soon become apparent, and beneficial if you can listen and learn."

He looked a little confused but answered her directly.

"I don't see why I would not have the ability both to listen to all you have to say and also to learn from what is said."

"I am concerned that the man might be overly concerned with the place, the environment he is being taken back into."

She glanced at him. He still shook his head.

"The place where I live will be familiar to you." She waited as she drove but gained no response. "And so," she continued deliberately. "Its location has the ability to destabilise you and throw you into a confusion, which might befuddle all logic."

He now seemed concerned and looked at her.

"I don't know how to answer if I don't know into what I am entering!"

She turned off the car's lights now they were into the full light of early morn.

"Are we going back to Cornwall?" he asked very softly.

"We are Aaron." She didn't take her eyes off the road ahead.

"I only know one place in that part of the country."

She did not speak and time passed in silence.

"Where?" He said, more than five minutes later. "Exactly?"

She slowed the car and shortly pulled over into a lay-by. She turned off the engine and, still not looking at him, spoke.

"I have lived in a small bungalow for the last year. That has been my home since my husband died and it happens to be placed exactly opposite the apartment that you and your wife hired for your holiday almost two months ago."

He now looked at her through tears but could not speak.

"I know this will cause much distress to you and I apologise, but we must be strong." He went to speak, but shook his head in despair. "I know you think that what I say is easy for me but it isn't, for I have been where you are; I too have visited the place in your mind, where you find yourself now. Therefore, whilst I know the journey is yours, and yours alone, I can give you my strength to help you through this most difficult of times. I can help you reach the other side Aaron, if you trust me."

"How can going back there be of any help to me?" His question was said through brimming tears, and almost child-like in its offering.

She hesitated only for the briefest moment.

"I know that, at this time, you cannot see any logic in the words I say, or even what I ask you to do, like the physical journey we are on at present. There are reasons, though, for all these things. You will realise this when you begin to see, but it will take time to see because this picture, your picture, is not clear at present. You have so many conflicting thoughts running at breakneck speed, bashing into one another and making no sense; coupled together with all you had to suffer at the trial, the media attention, the hatred. This has to have you at sixes and sevens. It is only when we clear the mist, when we can manage to wade through the miasma which has been created by all you had to endure that you will begin to put that picture together, to be able to see clearly the many roads ahead and then deal with each road in turn, in a reasonable and rational manner. When we can do this, start to make sense of that picture and join up all the roads that link this picture together, we will, finally, discern the truth that was there all the time."

Aaron was looking at her, his eyes beginning to dry. He wiped the residue away and took a deep breath. He looked up, at the road ahead. He frowned a little but only for a short time.

She let him think and waited, ready to aid if she could, but resolved to work with him, in his time and when he needed.

His thoughts were a jumble and he needed a drink. He shook his head and felt the need to cry but cast out that emotion as quickly as it appeared. To go back to that place was daunting but he knew it had to be done now. How could he face it? He didn't know but he knew he had to. Something was pushed into his hand.

"I took this from your car. I hope you don't mind?"

He looked at the bottle of Irish whiskey and then at her. She smiled back. He laughed out loud as a tear formed, but he wiped it away as quickly and smiled again at her.

"How the hell did you know?"

"I know Aaron; I've been there, remember?"

He took off the cap and raised it to his lips. He leaned back as he swallowed, shook his head a time or two and looked at her.

"Okay," was all he said.

She started the car and pulled back on to the road.

CHAPTER TWELVE
Pap!

"We've 'ad a call," was all he said as he jogged back to the car.

All the journalists showed an interest in this, and now began to clamour round.

"Come on." He ignored their requests and began dismantling his camera and tripod, bundling it all unceremoniously into the boot. His two friends began to do the same but the look of uncertainty was difficult for them to hide.

"What you got then?" Another reporter stood forward from the crowd of media that had stood by the gate to the cottage, but now were converging on the decamping trio. "Where you goin'?"

"Just got a call John, from the office, to leave this one for you geezers."

"You know somethin'!" The accusation was harsh.

He ignored him and started the engine. The other two quickly got in and he sped off down the lane, away from the cottage they had camped in front of for two weeks.

"'E's not there!" he pre-empted all questions from his fellow journalists. "I went round the back, cut an 'ole in the glass and poked the curtain out of the way. The iPod and the light are on a timer. It won't take that lot too long to realise 'e's buggered off and so we use this time to our advantage."

"Where we going?"

"The village. That car, whoever was drivin' it, 'ad to go through the village so we start there, at the pub, the locals; talk to anyone what saw somethin' unusual? We might get lucky."

CHAPTER THIRTEEN
Eye-Opener

They drove slowly through the countryside for almost an hour, hardly speaking now as he began to recognise the area. It took only several more minutes for them to reach the bungalow that was her home, driving around to the back, although Aaron could not take his eyes from the house opposite.

The car was reversed into the garage, the door closed and locked as Alki showed Aaron into her home, through the kitchen area and into the front living space.

It was Spartan though clean, with shelves and shelves of video tapes together with lever arch files which lined the walls of the lady's living room.

She drew the curtains, aware that the front window looked out on to the holiday let across the road. She apologised, and offered him tea which he refused. He seemed a little nervous, awkward, and looked as if he felt out of place.

"You're welcome here Aaron. There is lots I have to show you, and I shall, but not just now. We both need to rest and that is what we shall do, for at least a few hours."

He nodded his agreement and smiled as he was led down the short corridor.

Aaron was shown into the spare bedroom, Alki went to hers.

It wasn't long before they both were asleep.

It was a few hours later that they met again in the kitchen, in the mid-afternoon of the day.

"It's best in here Aaron, as there's only one window, and that looks out onto the back area. The lounge overlooks the road and also the house opposite and so there is a risk that anyone passing or approaching the house might see in, and then we would be done for before we'd even begun."

He agreed and so they sat down together to partake of tea amidst yawns and stretches with light banter.

"So, what's with all the tapes? Do you like TV so much you have to record all the episodes you might miss?"

"A bit like that, although there are some family video's and other stuff in there."

"And what sort of TV addict are we then, eh? EastEnders? Songs of praise? Star Trek?"

"Er, no! I'm more an Antiques Road show / Proms sort of person."

He smiled a little and raised his mug.

"To us. May our investigations prove fruitful and our seekers simply go round and round in ever decreasing circles!"

She drank with him.

"So, what's the significance of you living here then?"

She put down her mug and looked him in the eye.

"It was no accident, me coming to this place."

"I believe you," he said. "I have to tell you, though, that whatever my involvement in whatever has gone on or is even continuing to go on, is now beginning to frighten me. I need to start getting some answers Alki, and I need to start having this 'picture' you've talked of, begin to take on some sort of shape, because, at the moment I am completely lost!"

She continued to look at him and could see the fear of what is unknown written across his face.

"Then we begin," she said.

He mouthed more than said a word of thanks.

"I knew things were happening and I knew I was in the right area. I had watched several couples that had booked the same apartment you had but, after a short while in most cases, knew that they were not right."

"How did you know they were 'not right'?"

"I'll come to that soon enough."

He nodded.

"I kept eyes on many holiday places in the area, whose patrons fulfilled certain criteria. It was only after serious scrutiny that, one by one, they were discounted. You and Rose fitted the brief, and that is why I built a dossier around you, and then, over time, got to know you both."

He had many questions and she did her best to answer them.

She told him that she had been aware he and Rose were coming to stay and, after waiting some time had gone and vetted three other couples who also were arriving that day but in different areas. Two of them had been discounted due to age, accompanying relatives and such. And so, on return, she had concentrated her time on him and his wife. She had found them to be prime candidates and so had followed them.

"Prime candidates?"

"I believed that women of a certain age and a certain, specific look were at risk. That was the criteria used to narrow my investigations anyway and it led me to you."

"So you found us to be of the kind you thought might . . .?" He left the question wide open and waited.

She nodded and picked her words carefully.

"You were possibles. I have had possibles before and they amounted to nought. I didn't think that you were any more possible than others but, still, I carried out my surveillances."

"What did they reveal?"

"They showed that you were being taken notice of. They led me to believe that you might be the ones that they moved on!"

"They?"

"I will come to all these questions in time."

It was obvious he desired the answers straight away, but he held back his feelings, allowing her to continue.

"They had watched you from your arrival, and I believe they had, possibly, known of you since booking the apartment."

"Then all we do is find the owners and broach the subject with them."

"It is not that easy. They go through a broker and that is where the info, it seems at least, could have been purloined."

"They knew about Rose and me?"

"And also who you were, where you came from, which friends you had, your parents, children, everything about you."

"But why?"

"Because of what they wanted from you."

"The death of my wife?"

She hesitated as he turned to melancholy. The moment passed and he regained his composure once more.

"It might have been more than that Aaron," she said.

He looked at her through moistening eyes.

"How so?"

"What has been going on could be something more than the deaths of our partners."

"You mean, it could be to do with us, you and me?"

She nodded but then stood and went into the lounge. She returned with a framed picture, that he'd seen mounted on the wall.

"This is the best picture of my Reg. It was taken only a month before his death."

"Handsome man."

"Oh yes, he was handsome alright; the life and soul of every party and all the women wanted to dance with my Reg. But he always made a bee-line for me, to the disgust of all the beauty's that would have it otherwise. Very attentive my Reg was, even though he was seventeen years my junior."

"Okay. Handsome guy, attentive; I get all that, but what has it to do with us?"

"Trained to be a dentist you know; but he flunked the exam and so packed it in. Just like that. He said; 'Sod that, I'll find another, better way to make a living'. And he did. Me!"

"You? What do you mean?"

"He had magicked away nearly four million pounds of my inheritance. We were almost penniless when he died."

Aaron was shocked.

"Take a good look at him," she said. "He left me with debts I didn't even know we had. I had people knocking on the door day and night, asking me to make reparation."

He could see she was getting a little upset.

"I need to rest Aaron," she said. "It has been quite a few days for me. I daresay it has also been quite a few days for you too and so, if you don't mind, I shall turn in." He nodded. "Please help yourself to whatever you need. I would ask, though, that you moderate the intake of Irish as I wish for us to be away quite early in the morning, if you wouldn't mind."

"Of course." He said, and stood. "Might I ask where we are going?"

"Oh, just a short trip, through the countryside. I have something to show you."

She found him sleeping in the chair, bottle on its side on the floor.

She woke him and, after he quickly showered during which time she made toast, they were off.

It was about an hour before dawn and she drove quickly through the small country lanes, neither of them talking, both deep in thoughts of their own.

A little more than ten miles later saw them parked on the grass verge of a country lane, overlooking a fallow field which stretched away before them into a small valley beyond. She left the motor running and kept the heating on, but had turned off all lights a hundred yards prior to reaching the spot. She stretched to the back seat and took a pair of binoculars from their case and used them to look down across the field into the dark.

"I wouldn't have thought you could see too much with those at this time in the morning!"

She adjusted them a little, looked again and passed them to him.

"I need you to watch," was all she said. He lifted them up and chuckled.

"It's almost pitch!"

"Just point them at the foot of this field. Can you see the stick standing proud of the hedge close by?" He could. "The top of that stick is where you should be aiming, and as the sun comes up you will see, beyond the stick, at the bottom of the field, why we are here."

She picked another case from the rear seat, opened it and took out a video recorder. She opened the cover to the lens, turned it on to look in the same direction. She turned off the TV viewer and looked into the view finder instead. Satisfied with this she turned it round to face her for inspection.

"What's that?" He asked, pointing at something on the front, by the lens.

"Tape, where the red light shows that you are recording," she told him. "I don't want to risk discovery by showing a red light, small though it is."

"At this distance?"

"I don't take chances Aaron, even small ones."

He was impressed.

Neither spoke again for ten minutes as they waited for the sun to rise. Alki was recording and Aaron was looking in the direction she'd told him.

The dawn came quickly, but not before lights began to appear at the location they were looking.

It perked him up and he heard Alki murmur something, he thought it to be invective, but then he was concentrating.

He adjusted the lenses only slightly and surveyed The Barn house conversion that was quickly coming to life as it also became lit from the coming day.

He could now see movement within the home and he flicked from window to window, straining to see.

"They will step out shortly," Alki whispered to him, as if she might possibly be heard. "The door to the right of The Barn is where they shall emerge. Get ready, for you will only get a glimpse."

"What am I looking for, "he asked, almost nervously.

"Please Aaron, just look."

He nodded in the semi-light, not realising she would not see. Twenty seconds later and the huge single door of The Barn opened inwards, casting a long shaft of light onto the yard beyond, illuminating two parked cars.

"Now see," she whispered to him.

Two men came from the house, the first jumping into the furthest car, a convertible sports car, and starting the engine, the lights of the vehicle lighting up the courtyard even more. But it was the second, older man that caught Aaron's attention as he stood at the door, closing it whilst lit in the pool of light from the kitchen. Then he turned and was caught in the car's light as he passed by and got into the second vehicle.

Both cars now pulled off, going the other side of The Barn and out of their view. Alki handed the video camera to Aaron who took it. She set off, eventually putting the lights on as she picked up speed.

"He's had a haircut," she said as she took the first left turn and gunned it down the lane. "They don't come this way," she said, "but it makes sense to take no unnecessary chances."

Aaron held the camcorder and simply looked at her, eyes wide open.

"That was your . . ." He looked ahead, seemingly unable to finish his sentence.

"Yes. Looks good for his age doesn't he?"

"How can that be?" He shook his head and turned to her again. "But it was him, wasn't it?"

"Yes," she said. "Oh yes Aaron it was. That was Reg, my dead husband!"

CHAPTER FOURTEEN
Inklings

The air was thick as they sped along the country lanes, Aaron full of questions and Alki smiling, sometimes even laughing out loud as she answered him.

"It really is no big deal. He simply faked his death so he could get out of our relationship!"

"Faked his death?"

She glanced at him and could see he was incredulous.

"That's how I felt Aaron, barely able to believe it."

They arrived back at the bungalow and the car was quickly garaged. Shortly after they were in the kitchen, hot mugs of fresh tea in hands.

"Why didn't you tell me beforehand?"

He leant against the sink, a wry smile on his face.

"I needed you to see, so that when I explain things about him you will have that indisputable evidence that he is alive emblazoned across your mind."

"But why would he want out of his life with you? You made a very handsome couple, as well as the millions you had."

"I was quite a beauty then. I wore high heels and short skirts and all men looked, even though I was significantly older than most.

"You do have a look Alki."

"Had! But now I wear flats and grease my hair, accentuate the many lines and redden the nose so that all who observe me see age, non-concern with looks or clothes or blusher or make-up. They see an old woman who cares not for vanity or other such youthful frivolities."

"But you are still beautiful."

She turned to look him straight in the eyes.

"Fancy me do you?" She flung this. "He did too, but he fancied the money a lot more. Fancy me enough to take me to bed do you?" He backed away, unsure, shaking his head. "Course not. I'm old, not young anymore, not like the women a young man can get if he tries!"

"I didn't mean that. You are still beautiful, despite what he did to you. I meant no harm." She seemed to calm at his words.

"I'm sure. I'm also sorry for so harsh a rejoinder. The pain often gets too much when certain things are said. Please forgive me."

"Nothing to forgive." He smiled at her and she tried also to smile but failed and turned away.

"You wanted to shock me into believing you, didn't you?"

"That element is vital, sadly Aaron, to enforce what I show you, that you might grasp it and its meaning first time."

He didn't seem to understand. She explained.

"Time is of the essence my friend. What I have to say to you, to show you, I need for you to understand straight away. We have not the luxury of time, of my explaining at length everything I bring to your attention. I need you to trust me and, therefore, trust what I tell you, show you, and enlighten you with straightaway." He seemed to concede the point. She took a deep breath. "My ex-husband," she stressed each word in turn. "He, I believe, is instrumental in your wife's death!"

Aaron had raised his mug to drink but now, slowly, lowered it.

"What?" he said softly, almost in a whisper.

"I know," she held his eyes with hers. "Please remain calm. I know this must be difficult for you Aaron, but I believe your wife was . . . murdered!"

"She fell beneath the . . ."

"I know. I saw and heard all the evidence."

"They tried to say I pushed her!"

"I know. I also know you didn't!"

"I didn't push . . . What? How do you know . . ."

"I just do; also, the barrister had no real evidence."

"Were you there, in court?"

"Only the first day. Sadly, I had to leave as there were people there that could have recognised me if they had gotten close enough, and so I abandoned the trial in favour of Alex, and others, going in my stead. They recorded the whole thing so that I could build up the picture without actually being there.

"Alex?"

"Alex is my brother in law, well, ex brother in law actually."

"How does he fit in with all this?"

"Alex is a P. I. And I asked him to help when I knew things were happening. He's an ex-cop and so knows his stuff."

"You said others?"

"Just a couple of people Alex uses from time to time. But with all the recordings they made, and the masses of TV footage, it kept me abreast of the situation all the time. It also left me free to look around during the day, knowing that people I was interested in were there in court watching proceedings, and that Alex and the others were there watching them!"

"Alki, you need to explain to me why, how you might think that Rose was murdered. It is one thing to lose the woman I love, but to find out that she might have had her life deliberately taken is something that . . ." He struggled for the words and Alki could see he was visibly shaken.

He put down the mug with shaking hands and turned away from her to stand, holding the sink. She could see his shoulders begin to shake and heard the muffled sobs he could not hide.

She came to his side, putting a hand on his shoulder.

They remained like this for a time, until his sobs subsided and she helped him to a chair. He took a handkerchief from his pocket and wiped the tears away as Alki filled the kettle and switched it on.

"I don't need tea at this time," he said.

Without a word she reached behind the kitchen curtain, turned and placed a bottle before him.

"I know," was all she said.

He looked up at her and shook his head, a faint smile of incredulity trying to emerge through his tears.

"You never cease to amaze me," he said as he unscrewed the top.

"Not too much Aaron, you've only had toast this morning, and you had a skinful last night.

He looked at her and shook his head now as he poured himself half a glass.

"Sorry Alki, I forgot to tell you. I was so exhausted I fell asleep after two shots and the bottle must have fallen on the floor. I'm afraid your carpet must be sodden."

She looked at him sceptically, then stepped through into the lounge. She came back within seconds.

"I am sorry for doubting you, the carpet is sodden alright, but rather the carpet than you, for you have a lot to take in."

He tried to smile at her, wiped away the remaining tears and drank from the glass, grimacing as he swallowed. He now looked up at her and she held his gaze as the Irish began to reach inside. She slowly sat and began telling him about her husband, Reg.

CHAPTER FIFTEEN
Reg

They had married when she was seventy and he was fifty-three; a marriage seeming to have been made in heaven, and one Alki had not foreseen.

She drank tea whilst he now sipped Irish.

She had made up her mind that, after her previous marriage, which had lasted twenty-two years, she would never marry again. But when this man had come along and, seemingly, could not take his eyes off her, then her resolve slipped and, after just six months, married again.

"I was happy for the first time in my life. He was my constant companion and I loved being with him, and I mean all of the time." Aaron only just saw a flicker of emotion in her eyes before she quickly moved on.

They had moved to Norfolk on Reg's request and rented a place while their old home, Alki's previous marital home, was being sold. Reg had given up work in favour of playing the stock exchange and it seemed he was doing quite well.

"For two whole years we lived like this, in each other's pockets, him spending an hour or two on the phone every other day with me seeing friends and generally waiting until he'd 'done the deal', and then we were together again, inseparable the two of us. We both just seemed to thrive on it." He could see her joy from the sparkle in her eyes, but it quickly left. "It was one day in summer, just after our second wedding anniversary that the 'accident' happened."

She explained that she had been in town while Reg busied himself, as always, on the computer and phone, dealing with agents in London. She had spent her time with friends, talking trivia and drinking coffee when she received a call from the local Policeman in the village where they lived. It was he who had told her that Reg had been involved in an accident. She had driven quickly home. It was explained to her that the old tree in their back garden had collapsed and her husband had been crushed to death.

"I was taken to hospital due to shock. But when I recovered sufficiently enough it was explained to me that he had not suffered, but that he had probably died instantly. The coroner's report also showed he had died purely accidentally. The tree surgeon, though, had evidenced that it shouldn't have fallen, as the tree had been healthy enough, but his voice was not heard and so the accident was deemed to be 'an act of god'."

"So, it was the tree surgeon that made you suspect something was not quite right?"

"Yes, it was what he had said about the tree being healthy enough to stand for a good few years yet."

"But, you said no-one believed him."

"No, I said nobody listened to him, including me." Aaron spread his hands wide and frowned at her. "We didn't listen or give credence to his evidence that it shouldn't have fallen. Facts take precedence over evidence. The tree *had* fallen and that was that."

"So, it had fallen but shouldn't have?" She nodded. "But why did it fall then? How could it have fallen?"

"Those are the questions that were not asked, due to the 'accident' being deemed to be an 'act of god'." He frowned at the apostrophe signs she made.

"'Accident?'"

"Yes Aaron," she answered.

"So you are saying it wasn't an accident?"

"Correct."

"Are you trying to tell me that someone made it fall?" He now laughed, seemingly at the stupidity of his own question. Alki did not laugh.

"Not just 'someone'," She said. "Reg and his cohorts!"

"What?" She nodded.

He took a breath and looked at her for a while. She waited.

"You're serious?" She simply nodded. He thought for a moment. "Cohorts? Do you mean the younger man at The Barn?"

"And others," she said. He looked at her, seemingly non-plussed. "But let me come back to that."

"Alki, you can't seriously think Reg . . . You are saying your husband made the tree topple and . . ." He shook his head, struggling to explain himself.

"I know it seems strange and, because of that, it's not understandable to you at this time, but let me come back to it a little later; I think you won't then have as much difficulty in taking it in." He slowly nodded in agreement, a very faint smile on his frowning face. "Just keep in mind the shock you experienced when you saw Reg at The Barn." He lost the smile almost immediately. "If I had simply told you about his demise and then said he was alive, you would just have been puzzled and seriously sceptical. The fact that you knew what he looked like, and then saw him in the flesh was what sealed the truth for you, in that instant." Now he nodded and the frown also disappeared. "Good. Simply suspend your disbelief for a little while longer Aaron and I guarantee the puzzle will evaporate before your very eyes."

"Alright Alki I will. But I would have you know that I have never put as much trust in a person before as I am putting in you at this moment, and I barely know you."

"I know what lengths you are having to go to but you will reap the rewards, I give you my word."

"Okay," he said. "Tell me what you found."

"It was the 'act of god' bit that was the catalyst."

"How so?"

"Well, god doesn't do things like that, apparently."

"God? What do you mean Alki?" He looked at her sideways, sceptically. She saw the look and laughed.

"Hell, I don't believe in god any more than you do!" She paused. "You don't believe in god, right?" She looked at him quizzically. He smiled and shook his head. "Thank god for that!" There was a pause, then they both laughed out loud. She carried on. "But something happened, which helped me through that time and made me think about it, think about it seriously enough to consider it might not have been an accident, that it might not have been one of these so-called 'acts of god'. It set me on the road to begin considering if it might have been deliberate."

"Deliberate?" She nodded. "Okay," he said. "What was this 'catalyst?'" He still looked at her with a smile of disbelief.

"I was high on drugs and drink through most of that time but, one day, these religious buffs came to the door. I normally fob them off with an excuse, but instead I decided to have a go at them. I was angry Reg had been taken from me and so, in my drunken haze I told them about Reg's death and asked why god would do such a thing; why this 'act of god'? I said. Why the hell does he have to be so selfish and take my Reg? They kept calm despite my vitriol and told me he didn't do the things that people call an 'act of god'. They then showed me in their bibles that he didn't. I looked at what they said, spent some time on it, then argued, cried a little, shouted a lot, slammed the door on them, drank some more and then slept, but woke after about three hours and thought about it again. They came back exactly a week later and showed me, in my old bible this time, that these 'acts of god' had no basis in 'god's word', I even marked it in. I realised weeks later that it was my not wanting to believe or accept what had happened, together with the drugs and alcohol, that made me latch onto this, but it was the catalyst that led me to where I am today."

"Why?"

"Because I wanted to know why he'd died, and now, because the old 'act of god' thing didn't cut it anymore, I needed answers. It was their religious belief that caused me to get my act together and probe further. Thank god for religious loonies!"

"What did you do?"

"I researched trees, particularly the birch that had been in our garden, and why they become diseased, what the signs were of that disease and also why the tree might fall without us seeing, knowing it was at risk. In addition, I also sought out the tree specialist from the trial and quizzed him about it."

"What did you find?"

"I found that, in this instance, there was no 'act of god' because, when I looked, I found truths, I really did. This specialist showed me enough to prove the tree was not diseased; well it was diseased but, not enough to make it fall. My research, together with his facts using pictures of the tree after it fell, and pictures he showed me of trees that had been weakened enough to topple by themselves, were enough to prove to me that there was something not quite right here; the tree couldn't have fallen by itself, it had to have been manipulated!"

"So why didn't they listen to him, he was the expert?"

"Because it had come down! The questions concerning why it had come down were of no consequence to the powers that be."

"But why?"

"Because the tree surgeon, when asked specifically, had to agree that there was a possibility it could have fallen, even though, as he told me, the probability of it falling at that time was virtually zero. And, it would seem, because of the statements of the other two professionals, the policeman and doctor, that no doubt was thrown on the feasibility of the tree falling."

"Okay. But what about the body? It wasn't Reg!"

"Correct."

"But didn't you have to positively identify him?"

"They tried to put me off doing that but I insisted. I wished I hadn't as there were no features left to distinguish him. The only way to formally identify him was by his teeth."

"But, surely, that would give the scam away?" He stopped and now looked at her. "Reg had trained as a dentist, I think you told me?" She simply nodded. "So you're saying that Reg . . . But, even doing dental work on a body . . . Surely there would still be giveaway signs?"

"If they had a doctor, a policeman and a former dentist working together on this I think they might also have put into place anything else needed to guarantee the success of the scam, enough anyway to overwhelm any doubts a lowly tree surgeon had." He gave this some thought and, eventually, had to agree.

"Would you say then, that this is a gang working together?" She nodded. "But why?"

"Why?"

"Yes! What's the reason? Why would anyone go to these incredible extremes?"

"Now you are at the position I found myself in when I first discovered Reg alive. The difference between you and me being that it took you just over a day, for me it took months. And then there was the period of time it took for me to recover from the fact that he was alive, with the constant thought running around my head, 'why?'"

He took a slug of liquor and leaned back.

She said nothing and they remained silent for a time.

He drained the glass and poured himself another.

"Hell! Do you want one, you must need it?"

"No," she said. "There was a time, a long period of time when I did because I could not face the truth without it, but now my head is clear."

"How the hell is your head clear? Mine is buzzing!"

"Time Aaron, time is the great healer, and I would ask you keep that in the forefront of your mind."

"I will," he said whilst standing and putting the bottle on the window sill, behind the curtain. "So, how did you find him?"

"Things he did?"

"Reg?" She nodded.

"Reg loved me, of that there can be no doubt. In relationships you can act your way through for a time, but in close proximity to one another for such prolonged periods, the cracks cannot help but poke through if you are merely playing at it. There were no cracks in our relationship for we never stopped laughing, making love, chatting, and watching old movies together. No matter how good an actor you might be, if you do not love the person you are with, after a time you will give yourself away. I know this because of my first so-called marriage."

She seemed a little melancholic and so Aaron waited. The moment passed.

"I suffered a breakdown after Reg's going, and the doctor prescribed heavier and heavier pills for the depression. Problem was that I was drinking, as well as taking double the dosage. Bad move that, but not just for me."

"What do you mean?" Now she smiled a little.

"Reg loved me still and, I believe anyway, could not bear to see me go downhill in this manner and probably die from the effects of drugs and alcohol eventually, so he did things."

"Things?"

"He called me, twice, on the phone. He did not speak, but I heard noises that told me it was him. I also came home one time and was certain that he'd been in the house as some of the pills had been taken; I hadn't changed the locks. He probably assumed I would put it down to forgetfulness due to the alcohol and drugs, but by this time I was playing a game; alcoholic and pill taker to the public, but teetotal and pill-putter-down-the-toilet in private. I was clean, and playing a game of abandonment of life for all to see. I knew Reg well, very, very well and knew he would not just stand by and allow me to destroy my life, not in this way, not if he truly was still alive."

"How did you know for certain he was alive at that time."

"I couldn't be absolutely certain, but I was beginning to believe, seriously, that he might just be."

"So, you just believed he was alive?" She nodded. "But why?"

"The fact that the tree did not fall, it was pulled. That is what led me on to find out the truth of the matter."

She told him that she had inherited money from an insurance policy she didn't even know was in place and, because of that, had also been accused of being a leech by, supposed, one-time, friends in the village. She had spent a year investigating various aspects of his death, during which time the doctor who had pronounced him dead had moved from the area together with the police officer that had been called to the scene. She had enquired where these two professionals had moved to and, after a considerably hard time finding out where they were, also using the talents of Alex who told her that they had definitely tried to hide their tracks, she had sold up and followed them, renting the bungalow opposite the holiday home where Rose and Aaron had stayed.

"It was then that I stumbled upon the single clue that led me to where Reg was."

"Do you mean The Barn we went to this morning?"

"Absolutely," she said.

She told him that, due to the discovery of the policeman's and the doctor's destinations, she had only the area, Cornwall, to go on. Alex, likewise, had drawn a blank, and it was only sitting in a cafe a couple of months later that she overheard a young couple talking about a number plate they had seen on a classic car; a cherished number she recognised. She had excused herself and asked about it and been told that it belonged to a Jaguar XJS.

"LAD 01R."

"LAD?" Aaron said. "Why would he want a plate that said 'LAD'?"

"That was the number plate of a car Reg had as a young man. He spoke of it many times, the R is obviously for Reg. He also told me it had gone to the scrap yard after he'd written it off in the snow."

"If it had been written off how could the number plate be used?"

"I did some checking and, apparently, you can ask for unused, old licence plates to be used on other cars as a cherished number."

"And you thought it might be him?"

"I did a search for it and it turned out the number plate had been bought, and put on his favourite car of all time! And that was what led me to 'The Barn', as it is so imaginatively called, which is where I saw him for the first time since his supposed demise."

"And so, did you find out the reason for the charade, the reason he wanted to disappear in the first place?"

"No, and I am still unsure as to what the whole thing is about. Of course, he stole almost four million pounds from me and that alone could be the reason for the deception, but he had it anyway; I allowed him total power over all our finances which is why he was able to pull the wool over my eyes so easily. But I look at him now and realise, he is not using the money in the way he did when he and I were together. He was flamboyant with cash then and I didn't mind, there was enough of it and it wasn't as if he bought a new jet each year. No, he was living the dream and he was also with me, the love of his life. His lifestyle now is nowhere near as ostentatious, apart from the Jag and the number plate that is, but that always was his dream. He lives a fairly low key, ascetic life and that is why I am still at odds as to why he did it."

Aaron thought for a while. Alki put the kettle on and looked out of the kitchen window. Aaron spoke.

"If you want to disappear then you have to keep a low profile, because if you didn't and were caught by the authorities for any minor misdemeanour, you would be found to be beneath the radar and an investigation would be carried out and all the evidence, dental, medical, DNA would be scrutinized; it would give the game away and he would be caught."

"I agree and so can see, to a certain extent, why his life now is what it is. But it doesn't explain why he did not stay with me, the woman he definitely loved, and continue to spend money, have a good time and maintain the lifestyle he had learned to love so much."

"Didn't you say he spent all the money, or lost it in stocks and shares?"

"That was what he wanted it to seem like but, after numerous forays into that part of his life, we managed to discover it had all gone into offshore banks in dribs and drabs. It definitely was not lost in stocks and shares."

"So if he has it, why doesn't he live the high life?"

"That is the big question, and one that I have deliberated on many times."

"But, tell me, how did finding your husband alive and well after more than a year's searching lead you to Rose and me? Where do we fit in with all that has gone on in your life?"

Alki brought the tea to the table and began to pour.

"I think it's time I showed you a little of what kind of surveillance we have carried out over the last half year, since I have been here."

She picked up her mug and went into the lounge, Aaron followed.

CHAPTER SIXTEEN
Video

She went to the windows and checked each of them, that the curtains were blocking all access from outside. Satisfied, she came to the TV and turned it on together with the VHS player. She then went to the wall and selected a folder, turning to a particular page which she perused for a moment, then, placing the folder back, picked out three separate VHS cassettes. She placed the first one into the machine and came to sit on the settee next to Aaron who sipped his hot infusion with a somewhat amused smile on his face.

"Seaside is it? Bognor Regis with the family?" She ignored the comment.

"This one was taken some five months ago, just after I found out that Reg was alive and kicking and living at The Barn. After waiting and watching for a few weeks, I'd seen one or two things that made me wonder and so I decided to video from then on. This video was about the third day of recording. I think you'll find it interesting."

She pressed play and then sat back to watch, but not just the recording.

The screen came to life with a shaky view of a bush, which the camera was seemingly being pushed through. It eventually opened out, looking on to a high street, the main focus being the public house opposite.

"The couple you will see had come to stay in the apartment you and Rose occupied, about four months before you. Notice their age, height, weight and hair colour, but then keep looking to left of frame." Aaron nodded without taking his eyes from the screen, all trace of a smile now gone.

He waited only a while and then saw a couple approaching the pub from right of screen. The camera zoomed in and he could make out they were around late thirties, early forties. She had blonde, very curly hair and wore big round sunglasses, sight of the female being mostly blocked by the man whose arm she held. He was a little taller and dark haired, sunglasses raised on to the top of his head. They walked into the bar, the man opening the door, allowing her to go in first. Aaron kept looking, shifting his gaze to the left now. Straightaway there appeared two men. He gasped and sat upright.

"That's your husband!" he cried.

"It is," she said, leaning forward and ejecting the tape, quickly replacing it with another. "This happened almost two months ago."

She pressed play and instantly Aaron recognised the first pub he and Rose had visited, just down the road from their holiday apartment, the Wyndsor Arms. He watched and saw another, similar couple in almost all respects to the previous couple, come into shot and then go into the pub. This time there were no other people following them in and he turned to Alki. She was watching him.

"Keep looking. You'll see a car shortly."

He looked back and saw, almost immediately, a Jaguar XJS pass slowly in front, both occupants looking to their left, peering into the pub itself.

"What the hell is going on Alki?" he asked. She stopped the tape, ejected it and again replaced it with another.

"This one took place only a week before your, er, incident." She pressed play.

The shot came up and he recognised the interior of her car. The camera slowly rose above the dashboard to reveal another pub.

"That's the Lavender Screw," he said softly.

"It is Aaron." She still sat back watching his reaction. He remained rooted to the shaky image.

He could hear the throb of a car engine and yet the screen shot was of the pub's front door at twilight. He heard the engine turned off and two car doors being shut. A couple walked into view from the right and with their backs to the camera. They linked arms and headed for the door.

"That's the same girl as the first one," he said.

"Yes, we thought so too," she answered, never taking her eyes off him.

They watched as the couple entered the pub and Alki reached forward for the remote.

"I have to fast forward here for a short while, but you'll see why in a minute."

"It seems to me that they were eyeing up each individual couple, to see which one of them fitted the bill."

"We also thought the same Aaron."

"But for what?" He looked at her but she didn't answer. "And why did the same girl appear twice? Because that wasn't the same man."

"Watch now Aaron and see what happens." She pressed the button and the image flickered back to normal speed.

He watched and the seconds ticked by.

Another couple came into view and they entered the pub. Seconds later a man entered screen from the left and went in also.

"See anything?" she asked.

"Nothing, only the couple, and the man after them going in."

"Watch again, only this time ignore the couple, they are of no significance, just concentrate on the man."

He waited as the tape was rewound.

The couple went in again and the man came into view. Aaron watched him disappear into the pub and turned to face her.

"What am I looking for?" he asked.

"Watch again," was all she said.

This time he saw something.

"Hey. That's . . ." He stopped.

"What?"

"It's your bloody husband!"

"Correct! He'd donned a disguise, but if you know him, and you are getting to know him Aaron, there are things that give him away. Now watch as he comes back out, two minutes later."

She fast forwarded again and pressed play.

They both watched as Reg came back out and stood in the pub doorway, looking left then right. He had a moustache and glasses, and seemed to walk in a different manner. He stepped out after a short while and turned as the first couple emerged together. They stopped and spoke, all three, for only a few seconds and then, Reg, after shaking hands with the man and hugging the woman, walked back out of shot to the left, the couple clinging to each other as they walked back to their car.

"They are obviously very familiar with each other," Aaron said as she stopped it playing and took the cassette out. "They were in cahoots it seems, and looking for a prime candidate it would appear. But for what reason?" Alki nodded in agreement.

"That is the main question, and one we do not yet feel we have the complete answer to. Let me show you a little more of our observations since we have been here. Maybe that might shed a little more light on the subject?"

The afternoon was spent entirely on video tapes, and Aaron saw many different couples, mostly around the same height and weight as himself and Rose, some with longer or shorter hair, others with different hair colour, but all being followed at some stage or other by her ex-husband or some other person that she would point out from time to time.

It was well into the afternoon that Alki began to change tack.

"Most of the people you've seen went on from the pub and we followed a lot of them. But most was during the day, and this is what I want to show you now."

She picked out and placed a stack of tapes next to the player, inserting one of them. She pressed play.

It showed one of the couples he had seen before, coming out of the pub. Then the camera cut to a narrow country road where the hedges were high. It was about this time that a small red van came around the bend and slowed as it passed them. Almost instantly a huge tractor followed in its tracks, and the shaky camera caught sight of the couple leaning into the hedge as the vehicle passed.

Aaron expressed concern, then fell silent as Alki loaded the next tape.

A similar thing occurred, with the van coming into view and the tractor quickly following, the couple captive in the hedge row until both vehicles passed.

It took four more similar showings before Aaron turned to Alki, stiff jawed.

"Have you got one of these with Rose and Me?"

"I have Aaron."

He turned fully to her now and looked hard at her. She returned the look, but with a soft compassion.

"Are you really telling me that you have footage of the death of my wife?"

She did not respond, still facing him.

"You could have shown this in court." His voice was soft and a little shaky. "I think videos and such are not admissible as evidence but it would have been an eye opener."

"Trust me."

"Trust you? Here you are about to show me evidence of something which happened in my life that has virtually taken any kind of life I ever had and destroyed it, and you say 'trust me'?"

"One more time, please."

He turned away from her, obviously fighting hard to keep his emotions in check. He nodded and spoke.

"This picture you are building for me Alki." He tried to face her but could not. "It is taking on a more and more hellish look with each piece you put into place."

He indicated for her to get the tape.

She didn't speak, her eyes moistening as she took a single cassette from the wall and placed it into the machine. She went to say something but thought better of it. She sat next to him, leaned back and pressed the button. The TV came to life.

It showed a couple, Aaron and Rose, coming out of their apartment, full of joy with laughter and jollity dominating.

She saw him twitch, and heard a rushed intake of breath.

He watched.

He saw himself and his wife, backs to the camera, turn onto the road, head into the village and turn left up the hill, the lane becoming narrower and narrower.

The red van came round the corner and they both lent in to the hedge, then . . .

The images became a blur for Aaron but he could make out, or at least it seemed, that he was thrown into the hedge.

The tractor hit her!

He blinked through teary eyes and shook his head.

"Again!" His voice was husky. Alki rewound the tape.

He watched a second time and saw the tractor make impact. This time he held the tears, almost.

She rewound the tape at his urging and pressed the button once more.

He stood now and watched again, this time intently, and then yelled as if to berate the world. He mouthed furies at hell and cursed god forever. He sat, then stood and cursed again, and again. He apologised, then held his face in his hands and turned to left then right. He cried, though yelling bitter recriminations at everyone he knew, and those he didn't.

Alki sat, in tears also, as he slumped to the floor and bellowed oaths through a flood of tears which could not be stemmed.

CHAPTER SEVENTEEN
Revelation

"Alive?"

Alki had risen, poured a drink and handed it to him. He refused, using several expletives.

A few minutes later he stood and shook his head, as if to free himself from something. He turned to Alki and spoke.

"There is no mistake here, is there, no contrivance?" She could see, even through the drying tears that he was hopeful.

"No," she said, simply.

"Fine," he said. "Show it me again!"

She rewound the tape and pressed the button.

He watched as a couple left their flat in the morning, turning right and going past the Wyndsor Arms.

The video then jumped to them going uphill.

Aaron slid off the settee and now perched close to the screen.

He watched as a red van, exhaust blowing, turned the corner uphill. He saw the couple move to the side, into the hedgerow as the van slows and gives them a wide berth, passing with almost two feet to spare, and then speeding off downhill. He saw the couple spring back into the road, both still smiling and joking as a tractor turns the same corner and bears down on them, at speed.

He watches the woman turn and see the vehicle as the man is pushed into the hedgerow. The tractor drives past him; the woman runs ahead of it but turns, almost the instant the tractor hits her.

Aaron moves closer to the screen. Alki sits forward now, eyes firmly on him.

He sees the woman grab the bar at the front, as she is dragged beneath the engine and the vehicle hurtles on. Brakes seem to be applied and the woman thrashes as she is pulled along. He sees a shape fall, to be dragged under the rear tractor wheel and crushed, as the vehicle comes to a halt.

Aaron now watches even closer and sees the driver clamber forward, and then jump down from the top of the engine.

He sees him reach down.

He sees him pull the woman clear!

He sees her stand, hug him, then go through the hedge to the right, taking something from beneath the tractor with her!

Aaron slowly stands up as Alki turns the tape off. He walks to the window, turns and faces her.

She sees that he is no longer emotional but taut, his body shaking, eyes flicking this way and that, his mind working feverishly to make sense of what he has just witnessed.

"I have never wanted, ever, to take a human life . . ."

She remained sitting, perched on the edge of the settee. She felt for him but knew he had to deal with this himself, in his own way and at his own pace.

"Would it be alright for me to have that drink now Alki?"

"Of course." She got up and took it to him, pouring one for herself. She remained standing as he sipped, obviously reliving the whole event, questioning each segment as it flashed through his mind.

"She's alive?" He said, and downed the remainder in one. "I don't know which is worse now, knowing she died horribly, or knowing she didn't!"

Alki took a sip and refilled his glass. He sipped again without acknowledging.

"Why?"

Now she spoke.

"This is what we have to discover Aaron." He nodded in agreement but she could see his head was elsewhere. "With your help, together with the information I have garnered over the time this has been going on, we shall find their reasons and their goals."

He nodded in agreement and sipped the alcohol.

They stood like this for almost an hour, refilling glasses and speaking occasionally. She could see he needed time and so gave it, not speaking unless he asked her something, listening to him when he made a statement but answering only if it were required. Three glasses later Aaron finally smiled at her.

"I think it's time I looked my wife in the eyes," he said, and went back to the video player. He turned it on and rewound the tape, sat on the coffee table close to the screen and pressed play.

He came to the part where the tractor emerged. He saw her run, then turn to face it, grabbing the bar across the front and allowing her body to be dragged under, suspended with both hands gripping the bar. He stopped the tape, rewound it and played it, again and again until he was sure she did not get dragged beneath the vehicle!

She didn't!

Now he allowed it to run on.

He saw her grab the bar and dragged underneath, the tractor still travelling forward. He stopped and replayed that section too, again and again.

He allowed it to run on.

Whilst suspended, holding onto the bar, he now could make out she was kicking something beneath the engine to her left. Something gives and a shape falls, being pulled under the rear wheel on the offside. He rewinds again and plays. Sure enough, there seemed to be a package of sorts, a large package, strapped beneath the engine of the vehicle. He watches again as she kicks and, apparently, frees the object which then falls in the path of the right rear wheel.

He stops the tape and stands. Alki proffers a glass but he refuses. He murmurs a few things she can't make out and then returns, to play it again; two more times.

He allowed it to run on.

He sees the package dislodged, fall, and the wheel crush it as the vehicle judders to a halt. The driver appears above the engine and begins to scramble over, jumping down in front. The woman begins to pull herself forward, dragging her legs out from under the vehicle. The driver now helps her and she stands. Aaron sees her smile at him, gives a hug and then scrambles through the hedge to her right, taking some sort of paraphernalia with her that had been beneath the vehicle.

He stops the tape and grimaces as he rewinds.

"She knew him," he said. Alki nodded. "She liked him!" Alki simply looked away.

He played it several more times, scrutinizing each of the sections.

He could now make out the contraption under the tractor, which had been used to carry what he now knew to be another body, probably dead. It was swiftly unfastened and the woman took it with her when she disappeared through the hedge. He shook his head several times as he played this section over and over again, bleary eyed and tearful.

He allowed it to run on.

As the woman left, through the hedge, he saw the driver begin to shout with emotion, though his body language was completely without. He saw him look beneath the stationary tractor and heard a male voice from the other side.

"It's me . . . It's . . ."

Aaron heard his own voice and fell backwards.

CHAPTER EIGHTEEN
Anger

He awoke in the morning, a pillow beneath his head and a soft quilt covering his body.

His shoes and socks had been taken off but, apart from that, he'd slept fully clothed.

It was still dark but the dawn was not far off. He looked around and straightaway saw Alki asleep on the settee, a bedspread covering her.

He quietly got up and crept out to the kitchen, noting the empty bottle of whiskey on the floor.

He put the kettle on, sat at the table and began to put the previous day's revelations into sequence in his head.

He thought back to the previous day, early morning, which had revealed Alki's husband who had not died after all, but faked his death and moved quickly away to another part of the country to make the facade complete; yet, it seemed, without thought of the unique expertise of his wife. Aaron's smile was wry.

Then he had been informed that his wife's death might not have been accidental, and that Alki's ex-husband might also have been instrumental in her death. And also to find out that there might be a recording, a video recording of his dear wife's demise, only to find out that, not only was she not dead after all but that she had been complicit, together with at least the driver of the tractor, in plotting her own, fake death.

He now mused over these things and only became aware he had shouted when Alki appeared at the door to the lounge.

"How are you Aaron?" she asked.

"Not dead," he answered, getting up to make the tea. "And that's about as good as it gets today!" He put the kettle on again, realising it had boiled long ago.

They breakfasted after showering and Alki asked the question again.

"How are you, really?"

He looked at her and shook his head.

"I feel . . . Like I've been . . . I haven't the words."

"I understand," she said. "But I can say these words Aaron, for I have been there. I know what you mean!"

"Do you?" He questioned. "Well, how about this then." He seemed angry at her. "I feel like I have just been . . . Just been damn well raped!"

"I see."

"Do you? How could you 'see'?" he shouted a little. "I have just seen my wife come to life in front of my eyes, only to see her hug the man who had driven over her and who had playacted to me the sorrow that he had killed the only creature on this planet that I gave a damn about!"

"Yes. I felt that anger also."

"What?"

"With my husband. When I saw him alive, for the first time after his supposed death, the first thing I wanted to do was kill him!"

"But you saw him! I haven't seen my wife. I still don't know she actually is still alive! What if they have killed her? What if the plan was to kill her with the tractor, eh? What about that?"

"We saw that they planned everything, not to kill her but to make it seem as if they had. They knew what they were doing."

"What if they killed her afterwards? As a safeguard maybe, to destroy all evidence!"

"Go to all that trouble, just to kill her afterwards?" She looked at him. He did not seem impressed. "It is possible Aaron," she went on. "But not truly probable although, I admit, it was a calculated risk!"

"It was a risk you had no right to take. They might have wanted to kill her and so you had no right to play god and decide they wouldn't!"

"My husband's 'death', the fact that he emerged alive made it the right course of action to take."

"Your husband's supposed death could have been a one-off trick that he and his compatriots played to get them into a position which you know nothing about, and so Rose could have been set up to die. You had no right Alki!"

She could see he was getting more and more upset.

"You didn't have to show me Alki. You could have moved me into it a little more easily than that!"

"I could, and I could have walked away and never shown you anything, allowing you to wallow in self-pity inside a bottle. Instead I gave you a chance to live again, through pain and suffering, yes, I admit that. But at least now you know the truth and you can choose to do something about it, or just walk away."

"I never realised someone I thought I knew could be so evil as to fake her death, especially in so elaborate a manner."

"My husband also did such a good job on me that, like you, I bought it hook line and sinker. If not for him loving me as much as he did, and me acting on the fact that he did love me, I might well still be in the dark."

"But you said it was all luck! You only made yourself believe he had called and hung up, and also let himself into your apartment to take the pills away that were killing you?"

"True. I did realise, in hindsight, that there was a lot of wishful thinking going on. But there was one thing that was just too coincidental, and it was this one thing that made me think. It was this that led me, eventually, to him."

"What?"

"Something that only I would see; something that was peculiar to just Reginald."

"Peculiar?"

"Something that he always did, probably without even knowing he'd done it." She thought for a moment. "For instance, he would always leave the toilet seat up."

"Most men do that Alki."

"Hmmm, I'd noticed."

"Sorry."

"But there was one thing he did that was peculiar to him, just him, because I have never known anyone else that did it. It was something that happened in his throat prior to speaking, but only on the phone. He never did it at any other time. Even when I pointed it out to him he dismissed it. He never seemed to realise he did it, but he always did; and that is what I heard at two distinct times on the phone, and then the phone went dead."

"Really?"

"Oh yes."

"Do you think that's enough to go on?"

"I have never heard you do it. But more than that because, ever since that time, I have listened specifically for that sound whenever anyone has called me, or when I have heard someone else make a phone call. I have not heard that sound since. It was him Aaron, and only I know it."

"Well, if you're sure." He didn't seem to think it held water.

"Rose must have had some idiosyncrasies?"

"Well, she never left the toilet seat up if that's what you mean?"

"Of course not, she was a lady."

"She was, but how do you know that?"

"I knew her Aaron. I got to know you both." He nodded, then dropped his head. "There had to be something about her, the way she did things that you, only you would be aware of?" He looked up at her.

"I would imagine you are probably right. But I can't seem to think of any at this moment in time because all that I want to do is watch that tape again, only this time to see the damn tractor actually, really, run over the bi . . ."

He fell silent but held on to himself. She said nothing.

"I could have been convicted of murdering her. You had the evidence to prove I didn't! Why didn't you bring this out at the trial?"

"I could have Aaron, but if I had then I would have come into the spotlight and my investigations into why my husband did what he did would have all been for nought. They would have seen me you see, become aware that I was on to them and then evade me and all my attempts to find them from then on."

"This was murder Alki! I could have been sent to jail for a very long time. Only this tape could prove I was innocent! You could have given it to the police, they would have taken it on from there."

"They had the young police constable working for them, we know that, but Alex reckons that they must have had someone else working as well in the Force and so, had I given it in, there was a serious chance for it to have gone missing, or been lost."

"Lost! You could have made a copy!"

"The problem was Aaron, that I would have given away my presence. They would have questioned the whys and wherefores concerning the existence of a video of this accident, and so it would not have stopped there. My cover would have been blown in no uncertain terms. So I waited for the verdict and you were not convicted, and so my decision to wait was vindicated."

"Yes, at the possible cost of my going to jail!"

"If it's any consolation Aaron, I would have mailed several copies to the media in the event you were found guilty. It would have destroyed my chances of finding out what was going on, but I would have given up that opportunity and not have stood by and watched you go to jail for something I knew you hadn't done."

Well, that's a comfort I must say." Alki thought he was being sarcastic.

"Have you ever thought that you might be just a small cog in a much bigger machine Aaron?" she asked. "I too, might be just a small part of a wider, farther reaching scam? My Husband's elaborate scheme to fake his death, move away whilst hiding from the world and then begin all over again, far away from the first charade and set up another, even more elaborate fake death, says something to me that I believe you have not yet considered."

She could see that Aaron had listened attentively and now, after a short period of silence, his jaw slowly relaxed. She continued.

"I believe that all this, my husband's fake death, your wife's fake death, is part of something bigger, far bigger than the likes of just you and me."

"If so, then how could they have let themselves be found out by 'just' you?"

She saw the lost look again on his face and paused awhile.

"Alex." She said, her voice a lot softer now. "Whilst I did a lot of the detective work myself, I did not do it all alone. If not for my ex brother in law I would not, could not be here where we both find ourselves at this time. He was instrumental in many ways, at crucial times and also in piecing it all together. He went to the court case in my stead, when there were people there that would have recognised me. Without his expertise, my ex-husband would have got away with it, and so would Rose! A good man, despite what people say. You'd like Alex."

"So, what do people say then, that I should like him in spite of?"

"He's an ex copper, but he got mixed up with some illegal stuff when he was in the force and was booted out because of it, that's all."

"So: ex-husband; ex-brother-in-law; ex-copper? It seems there are more ex's in this than you can shake a stick at."

"He is a good man Aaron," she said. "Alex is very skilful, and it was only due to him and his abilities that I found out where the doctor and policeman had gone to."

"Does he not have any ideas what is going on then?"

"He didn't. I've not seen him in a month, but he was invaluable."

"So, he's not helping you now?" She shook her head. "And so," he went on. "If you are right, that this thing is bigger than just you and me, and if we are seen and recognised by them then that would be enough cause for concern for them to fly the coop, and so we would lose any chance of finding out just what the hell is actually going on."

"Correct. I have been lying low now since my husband disappeared. I did not challenge whether or not the body that purported to be my husband was actually my husband. To have done that at that stage would have caused ripples big enough to give them doubts as to their security. The same goes for Rose. If we pose the question and cause an enquiry into whether the body the authorities consider to be her is actually her, before the real truth becomes known they will be alerted and, because they are such a finely tuned unit, will react accordingly and probably disappear. We need to find out what we can find out now, before our investigations alone give them cause to wonder. Once they begin to have concerns, any concerns, they will put escape plans into operation. We have to play this softly softly until we are ready to pounce."

She made some more tea and then sat down opposite him in the kitchen.

"I know it's early on, that you have only just come to terms with the knowledge that your wife is still alive." He looked up at her and shook his head. "I know you must think me callous Aaron, but there is a reason for haste. I would not have sprung all this on you in so short a time if there weren't."

"What's the problem now? Why the haste? Your husband faked his death and buggered off; my wife faked her death and buggered off! Alright, they both nicked a lot of money off us but I couldn't care less, and I don't think you could either. I just think I'm better off without her, and so are you if you want my opinion!"

"I understand the anger but I need you to understand that the anger will fade, you will get past it, and when you do you will want answers. The reason I need you to reach that understanding now, which is months before I ever did, is because they are on the move and if we do not find out what is going on in the next few days we will probably have lost our chance forever."

He didn't speak but looked up at her, a slight frown still on his face.

"They will move swiftly and silently, and I do not think we will be blessed with luck in the same manner or amount that I received the last time."

He took a moment to think. She waited, never taking eyes off him. She heard him curse and saw a tear fall. He wiped it roughly away and turned to face her, jaw stiff, strength now in his eyes.

"So, what makes you think they are moving?" he asked. "And could you please explain to me just who 'they' are?"

She began to do his bidding.

CHAPTER NINETEEN
Videos

"Okay." She now sat down at the table and leaned forward. "Towards the end of the trial I was here – Alex was at the trial taking notes and taping it – and I kept the terrible twins under surveillance most of the time. I was there before they went off in the morning and also when they came back at night, about nine pm."

"Alright. Terrible twins? Who the hell are we talking about?"

"Sorry. Terrible twins? Reg and his younger compatriot from The Barn."

He laughed a little at her feverish manner. He could see she was incensed.

"Give me the cast list Alki," he said, not ungenerously. "Let me know who all the players are in this murder mystery. You're Sherlock and I'm Watson, that's a given. Now, who the hell's playing Moriarty, Moran and the rest of the baddies?"

She now laughed too, realising how intent she must have seemed.

"Forgive me. This matter has been a constant for me, in my life now for more than two years. I know all the players inside out."

"I understand Alki. So, who are we dealing with?"

"Reg seems to be the head. The young man you saw at The Barn yesterday, his name is Toby; Alex is almost certain that he's the policeman they used in Norfolk and here although now he must either be on a sabbatical, or left the force because he seems to be no longer active as a copper. The tractor driver, his name is Luke, is a player as well. I have seen him a number of times at The Barn, and he was also at the trial." Aaron nodded in agreement. "Now there is also Rose, whom I have not yet seen anywhere since she supposedly died."

"Didn't you mention others such as a doctor and dentist?"

"The dentist is Reg. As I told you, he went through the whole dentistry training then flunked the exam, long before we got together. The doctor is in this area, but he seldom appears. It seems he is brought in only when needed, as in the case of your wife's supposed death."

"That seems logical. Any more in the gang?"

"That's the lot, at least as far as I know."

"Thanks. That clears a few things up. So what's it all about Alki?"

"I don't know, but the answers are there for us to find, so we have to look for them together."

"So, where do we start?" He smiled at her and she smiled back.

"How do you feel Aaron, really?"

He could see she was in earnest.

"I'm sorry if I unnerved you, I'm sorry too if I frightened you. Rose was my life, and so finding out she was a lesser person than I knew her to be is a punch in the stomach, the like of which I've never experienced before."

"I can only tell you Aaron that, to date, you have exceeded all my expectations." She glanced at him. He now looked back at her. "Yours has been a journey of very quick and numerous revelations. You have handled them extremely well. I knew it would be difficult, for I went through similar revelations, but mine were over time, yours have come thick and fast and I have only admiration for the way you are handling yourself."

He still looked at her, now with a faint smile.

"Thank you Alki, that's very gracious of you." His smile faded. "I shan't pretend it's been easy and yet I'm anxious to know more, although, it seems, the more I know the more questions emerge."

"It was the same for me with Reginald, the situation I found myself in was unbelievable. The difference between us is that I found out over time, a significant amount of time compared to you, and so I had the benefit of easing into it a bit at a time; but I was on my own. You have found out very quickly, but with someone who cares alongside you. Having been where you are approaching now in your head, I would almost certainly choose your route. I know that what I say will have little value for you at this time because I know where you are and how you feel. But time will give you the space you need, for you to heal, and you are a young man and so you will heal, especially with me to aid you in whichever way I can."

He listened and looked her in the eye, but didn't speak.

"Rose's idiosyncrasies might help in our search for clues?"

"If you say so," he said.

"Could we review the tapes?"

He seemed at a loss.

"If you think we might benefit."

"It's a good place to start. It might trigger something."

"Okay," was all he said.

She showed him two tapes

The first tape showed a couple walking into view and going into the Wyndsor Arms, followed by two men, one of which was Reg.

The second tape showed a couple walk into the Lavender Screw followed by a man they knew to be Reg.

Aaron recognised both video's from before.

"Do you remember me saying that the women were the same in each video?"

"I do."

"Look closely."

She played them both again and he watched intently. He shook his head.

"Can we play them again?"

She did so and he moved closer, sitting once again on the coffee table.

He watched the couple come into frame from the right, and then went into the pub, the man opening the door for her. The second tape was played and he scrutinized that also. He saw Alki's husband, in disguise, and then the couple emerge, the woman hugging Reg.

Alki was watching him and now leant forward as Aaron slumped a little.

"What do you see?"

"Is that Rose?" he asked, with a shake of the head.

"I think so." She answered him.

"The dates on the tape are correct?" She told him they were. "Then that means she came down here a month before we both did as a couple, and a week before as well. What does that mean Alki?"

"Have you got your diary with you?"

"No, but I think I might be able to link the dates." He looked at the calendar on his phone and checked. Slowly he nodded. "I was away, both times. The weekend one we went paintballing, it was a lad's weekend, and the one midweek was Charles's divorce do, we all stayed the night at his." He shook his head. "Why?" He seemed at a loss as he checked his calendar again. "She said she was with Sonia, both of those times. What the hell was she doing down here?"

"I think she came to do dummy runs to the lead up to the actual 'accident'. We have footage that shows other couples, on different roads, but also the same road you were on, with the tractor hurtling past them and their reaction."

"What good would that do them, with different couples, it was me and Rose the scam was all about?"

She didn't answer him straightaway.

"Aaron. Let me show you the tape where your wife is supposedly hit by the tractor."

He agreed, a little reluctantly.

She let it run for him and he seemed unimpressed. She showed him again, pointing out the precision needed to grab the rail, and also to kick the body free to be crushed by the wheel of the tractor.

"In order to carry out this stunt, because stunt it is, it had to be practiced many times. I firmly believe that Rose came here at least twice, probably more, in order to familiarise herself with the stunt and so minimise any chance of an accident when it needed to be performed."

"Performed?"

"It has all been a performance Aaron, the tractor stunt is just the pinnacle. One thing I believe, though, is that the body was probably released by the driver. It seems that, despite all the training, it still went wrong and needed your wife's quick thinking to make the body fall."

"How do you make that out?"

"The kicking we see her do. It was obvious that the release mechanism had stuck so she improvised, and it worked."

"She always knew what to do, she always had a solution to any problem."

"She seemed to be a very clever girl, your Rose." He looked at her with narrowed eyes.

"Hardly 'my Rose,'" he said. "His probably!" She could hear the unmistakable tremor in his voice and saw him turn away from the screen.

"Why do you say that Aaron?" She asked. He simply shook his head. "Do you believe she didn't love you?" He turned to face her.

"Oh, come on Alki!" he said. "I'm not seven!"

"I know this will sound insane but, despite what Reg did, I firmly believe he still loved me then."

"How can you say that?" He shook his head and looked down. "He orchestrated his own death to leave you, as did she." He pointed at the flickering image paused on the screen.

"Yes she did, but there might be more than just that fact." He looked up at her with a frown. "We know they both did it, but why, if they loved us that is?"

"She might have loved, but not me; him probably!" He pointed again at the screen.

"She knew him Aaron, obviously, but I doubt she loved him."

"She hugged him!"

"Yes, she hugged him." She rewound the tape a little. "But look what happens after the hug." She pressed play.

The tape resumed and they saw Rose helped from under the tractor, she then hugged the driver, spoke and left.

"What did she say?" Aaron asked.

"What do you think she said?"

"Probably, 'I love you'!"

"Do you think she hated you Aaron?"

"She can't have loved me, not when she goes and does something like this!"

"Like Reg did you mean?" He looked at her but said nothing. "Reg didn't hate me, and I don't think Rose hated you."

"What makes you so sure?"

"Her actions."

Aaron threw his hands into the air, looked to the heavens and then faced her.

"She plans her death, comes down here several times to practice it, keeps me completely in the dark and then throws herself underneath a moving tractor! Her actions?" Alki held his gaze. "Then lover boy helps her up, she hugs him, whispers sweet nothings to him and buggers off, leaving me to believe she died the most horrible death imaginable!"

Alki could see the deep emotion welling up inside him, close to engulfing the man. She paused awhile, allowing the moment, and giving the man space to breathe.

He seemed to fight his feelings and slowly brought them under control.

"What do you think she said to him Aaron?"

"I don't know; I don't really care!"

"I think she said, 'take care of him'."

Aaron looked at her and went to speak, stopped, then shook his head.

"I do, but look for yourself."

She rewound it again and played.

He watched and rewound it, then watched again. He did it once more and then slowed the replay, going through it frame by frame at times. He eventually stopped and turned it off, not speaking.

"I think she did care Aaron." He didn't seem to want to agree with her. "Look at this." She turned the video player back on and rewound it to the spot where the tractor appeared. "Now, watch," she said, and pressed play.

He watched, as asked, but with little enthusiasm.

She stopped it mid frame.

"Just watch this little bit, closely," she said, and set it going again.

He did as he was asked but saw nothing. She replayed it and now pointed it out to him.

"If you watch carefully you will see she pushes you, so that you fall into the hedge and out of the way of the tractor. She saved your life!"

He shook his head, fighting back tears and looked at her.

"Play it again, please." He sat forward.

Three times it was played, and now a slight smile appeared on his face.

"She did push me, and she told him, whoever the hell he is, to take care of me, at least that's what it seems she said."

"What do you think it means?"

"I'm not sure I . . ."

"Two very separate people go out of their way to make their partner, and the world, think that they are dead! They both choose to 'die' by supposedly being crushed to death. And, on top of all this, they both demonstrate, in no uncertain terms, that they still love their spouse."

"You say she loved me?"

"As Reg did me, it was just that she had a hidden agenda, as Reg did. And it is that agenda we need to access, to find out just what they are doing, and why they did what they have done!"

He sat, close to the screen and looked at the image which flickered there, tears now rising again.

CHAPTER TWENTY
Surveillance

"I did some research, checking Reg's movements, appointments and all places he'd been prior to his 'death'. Nothing bore fruit, apart from his dentist. He'd visited him a month before, and this was of huge interest only because he hadn't told me, and Reg always told me everything."

"What did you find out?"

"He had some dental work done and insisted that the work had been photographed for him.

"Didn't that seem a little odd?"

"It seems not; apparently he always did it." Aaron raised an eyebrow. "Reg had insisted all work done on his teeth be recorded photographically. Reg had told him that, as he'd been a dentist himself, he wanted to check all procedures to ascertain he was getting the best treatment possible; he went private, obviously. But the most telling fact is he didn't tell me he was going that time. He never did that!"

"It doesn't seem that important to me."

"And I understand why." She seemed to pause, hesitant and unsure. "Aaron," she said. "I need to tell you something, and I am hoping you won't be annoyed."

"Just tell me Alki? I doubt you have anything left to say that will make me feel worse than I have felt over these last couple of days."

"Well, I hope not." She shuffled on her seat. "Do you remember me saying that I knew both you and your wife well?" He nodded. "I couldn't have got to know you well, just from the day you came here up to your wife's supposed demise, could I?"

"Seeing as that would be just over a day, I suppose not," he said, a little unsure of where this was going.

"During your trial I investigated your wife," she said.

He looked at her, hard.

"Don't forget, I was privy to all the facts these tapes held, and because of what had come out in those tapes I felt there might be something more in both your pasts that could be of assistance, but specifically Roses."

He nodded now, sat back and listened.

"As I've just explained, I did similar enquiries too when Reg supposedly died, and thought the same might bear fruit with Rose."

"Okay. What did you come up with?"

"She went to the dentists just a couple of weeks prior to coming down here on holiday with you."

"So what does that prove?"

Alki took a moment.

"To prove a person's identity, dental records can be checked."

"I know that Alki, but I still don't get it."

"If we chose to have those two bodies exhumed and their dental records checked, I feel sure that they would match with the dental records of the real people!"

"How? Why?"

"Reg was a dentist, don't forget. I believe he may have carried out dental procedures on those bodies, whilst still alive, to match the records of himself and Rose!"

"So that if they were checked . . ."

"They would match!"

"So, Rose went to the dentist . . ."

"For a check-up, so that the condition her teeth were in at that time, extractions, fillings and all other discernible work, would be recorded."

"So Reg would have matched her teeth in the would-be corpse?"

"Exactly!"

"But what about DNA?"

"The doctor who pronounced Reg dead provided a blood sample for DNA testing, and it proved accurate!"

"So he did a switch!" Alki nodded. "But if we have a DNA test done on the bodies, have them exhumed, it will prove they are not Reg or Rose!"

"Only if their DNA had been registered before their death; Reg's had, but Rose's hadn't."

"You even checked that out?"

"I try to be thorough Aaron."

"So, having the bodies exhumed would not be the way to go it seems."

"I am so glad you are of an intelligent nature Aaron," she said. "That way would seem reasonable, until you begin to untangle it and understand the kind of people you are up against. That is the very reason they took these precautions."

He smiled at the praise.

"Then what is the right way forward?"

"We follow the terrible twins?"

"The terrible twins? But they go separate ways, or so you said."

"They do," she replied. "Can you ride a motorbike?" He now smiled at her.

"First driving test I ever took!"

CHAPTER TWENTY-ONE
Chase

They stood together in the garage, the motorbike having been revealed.

"Where did you get the Morris and the Bantam?"

"They were my uncle's, from my Father's side."

"Did you not think they might be traceable?"

"How do you mean?"

"You traced Reg because of his treasured number plate, and the classic car he loved, would not he do the same with these classic vehicles?"

"Oh, I see. No, he didn't know about them." Aaron looked at her, puzzled.

"He didn't know about these beautiful, vintage vehicles?"

"Oh, no! I didn't even know about them myself until Reg 'died'."

Aaron smiled, but looked at her for explanation.

"My father had them when his brother died and my brother had them after father passed away, and it wasn't until Reg left, or died whichever you prefer, that he gave them to me."

"Why was that?"

"They both disliked Reg and, before Daddy passed, he told Baddie, apparently, to keep the Morris and the Bantam for me, only me not Reg you see, and so when Reg died he gave them over."

Aaron was shaking his head and smiling.

"I'm sorry; Baddie?"

"Yes. He got the Austin though, and the Bonnie so he didn't lose out."

"Bonnie? Baddie? Would you care to enlighten me?"

"Sorry. Triumph Bonneville. So much better than the Bantam, but don't tell Alex I said so."

"Fine. Another motorbike. Baddie?"

"Oh yes, I forgot to tell you. Baddie, or Bad boy which he ridiculously prefers, is my brother, younger brother."

"I take it that is a nickname?"

"He was named Obadiah as a child, and so Bad boy became his chosen nickname. I call him Baddie."

"I'm not surprised. Couldn't he have used his second name instead?"

"Doesn't have one. Father deemed four syllables more than enough for any child."

"Was he religious, your father?"

"No, just a wicked sense of humour."

"Couldn't he have changed it, when he was older I mean?"

"He got used to it, and he adored my father and so would never have discarded his given name."

"Wicked sense of humour eh, just plain wicked sounds more credulous." He looked at her now, smiling a little. "So what's your middle name, or was too syllables more than enough for a female child?"

"No, he supplied me with the full four." She turned away and drank tea. He waited a while.

"So, we're not going to be allowed knowledge of this precious two syllable add-on then?"

She laughed, and beckoned for him to come closer.

"My father told me that when I was born he held me up and I pee'd in his hand. He, apparently, then said, 'what a lovely little drip'. And so, because of that unfortunate accident he gave me the second name, Venus."

"That's a lovely name, and it fits."

"Don't start that again!" He held his hands up.

"So what is wrong with Venus?"

"Nothing really, or even Ilka Venus, but when my father used to say it, mistakenly he lied, it came out as 'intravenous' and then he would add 'Drip' to make the joke complete."

Aaron thought for a brief two seconds and laughed out loud.

"Intravenous drip! I think I would have liked your father."

"You would, until he found something about you he could twist or manipulate and then you might not have found him so . . . humorous!"

She smiled at him, drank her tea and made her way back into the house.

Morning saw them gone before the dawn, Aaron following her on the Bantam as they headed for The Barn.

After discussion the night before it had been agreed that she would take the car and follow the younger man, Toby, whilst he would don crash hat and gloves and follow Reg in the XJS.

They both took up their agreed individual positions and, sure enough, just after dawn they began their pursuits.

She was waiting for him at the rendezvous point just over an hour later as he parked up the Bantam and went to sit in the Morris.

"I lost him almost immediately." Aaron nodded, as if understanding. "I got to the roundabout but he'd gone! How did you fare?"

"I followed Reg to the third roundabout which is where I lost him. I can locate him from there tomorrow I think." He didn't sound convinced.

"Do you really think this is the best way Aaron?" she asked.

"We need to find out where they go each day."

"What if we can't though, they are both very fast?"

"The Barn is the only logical place to look next."

"I'm a bit rusty in the old 'breaking and entering' protocols," she said. "But if needs must."

"What about looking at the property's ownership, and the cars they drive?"

"Already have. The Barn is rented by Toby, and I have checked out the owners whose families have lived in the area for centuries. The cars are both registered in Toby's name as well."

"So, we do need to find out just where they are going."

"We do Aaron, but how?"

"Let's go and hire a fast car, shall we?"

Early the following day saw them each stationed at the roundabouts where they had lost their targets the day before. Alki was in the hire car and Aaron in the Morris, deeming it to be quicker than the Bantam.

They didn't have to wait long before they were once more on their trail.

They got back to the rendezvous point about eight a.m.

"He was just too fast, even for the new car." Alki said.

"Yes, Reg is no slouch either and, even though I did catch him up at the next roundabout due to build-up of traffic, when he got past the roundabout and onto the carriageway he just went. I tried to follow on but there was absolutely no sign of him."

"I didn't even get past the first roundabout!" She shook her head. "I'm not a slow driver as you well know, but he's just blinking nuts!"

"I'm of a mind to rethink our strategy Alki. What do you think?"

"This isn't working and we are running out of time."

He turned to her and smiled.

"All the best stories would now have you declare you have a pilot's licence. Then, we would find the nearest airfield, hire a plane and follow them from the air!"

"I have actually!"

"What?"

"I have a pilot's licence."

"Come on Alki, stop messing about."

"Daddy taught us as youngsters, he taught us lots of things." She smiled a wicked smile. "I used to fly everywhere for Daddy; he had an Auster Arrow."

"Is this a joke? This has to be a joke?"

"No joke. We used to hire a twin engined Cessna - the Golden Eagle I seem to recall - and then fly to France for a few days. He always made me do the take off and land as I was the best at it; Baddie used to get so annoyed."

"Then what are we waiting for. Let's hire a plane and get following them?"

"It's no good. I haven't flown in ten, twelve years. They wouldn't let an old woman up without a serious refresher course, and they probably wouldn't even allow it then due to age."

"Really?"

"I am afraid so Aaron. Reg and I did try when we first married and so, when they presented me with all the red tape we both decided to give it a miss and go by train instead."

"Damn! I really thought we had a way out."

"Sorry."

They settled back and sipped tea from the thermos.

Morning saw them in their respective cars, heading off towards The Barn. They got to the crossroads where they would normally part but Alki stopped, Aaron pulling up behind her.

They got out and stood together, looking in the predawn light at the spectacle ahead of them.

Billowing smoke and flames were reaching high into the air.

"Good god! Do you think that's . . .?"

"Yes I do Aaron. That's The Barn, ablaze!"

CHAPTER TWENTY-TWO
The Barn

The spectacle of The Barn burning furiously in the pre-dawn light had unnerved them.

They had both travelled to the observation point to ascertain it really was The Barn ablaze. It was. There had been no sign of life, no cars on the drive, in fact nothing to suggest that anybody was in or around the vicinity. They heard the sirens and saw the fire brigade arrive; it was then they decided to go back home.

"So, what do we do now?" Alki sat, mug of tea in hand, shaking her head. "I should have expected something like this. They never leave a trail for anyone to follow. I should have realised this could have been on the cards."

"Do you think they suspected we were on their trail?"

Alki shook her head.

"Maybe," she said. "We know how professional they are and so, I suppose, it is a real possibility."

"But, based on your knowledge of these people, which is far in excess of my own, what would be your educated opinion? Have they sussed that we are on their trail, or is this cleansing operation simply a part of their prearranged plan?" He looked at her and waited for a response.

"I'm at a little bit of a loss at this moment Aaron," she said. "They have flown the coop here, as they did in Norfolk." She now looked up at him. "I fear we may have lost them, and also our chance of finding out just what the hell was going on!"

"Surely not Alki; we can't have come all this way just to give up now?"

"I don't know where to go from here," she said. He could see she was drained.

"I know. We just need to approach this from a different angle."

She nodded in agreement, but he could see her heart wasn't in it.

It was after two pots of tea, and a few little kicks of Irish when suddenly a smile appeared on her face.

"We have both registration numbers of the cars, don't we?"

"We do."

"Then why don't we?" She sat forward now. "Why don't we use the reg. numbers of both vehicles and trace them for speeding fines?"

He looked a little unsure.

"They both like to speed? Chances are they might have speeding fines, or even just one of them!"

He seemed to be listening.

"Both cars are in the boy's name. I think it's just a precaution, so that Reg's assumed name doesn't come under undue scrutiny."

"How would we find out if they had been speeding, and what good would that do us?" Aaron asked. "We know their registered address is The Barn already."

"Yes, but because it is an infringement of the law, it would have to state the location the infringement occurred."

"Okay. What then."

"Well, we go and wait at that spot and hope they come by sometime, and then we follow them."

"Alki, I've heard of long shots but, come on."

She looked at him and laughed lightly.

"What would you suggest then, that isn't such a long shot?"

He shrugged his shoulders and raised his eyes.

"So, how do we find out if they have been speeding then?" He said.

"I don't know, maybe Alex would." She said, picking up the phone.

"Thanks Alex," she said as she terminated the call.

"Any luck?"

He reckons there is a way, so he's put his kids onto it and they should be in contact shortly if they find one."

"His kids?"

"Yes. Britney and Ringo are both whizzes on computers apparently."

Aaron didn't seem to be impressed but, less than a minute later, they were both perusing the computer screen, having followed a link that had been sent.

It wasn't long before they found what they were looking for; a traffic violation, a speeding fine, and they could see it was the Jaguar!

CHAPTER TWENTY-THREE
Follow

They arose before the dawn and headed off to the Cornish south coast, approaching a coastal town in the dark and quickly finding the road on which the traffic misdemeanour had occurred. They found a place to park up, slightly away from the road itself and waited for the dawn, with tea being poured from a flask.

They had found that the young man, Toby, had been caught speeding along this road about six weeks ago. He had been issued with a fine and also points on his licence. Alki felt sure that it had been Reg who had committed the crime because it was the jaguar that had been driven, but that he had given the boy's name so as not to draw any attention to himself. Aaron concurred as they sat in the dark, waiting.

Time moved on and the dawn came and went. They still waited, until just after mid-day but neither car appeared, and so they decided to leave it for the day.

The following morning found them in the same place, tea being poured and chat in abundance. They kept the engine on to heat the vehicle and almost didn't see him, but thanks to a bad-tempered motorist blaring his horn which brought their attention swiftly back, they were just in time to see the Jaguar appear in the rear view mirror. They thanked their lucky stars, waited for it to pass then pulled out, leaving three cars in between.

They followed at a distance along the main road, and after about two and a half miles the Jaguar pulled off to the left, heading down to the coast itself on a dirt track. They continued along the A road and pulled up in the first lay-by they came to.

"I didn't think we'd be that lucky," Alki said.

"Me neither," Aaron agreed. "So, what do we do now?"

"Look at the map, see what's down there and work out how we can get close enough to see just what is going on."

They got the map out and found the track the Jaguar had taken, a single lane track which went down to the coast, to a small cove.

"That's going to be tricky, getting a close look at that place."

"I know," she said.

She took out her tablet and, minutes later, they were looking at an aerial view of the coast, and the A road they had been on as well as the little track which led down to the cove, showing a small cottage by the sea.

They scrutinised the Google Earth images and could see the single house quite clearly. It was a small indistinct cove, with only that one little house secluded away out of sight of the main road. There were rising cliffs to the western side, with access to the small sandy beach only by the track the Jaguar had taken, and with another cliff rising up to the east of the beach itself. There was a small car park halfway up the lane, obviously put there for the public to use the beach. After studying the images on the computer screen, and scrutinising the map, they agreed it might be best to go east along the A road from where the Jaguar had turned down, and see if they could find a place to overlook the cove from its westernmost cliff.

They found a place to park at the beginning of a coastal path which led southeast, away from the cove, but that had access to the cliff's edge at numerous points along the walk.

They quickly set off, armed with binoculars, and walked a little way along the path, scooting off towards the edge a few times, eventually finding a spot that overlooked the whole of the small bay, the house and also the bottom section of the drive. It was a secluded spot and so they set up, binoculars coming to hand, giving them their first sighting of the house that was their focus, some four hundred yards away across the golden sand. They could see two cars, the Jag and the Merc convertible, parked at the front of the house.

They spent only a short while there, happy with their new found spying position but with twilight approaching, decided to call it a night.

The following morning found them lying in the same position on the grass before the dawn, binoculars trained. They waited patiently, watching and waiting.

"So where do we go from here?" Aaron asked after a while. "We assume they used to come to this place on the coast every day, and now it looks like they are living here, but why?"

They could see the Jaguar and the sports car parked outside.

"We shall give it a little time Aaron," she said. "At least we have managed to keep with them despite their shenanigans, that is a plus in itself. Let's observe, and allow their actions to dictate ours shall we." Aaron silently agreed and poured the tea.

It was around midday when Aaron called Alki back from stretching her legs, beyond the ridge.

She came quickly, and lay down next to him.

They both could see two people had emerged from the cottage and now they strode out together.

"Jeez!" he exclaimed.

"Keep calm Aaron."

He seemed not to hear.

"It might not be her!" She put her hand on his shoulder.

"It's alright Alki."

She could feel him shudder.

They both now watched as, side-by-side, the couple walked along the beach. Alki could see that Aaron was upset and she now turned to him, but he was riveted to the spectacle being played out before him. He did not turn away and kept the binoculars trained on the couple who now strode out, heading in their general direction but much too far away to pose any threat.

Alki was videoing the events but constantly kept a watch on her companion as he continued to survey the scene.

It was only moments later when he took the binoculars from his eyes and cast his head down that she could see the emotion within, as he now backed away from the edge to stand and walk away. She remained where she was, zooming in as close as was possible on the couple now walking along the beach. She remained there, yet constantly looking behind her.

Alki watched as Rose, together with her own estranged husband, walked along the sand. She felt a little outraged to say the least but continued watching whilst they walked, sometimes arm in arm though mostly separately, yet always chatting. She saw that they had camaraderie of sorts and felt hurt within. This was her husband, albeit for only two years, yet it felt a lot longer than that. She continued to watch as they turned around and headed off back toward the cottage, eventually entering the dwelling and closing the door. She switched off the camera, wiped away a tear and turned to look for Aaron.

He stood by the car and wiped the tears from his eyes as he continually shook his head.

"How are you?" She asked.

"Alright?" He tried to smile at her.

"Do you think we've done enough for today?"

"Oh, I think we might have. Do you think it's time we visited the pub?"

"If you're twisting my arm."

Alki smiled at him and he smiled back, although she could tell it was strained.

She drove, and it was as well she did because Aaron broke down within minutes of them beginning their journey. She tried to comfort him but it seemed as if he was somewhere else within his mind.

It took a short amount of time for Aaron to dig himself out of the pit from which he seemed to be drowning. When he did he turned to Alki and apologised.

"I couldn't believe what I was seeing," he said.

"I understand," Alki nodded. "It is hard Aaron, I know, because I had to go through it as you are now."

"They both seemed to be . . . friendly, Rose and Reg together?"

"They did Aaron, and I also found it difficult to watch as your wife is very beautiful."

"What do you think is happening Alki?"

"I don't know, but I feel sure that we are on the verge of finding out."

They arrived at the pub shortly after and Aaron seemed to be his own self again.

They chatted for a short while but talked about things of little importance. Alki could make out he was still visibly shocked to have seen Rose alive. She could tell that the man needed time to get past this revelation. She ordered more drinks and they drank in silence.

She drove them home where she plied him with Irish whiskey through the evening and chatted about everything unimportant until he fell asleep. She put a blanket over him and whispered her heartfelt wishes that he might get well again, as she departed and went to her room.

She lay on her bed and thought of the day's events, particularly of seeing Aaron's wife and her own husband Reg, together. She remembered the times past, when she had gone through just what Aaron was going through now. She did not know how to help him for no one had been able to help her. She re-lived events in her own life and the pain rose once again. She could do nothing about it this time and so cried silently, with deep emotion.

She didn't know just when she fell asleep.

CHAPTER TWENTY-FOUR
Aaron

"He was gone before I got up, and in the hire car," she said on the phone.

She sat in the Morris and turned the key once again. The engine whirred for several seconds but did not start.

"Just keep an eye out for him. I shall have to use the Bantam because the Morris is dead."

She tried the engine once again and held it on for thirty seconds but still it did not fire. She gave up, closed the bonnet and took the motorbike out of the garage where she kick-started it and left it ticking over. She went back into the house and minutes later came out wearing crash hat and goggles.

She flicked the bike into gear and set off, pulling out of the yard and heading down the main road.

Seconds later another bike pulled out from a house further down from her cottage and headed the same way.

It was still dark.

She sped towards the main road but then cut out to her right along a small track, heading down this route for a few miles, having to avoid regular potholes but keeping up as much speed as was safe to do. Twenty minutes later saw her approaching the seaside cottage from inland, having cut out the dogleg journey she would had to have taken in a car.

A hundred yards before she hit the main coastal road she stopped, took off her goggles and peered out in the dim, pre-dawn light, looking to see if there was any sign of the hire car or Aaron. She didn't see anything and so carried on to the place from where they had observed the cottage the day before.

She got off the bike and scrambled up the bank, binoculars in hand. It was now beginning to get lighter and she surveyed the scene before her. The two cars were there, and a quad bike now sat beside them, but no sign of the hire car or Aaron. She stayed like this for a short while and then scrambled back a yard from the top of the ridge as her phone rang.

"Have you seen him?" She waited only seconds and then scrambled up the bank again, bringing the binoculars to bear. "Inland from the cottage?" She adjusted her view. "I see him!" She cancelled the call, put her phone and the binoculars away and went back to the bike.

Minutes later saw her driving the Bantam off the main coastal road and onto the small track, heading for the sea. Yards before the turn which would reveal the cottage she turned off the road and approached the hire car which was parked at the side of the dune. She stopped the bike, got off and removed the helmet and goggles, leaving them with the bike as she headed round the dune on foot.

She now climbed, approaching Aaron who was lying down at the ridge of the dune.

"I know Alki," he said quietly, without turning. "I was going to simply charge straight in there and ask her all the questions I have in my head, but I stopped myself in time, in favour of observing instead."

"You do realise that if even one of them decides to use a car, for whatever reason, they will come this way, see the hire car and know someone is here?" He seemed to nod in agreement. "They would then climb up here, recognise you and the game would be over."

"I don't really care at this stage; all I want to do is face her."

"I know Aaron, I have been where you are, remember?"

He now turned, coming back from the ridge to stand in front of her.

"I don't know how you can stand it, knowing Reg is in there, after what he has done and is continuing to do to you."

She could see he had been through a lot, and could smell alcohol on his breath. She shook her head slightly and held out her hand to him. He looked and then took her hand in his. It was not hard to see the emotion welling from deep within.

"It is alright Aaron," she said. "You have to do what it takes in order to ease the pain you are feeling at this time." He shook his head and went to speak. She stopped him. "It's alright Aaron," she said again. "Your sanity is more important than our knowledge of their caper."

They stood like this for a short time and she could feel the tremors increase and wain through his fingers. Eventually his fears subsided and he released her hand, his still shaking.

"Come with me," she said, "to a safe distance where we can talk for a while."

Without hesitation he nodded and picked up his bag.

"You must take the Bantam," she said. "Follow me Aaron, and take it easy for you have been drinking. If we encounter the police and they attempt to pull you over, simply go across country to lose them, abandon the bike and call me with your location; I shall come to collect you." He looked at her. "We cannot risk the police incarcerating you at this time for drink-driving. I need you; we need each other." He nodded and gave her the car keys.

Twenty minutes later saw them five miles west of the cove, in a little cafe on the seafront.

She gave him tea and could see that, after a few cups, he was beginning to come back to some semblance of sanity. Shortly after he raised his head and looked at her.

"Sorry," was all he said.

She smiled at him and waved away his apology.

He explained that he'd woken up in the chair and not been able to get back to sleep, and so had mulled over just what he should do after seeing his wife on the sands with Reg. He had drunk again and then slept a little but woke before the dawn, his thoughts riotous in his head. He told her he'd decided then and gone, Irish in hand, with the objective of facing her and gaining the answers he felt he must have. It was only upon reaching his destination that he had stopped and thought again.

She listened to him for over an hour, during which time they breakfasted and drank more tea. They then walked through the streets of the little town, browsing and chatting together until late afternoon. They dined and Alki could see he was recovering, both from the alcohol but more importantly the knowledge he had gained of his estranged wife. They chatted into early evening, eventually heading back to the car and the bike.

They made their way to the observation point, reaching it at dusk where they took up positions on the ridge, binoculars and video camera being employed.

Almost immediately they saw movement.

In the dim light they could see five people, two seeming to be female, come out from the cottage and embark into both of the cars. All lights in the cottage were extinguished and both vehicles headed off up the track.

"Quickly Aaron," she urged. "Run back to the main road and see if they come past this way?" He nodded and ran off.

She turned back and peered at the blacked out cottage through the binoculars. Less than a minute later Aaron came back.

"Both of them came by," he said. "Three in the Jag it seems, and two in the sports job."

"Do you think they'll be going out for a meal?" Alki asked.

"That would be my guess," he said. "Should we go and see? They couldn't possibly recognise the hire car, and in this light they wouldn't see who was inside either."

She agreed.

Five minutes later saw them in the nearby coastal town. They drove slowly through on the coast road and spotted, instantly, the two vehicles parked together on the main road. They parked up and, using the binoculars, began to study the numerous restaurants that ran the length of the main road, through the un-curtained windows. After a while Aaron caught a glimpse of something. He moved the car as Alki now watched, giving instructions until she halted him. There they were, all five of them. Aaron took the binoculars and gasped.

"What Aaron?" He shook his head a little and passed her the bino's. "Is it Rose?"

"Yes, it's Rose. But look at the second female," he said, seemingly shocked.

Alki took up the glasses and brought them to bear.

"I see her," she said. "What about her, she seems a little familiar."

"She would be," he answered. "That's Sonia, Rose's twin sister!"

They turned the vehicle around in silence and headed back.

"They'll be hours," she said. "This might be our best opportunity to have a closer look at where they're living now, don't you think?"

"I do."

"We'll park at our observation point and go down onto the beach and across the sands."

"No. I think we should take the car down."

"What? Down to the house?"

"Yes."

Alki seemed unsure but Aaron began to explain.

"Do you remember the car park at the bottom?" He said. She did. "I almost went into it this morning in the dark, but decided against it when I got there and so parked further up, where you saw it. The car park is for visitors to the bay, and even if Reg, Rose and the others of their little clique came back early they would simply see our vehicle as a sight-seers' car." Alki still seemed unsure. "It's a hire car and not known to them. Besides, it's getting on for half a mile from the house to our viewing point at the far side of the bay Alki," he said. "It would not be a good idea to walk from there and back again; even in this light, anyone who might be watching would definitely see us."

She thought for only a moment and acquiesced.

They drove back along the coastal road and down the track to the cottage which remained in full blackout. There were no cars in the visitors' car park and so they parked nearest to the exit, facing out, and made their way down the final hundred yards to the cottage itself. They approached slowly, listening for any sounds that would indicate occupancy. There were none.

They reached the dwelling and looked in at the window by the front door. The curtains were closed and Aaron tried the door itself. It was locked as he thought it would be. They worked their way around to the back which overlooked the sea. All the windows were curtained and the doors were all secured. They came round the other side where the quad bike was parked and, as they were making their way to the front door again, heard the sound of a car approaching, coming down the track. Alki's phone began to ring as they quickly ran back toward the quad bike and huddled together behind it. She glanced at her phone and rejected the call, turning it to silent in the process.

They could both see a vehicle slowly coming down the dirt track. It was the sports car!

"Damn! What the hell has he come back for?"

They watched as the car came past the car park and slowly approached the house, parking outside the front door. The driver, the young man from The Barn, Toby, got out and surveyed the area, glancing several times back towards the car park. They saw the passenger door open and Sonia emerged, stepping away from the car and looking all around.

Aaron backed them both away from the quad bike, heading towards the sea but keeping the house between them and the vehicle.

"Where are we going?" she asked.

"I don't know," he said in a whisper. "Away from here though."

"Do you think they know we're here?" She asked.

"They know something, and that's enough." He now looked up at the cliff nearest the house as the sound of another car approaching was heard. "That's the Jag," he said, and cursed.

"How do you know?"

"Sound of the engine, unmistakable."

She nodded and looked at him, then up at the cliff face.

"I'll never climb that Aaron," she said, almost apologetically.

"I know," he said, looking this way and that. "And they'll spot us if we go for the car."

"We can leave the car, get across the sands and make our way to the Bantam."

"We could, if I hadn't left the keys in the car," he said.

"Forget that, we'll just hot wire it!" Aaron looked at her in the dark.

"You can do that?" He could see her smile.

"Come on," she said.

They headed off across the sand, Aaron holding her hand.

"We're in dark clothes," she whispered to him. "The moon is partially covered and they have no reason to suspect we might go this way; our chances are good." She saw him nod, but frown also in the faded moonlight.

They were halfway over, and thought they were doing well.

CHAPTER TWENTY-FIVE
Interrogation

Alki and Aaron made their escape across the sands, heading towards the opposite bank where they knew the Bantam to be, even though it was up the steep incline at the end of the beach and almost half a mile away.

They were only halfway across when they heard a motor start-up in the vicinity of the cottage. They looked back and could see headlights switched on and the motor rev as it now began to cross the sands towards them. They hastened on their way, although Aaron could see Alki was not up to this and so he stopped. She would have argued but Aaron held up his hand.

"We can't escape them," he said.

"Then we've lost!"

"We did our best Alki, and there is nothing more either of us could have offered."

The motor got closer to them as they now slowly backed away. They could see it was the quad bike which approached and had two people sat upon it. Aaron placed her behind him as they now stood and waited.

"Alki. I must admit you found us quicker than I thought you would!" They were now in the full light of the headlights.

Aaron held her in his arms as she now turned towards the approaching vehicle.

"All that we know about you and your organisation is on its way to the press as we speak!" She yelled at him.

"Of course it is. I wouldn't have expected anything less!" He answered as the bike reached them and he got off.

Aaron stepped forward, shielding her.

The man stood, silhouetted in the lights of the bike. Alki and Aaron did not move.

He now stepped towards them.

"You've done some damage today Alki," he said. "A lot of good work has gone down the pan thanks to you sweetheart!"

"All we've done is to find out what a low life you actually are Reg!" She shouted.

"That's as may be darling. But we have to carry the can and sort out this mess you have managed to create. So, without further ado, let's get back to the house."

The man driving the quad bike now got off and waved what appeared to be a gun at them, and pointed.

They looked at one another and Aaron could see the fear in her face.

He held her hand firmly as they walked across the sand, back towards the house, being followed closely by Reg and his companion on the bike.

They were ushered through the small back door into the kitchen and made to sit, Reg and his companion whom they both recognised as the tractor driver, Luke, standing opposite. The inner door opened.

Rose and Sonia stepped into the room.

Aaron went to stand but Luke warned against it. Reg put his arm around the younger twin.

"Hi Aaron," Rose said, a slight smile on her face.

"Hello Aaron," Sonia said without the smile.

"I'd like to say it's nice to see you Rose, and you too Sonia, but I cannot lie!" Aaron sat tight lipped, still holding Alki's hand.

"You want me to shut him up?" Luke said, but Rose shook her head.

"He's just confused Luke. Leave him for now. Once we have managed to explain he will understand I'm sure." Rose's face seemed to soften as she looked at her ex-husband.

"Yes, please explain all this to me, I can't wait," Aaron said.

"It might seem, at this stage, there can be no explanation for what I have done." Rose continued. "But, even though you might find it strange, there are reasons for what we, all of us here, are doing, and they are beyond your understanding at this point in time. Providing you listen and you want to know, to understand, then we can explain and we will."

"I doubt, sweet girl, you can say anything to assuage our anger at this moment!" Alki did not seem to be in a mood to be toyed with.

"Let's have a cup of tea," Reg said, and then gestured to Luke to put down the gun. He complied, turned and busied himself with tea making. "At the very least we can be civilised for we are all friends here, even if some of us don't realise this yet." A phone rang. Sonia took it from her pocket.

"Yes sir," she said, and turned away from the assemblage, continuing to talk in soft tones.

"What's it to be Alki, tea or coffee dear?" Reg said. He picked up the gun, smiled and walked towards her.

"Has it been so long Reg, 'Dear'," Alki said. "You know I drink nothing but tea, Assam preferably."

"Oh yes, I'd forgotten that." Reg laughed. "Have we any Assam tea Luke?"

"Tons of it Reggie, though we call it builder's tea!" He now laughed, put four tea bags into the pot and then went across to Sonia who was still on the phone, following her through the inner door.

"Will that do Alki, love?" Reg asked, with a smile.

"Anything to please you, love," she replied with a sombre smile. "Heavy on the arsenic if you don't mind!" She said, almost under her breath.

"Oh come on Alki. I know I must have hurt you but I still, always, looked after you no matter what."

She slowly looked up at him and Aaron saw something appear on her face, in her eyes, that he had not seen before. He squeezed her hand but she did not respond.

"Yes Alki, it was me in the house. I took away the pills because I wanted you to be safe!"

"Why did you do that Reg?"

"You know why."

"If I did I wouldn't ask!"

"You know how I felt, feel about you. I looked after you in many ways."

"Did you phone?"

It took only a second for the smile to appear on his face.

"Was I that obvious?"

It was Alki who now smiled.

A moment passed. It was Rose that spoke.

"We have all been through a lot," she said. "I would not dare say that we or you have gone through more than the other. Suffice it to say a lot of suffering has occurred and I wished it could have stopped after mine and indeed Reggie's deaths. We have a mission to fulfil as indeed do you; ours is for our country and so is yours, albeit in a circumspect fashion. We have to go away and you two have to stay. None of our circumstances is enviable and yet we have to fulfil our part in this that is now upon us."

Sonia came back in through the kitchen door followed by Luke.

"Who was it?"

"The Boss!"

"Why is he ringing?"

"He wanted to know if the project has actually been compromised. I told him that we don't know yet."

"We only need two days, three at the most and we'll be gone." Reg now turned to Alki. "Did you involve Alex in this last episode?"

She looked him in the eye and said, with as much bitterness as she could muster.

"We have passed on everything we have ever learned to the media, and if we are not released, then by this time tomorrow it will be all over the newspapers, the radio, the television and, indeed, the world!"

Reg turned away to look at Sonia and they shared a look. He turned back to Alki.

"Darling. To date, we have heard the content of every phone call you have made, both from the landline and your mobile, even from this young man's device as well. All e-mails were scrutinized before they were allowed on their way. Even the websites you have frequented have been logged and passed on to people who work for us, to discern if they pose any sort of threat."

Alki seemed quite shocked at his words, Aaron also. Sonia took up the assault.

"Whilst I applaud your ingenuity in managing to follow us from Norfolk to here, I am more than a little annoyed at your niggling persistence in pursuing your goals, despite acknowledging that Reg could have had all the money, and you as well."

"I never said that!" She blurted. Aaron frowned and whispered something to her. She looked at him, quizzically.

"We have your house bugged Alki. We heard you say that several times to your new companion!"

She looked back at Aaron again who nodded to her. Sonia continued while Alki tried desperately to gather herself together.

"We've known about you for a long time now Alki, but never considered you a serious threat, until now."

Reg took up the baton.

"We found out that someone had investigated the doctor and police constable after my 'accident'. That was when it was decided, not by us, by higher up than any of us, that you had to be investigated. I insisted that it be done with concern for you and that every care be taken that you were not harmed in any way. I was guaranteed that this would be the case. In fact, I went further and asked for you to be made comfortable." She looked a little annoyed, but it soon gave way to a smile she attempted to hide. "Remember the lottery win?" She mouthed something though said not a word, then nodded. "How many times have you taken part in the lottery?"

"You know fine and well Reg that I never do the lottery. It is only for fools."

"But you did do it, just the one time, remember?"

"It was only because I won it in a raffle. I would never have done it normally. I was high on pills and alcohol at the time."

"You were love, but you won more than three hundred thousand pounds!"

Alki was at a loss for something to say. Instead she nodded in agreement, then hung her head low. Aaron now spoke.

"I also gained an amount of money." He sounded incredulous. "I gave all the money away though." Aaron looked directly at Rose.

"We can give you as much money as we want Aaron," she said. "We have absolutely no control over what you do with it!"

"So, it was you then Rose, that did that?" He asked.

She looked at him and simply nodded.

"Mine wasn't as much as that given to Alki, but the amount doesn't matter." He now sought her eyes and she looked at him. "I can only thank you Rose for that kindness; however, it pales into insignificance when compared with the harm I have suffered at your hand!"

She didn't seem able to speak. Reg stepped forward and took her arm. She looked at him, a kind of hurt expression on her face. He turned to Aaron.

"The point is, we know how much you know. The fact we have done nothing about it to date shows that we do not look upon you with any sort of malicious intent, Alki, Aaron. The fact that you are here, though, does present us with a problem I must admit. But that problem is for us to solve, not you." He paused awhile, seeing they were both taking this in. "We are at the end of an extremely complex project and cannot risk anymore interference. That is why we are simply going to let to you go and ask that neither of you say nor do anything more in regard to your investigations thus far."

It was clear they were both ready to bombard him with questions. Sonia, phone in hand, stepped forward.

"Everything your ex-husband has said is true Alki. We have no problem with either of you, even though you might have jeopardised this project. We need you to know a few things before we let you go but be absolutely certain in this; we offer you no harm, and you shall not be harmed. We simply need you to be convinced that what we are doing here is for the common good."

"Is that why that young man was holding a gun on us, on the beach?"

"What Alki says is true. If you are not offering us physical violence why have we been brought here against our will?"

"We were instructed, by our seniors, that now was the time to put this investigation of yours to rest."

Sonia's phone began to ring. She turned away, answering it as she went out of the room. Reg now continued.

"Even if you had gone to the press Alki, and given them all the information you have, you wouldn't have created the impact you think you might. Oh, there would have been ripples, of that I'm sure but nobody would have taken you seriously, believe me." They were taken aback by his words, Reg went on. "We made the decision to confront you now, instead of continually trying to stay a step or two ahead of you, which didn't seem to be working anyhow." He shook his head and smiled a little at his ex-wife. "Our project is now reaching its climax and it is vital that we divert all attention away from it, which is the reason you are here."

"I am not sure just what you are trying to achieve with all this rubbish you are spouting," Alki spoke slowly but with meaning. "There are things you can never explain to me, or Aaron, because they are so against everything I, we, believe in."

"We can Alki, we . . ."

"What about things like the bodies that were used to replace you Reg, and you Rose?" Alki now stood, Aaron also. "How the hell can you hope to explain those two little thorns in the side?" Reg went to answer but Rose put her hand on his arm. He looked at her and they shared a moment.

"Can I ask both of you a question?" Rose said.

"Of course dear," Alki said, with a slight smile on her face. "What can I tell you that you don't already know, according to dear Reg that is?"

"It is quite plain that you have a lot of anger. I cannot blame either of you, particularly you Aaron and I do apologise to both of you. My question is this." She indicated for them both to sit again. They looked at each other, and complied. "What did you think that I would gain from this subterfuge Aaron?" Before he could speak she held out her hand to stop him and now turned to Alki. "I offer the same question to you dear lady, regarding Reg. What, in your opinion, do you think he would have gained from the covert manner of his supposed death?"

Alki and Aaron were not a little surprised at this, looking at each other and then back to Rose and Reg. It was Alki that spoke first.

"I do believe, Reg, that you had more than the one reason I shall now state; although I am at a loss as to what that other reason, or reasons, might be. You gained money from me, of that there can be no denial; my enquiries discovered numerous bank accounts opened over the two years that we were together and, whilst they do not directly point to you, it is obvious who the beneficiary was. As I said, I firmly believe there are other motives which are the reason for my investigation, to discover why the hell you wanted to get out of a successful and harmonious and very happy marriage!"

Alki was now almost in tears, but she held on. Reg stepped forward and took the handkerchief from his top pocket, bent down on his haunches a step away from her and held out the piece of cloth. He said nothing but looked into her eyes. She took it and the moment passed. He stood.

Aaron turned to her and asked if she was okay. She nodded, smiled at him and yet still kept her head down, clutching the handkerchief. Aaron now looked at Rose and stood.

"I don't quite know how to begin," he said. "My world came to an end when I saw what I thought I saw." They could see that he too was just holding on. "I have asked myself why a thousand times although, at that time, the question was aimed at a god which I have never believed in. When I saw the evidence Alki showed me I asked why again, although this time I didn't know who I was asking the question of. You, like Reg, also took money from me. I fervently do not believe that was the whole reason. Like Alki I do believe there was an ulterior motive. After seeing all the things I have seen, hearing all the things I have heard, seeing you, seeing Reg, seeing this setup, I am more confused now than I have ever been in my entire life."

They could see the battle begin again, only this time he was not as successful. He sat down and Alki took his hand.

Rose stepped forward, holding her hand out to him. He glanced up at her and turned away as quickly. She withdrew her hand as Sonia and Luke entered from the lounge.

"Keep them in here Reg. Luke and I are going outside."

"What's wrong?" Reg asked.

"Not sure," she said. "Toby thought he heard something."

Luke took the gun off the side and tucked it into his trousers, hiding it with the jacket he wore. They both exited the back door.

CHAPTER TWENTY-SIX
Game Up?

Tea was made and offered, only Alki accepting.

Silence reigned for a time. Alki broke that silence.

"You ask us a question Rose, and yet you offer nothing yourself. Why is that?"

Rose looked at her but did not speak. Alki simply looked at the woman, unblinking, questioning. It was Reg who replied.

"All the things that I did Alki, taking the money, all the subterfuge which led up to my supposed death, were detailed instructions that I simply followed, and which led to where I am right now. They were all designed as a smokescreen to confuse anyone that might have investigated my demise. They were all real, insomuch as you were led to believe they were real, and so anyone looking would see only truth. Even if you had been questioned, interrogated, we knew you would have been convincing, you could even have passed a lie detector test such was the need for complete and total secrecy." Sonia and Luke entered from the back door, she closing it as Luke went into the lounge. Rose now spoke.

"The same applies to me Aaron. I had to make bets and create debts, all of which you paid after my supposed death. Just like Reg I had to create the illusion that I was out of control so that if anyone came and investigated me they would find everything true. You, like Alki, would have been able to pass a lie detector test. This must surely indicate to you, both of you, how important this mission that Reg and I have embarked upon actually is."

"You have forgotten just one thing," Alki said, quite softly. "What about the bodies? If they are exhumed they will surely give you away?"

"No, I don't think they will." Sonia said, looking up from her phone.

"They only have to check dental records and the teeth of the bodies!"

Sonia simply shook her head.

"We know all about Reg and his dental career," Aaron now joined in. "We know he will have worked on the victim's teeth, to be replicas of his own and Roses!" Sonia simply looked at them, a slight smile on her face. "But medical records will show enough discrepancies, even slight, that would demand closer scrutiny."

"All taken care of!"

"You've even fixed their medical records, as well as their teeth?" Sonia nodded again. "How in the world did you manage that?"

"I've told you, we work for a larger organisation than you can even imagine."

"But even so," Aaron added. "The bodies would not, indeed could not survive close scrutiny by medical experts."

"In such a case, if that were ever to come about, our bosses would simply have them cremated!"

"Wouldn't that look a little suspicious; two bodies that have already been buried, being mysteriously dug up and then cremated? Questions would be asked, serious questions."

"You're still working on the premise that we are a lonely, little two-bit organisation Alki. Our superiors would obviously prefer questions to be asked concerning two bodies being cremated by accident, than allowing those same bodies to go through meticulous scrutiny. Questions are always going to be asked, but answers, the right answers, do not necessarily need to be provided. That would be significantly more acceptable than risking the loss of a project such as this, which we are almost at the culmination of."

Both Alki and Aaron seemed at a loss for words.

Sonia broke the silence.

"If you truly love your partners, why not show just how much you love them by being genuine husbands and wives, and let them go?"

There was only silence.

Sonia spoke again.

"Their job is one of extreme difficulty. They go to, maybe, their deaths! They do this for their country, for the greater cause, and for you. If you truly love them Aaron, ilka, love them now, truly love them now before it is too late!"

The two both looked stunned. Alki spoke first.

"I don't see why you had to go to such extreme lengths. What can it be that you have to do that is so important you had to fake their deaths; and not just that, but also to seriously harm me and Aaron in the process?"

Reg and Rose came to stand side-by-side.

"We have a mission Alki, and it is one that only people who need to know, can know!" Reg said.

"But what is it that is so important you have to keep us out of it. I don't understand Reg, and you are not really making any sense."

"I have to agree with Alki," Aaron said. "This does not make any sense to me either!"

"It won't make sense!" Sonia's voice now rose a little. "How could it possibly make any sense to you, you are not in the loop; you don't know what it is we do or why indeed we do it. It is for the nation, it is for the common good and that is all you need to know!"

"No! It is not all we need to know." Alki stood now. "We have come this far, both Aaron and me, and we deserve some sort of an answer at the very least." Aaron now stood beside her.

Rose shook her head, seemingly with tears in her eyes. She looked up, at Aaron.

"We are both fluent in . . ."

"No!" Sonia stepped forward holding her hand up to Rose's mouth.

She now stood in front of her younger sister, facing her. There was a tension between the two, then Sonia turned to face Alki and Aaron.

"We know you have security clearance, to a level, the PM has assured us of that. But where Rose and Reg are going, that knowledge is definitely on a need to know basis only! The language in which both are fluent you two may already be aware of. But I can only stress, if you speculate on what that language is, anyone hearing, anyone outside these four walls hearing your speculations, might put two and two together and make their job even more difficult than it already is. It may even become the catalyst which leads to their deaths!"

It was obvious that Sonia's words were having an impact on both Alki and Aaron. Now they both sat down and looked at each other, concern written across their faces.

"You have stressed that this mission, their mission, is of the utmost importance." Aaron said. "And so, it would seem that we have to go along with all you have said. I must admit, though, I am at a loss as to what can be so hugely important as to fake people's deaths and to take loved ones away from their partners."

"There are many factions out there that would do damage to the free world if they could. There are many operatives, from this country and from others that work alongside us, who are doing what Reg and Rose have been trained to do, and will be on their way to do within the next few days," Sonia said.

"These two are sleepers darlin', they were prepped long ago and left alone to be good, honest decent citizens until the time they might be called. They were called and now 'ave completed their trainin' for what they're about to go and do." Luke added.

"Sleepers?" Aaron asked. "Does this stem from even before we were married?"

Rose nodded and allowed her head to fall.

"About two years before I met you Alki, I was approached." Reg said. "When we were married I firmly believed I would not be called upon."

"I also." Rose agreed. Aaron frowned.

"You knew, before we were married, that you would be leaving me?"

"I knew there was a chance Aaron. I did not know for certain and, like Reg, I believed I would not be called upon." She held his gaze and shook her head slightly. "I loved you and wanted to live the rest of my life with you."

"Loved?"

"I still love you Aaron." Her head dropped. "But my country needs me and so I must go."

"But why so dramatic in your leaving?" Aaron's face was pained.

"There are more than just terrorists at large in this world Aaron." She said. "Our job is vital which is why we had to 'die'. With us no longer existing it is so much easier for a new, manufactured, persona to be created around us."

"You haven't yet explained about the bodies!" Alki said.

"And just what do you want us to explain dear Alki? Sonia asked.

Alki hesitated, Aaron didn't.

"I saw Rose kicking the parcel beneath the motor of the tractor Sonia!" Aaron almost whispered. Rose now turned to him. "There was a body, and it must have been dead and not by very long!" He looked her hard in the eyes and she held his stare. Reg broke the stalemate.

"But of course we had a body, dead bodies." He looked at Aaron and then at Alki. "They were needed to complete the charade. What do you want us to tell you? They were needed and we got them."

"Isn't that a little callous Reg?" Alki asked. "They were someone's sons, daughters! Are you telling me you are such a monster as to deal in human flesh in such a flippant way, as if speaking of a lamb to be slaughtered?"

"Of course not Alki!" Reg curtly replied. "You know me better than that. Aaron, you know Rose better than that."

Alki would have replied instantly had not Aaron touched her arm. She looked at him. He now spoke.

"I know Rose and so I would have to agree with you. I do not know you Reg, but everything Alki has told me about you would lead me to believe you would not treat a human being in such a manner. And yet the evidence is there."

Sonia stopped both Rose and Reg from speaking and she now

turned both of them to face away from Aaron and Alki as she spoke in hushed tones. Five seconds later she spoke.

"I can see that the use of human beings, or rather dead bodies, how we came about them, why we would use them and all the other things about them that you might be concerned with bothers both of you." She looked straight at them. They nodded, eyes never leaving hers.

"It seems Sonia, you are the one to deal with awkward questions, am I right?" Alki asked.

"It seems Alki, you still do not fully grasp what you are dealing with here," she answered dryly. "To most decent human beings, the use of a body in the manner that you have described would be abhorrent. It is to us too. But if I could save one thousand lives with the loss of one life then would that, too, be abhorrent?"

"Human life is sacred Sonia," Alki answered. "Even one for a thousand is too many, I thought even you would grasp that?"

Aaron took up the argument.

"All of this grandiose talk. How great that what you are doing is for the common good, for the good of mankind, for the good of the western world; Sonia, it all pails into total insignificance when you treat a human life in this manner."

"Did you never hear of the soldier in the second world war whose body was used as a decoy, for Germans to discover with supposed secret files in a briefcase attached to his person?"

Both Alki and Aaron nodded their agreement.

"Whilst we are not at war in the old sense of the word, we are at war in the modern sense, terrorism being one of the words we would now use. In the same way that soldier allowed us, his country, to use his body to save many thousands, we used the same principle for both Reg and Rose."

"Please correct me if I'm wrong Sonia, but, if memory serves, that soldier was already dead and did not have a say in how his body was to be used." Alki said.

"You are correct of course Alki." Sonia agreed. "But do you also

remember the various lookalikes recruited during the war, for Field
Marshal Montgomery, for Winston Churchill and many others? These
recruits were all prepared to give their lives to maintain the lives of
our commanders; for the common good. The same has happened
here, nothing more."

"And so, you are trying to tell us that two people happily gave
their lives so these two could become anonymous?"

Sonia went to speak but Reg now stood forward. They exchanged
a look which Reg seemed to win. Sonia held up her hands and stepped
back. Reg now looked Alki in the eyes.

"I know Alki. I know you, and I know you won't be fobbed off.
I should have warned Sonia and the others what you would be like.
Sadly, I did not realise we would be here, we few, here in this kitchen
today. But we are, you are, and so we have to deal with this situation."

He turned back to look at Sonia, Luke and Rose. He seemed to
shake his head, then turned back.

"When I was first approached and I agreed, in principle, to be
recruited, I was told how this would work. I was dubious at first, as
I can see that you are Alki and I cannot blame you for that, you also
Aaron. They explained the scenario to me in various different ways
and I looked at all the evidence to support what they said. I even
went to London to survey the situation for myself, as they told me it
was. It took me a time, as it also took Rose the same amount of time
because I was there and instrumental in teaching her how this process
would actually work when her time came. I saw in her the hesitation
I had felt when it had first been explained to me." He could see only
doubt in both Alki's and Aaron's eyes. He went on. "What I can say
to you now is only as it was and so forgive me if it seems blunt." He
took a kitchen chair and sat down in front of them. "There are lots
of homeless people in this country. A lot of them are without hope
because of the way they have treated their bodies, particularly the
older ones; when I say older ones I mean around my age and, forgive
me Rose, yours also. Our superiors found a man approximately my
age; they actually found several but most were healthy, and yet the

one I am talking about was not healthy at all. He had terminal cancer and was told about this and offered a good, happy, cared for life until his end. He accepted the conditions we offered and so things were put into operation. His teeth were modified, his hair also coloured to match my own.

"What about fingerprints? You can't fake fingerprints!" Aaron interjected. Sonia threw her hands in the air and left the room.

"You can if the person whose fingerprints you are checking for has never had his fingerprints taken before in his life; how would you know which are mine and which are not?" He now stared at Aaron who went to speak again, but decided against it. "The main thing is this; he was given a very happy existence until his life ended. Our operation was geared for that day and, when it came about, the operation was executed." He now looked directly at Alki. There seemed to be tears in his eyes. "Tomas was my friend and I held his hand as he left this earth. He knew my mission and smiled as he left me. Later that day he was found by our neighbours beneath the tree." He now stood and turned away, wiping tears from his eyes.

"And you now believe we will swallow this hogwash?" Aaron said. Alki looked at him, pleading.

"How can we believe this Reg?" She said, quietly.

"Police records are for public scrutiny." He said. "If you chose to look in the police records in London, around the embankment area, you will find the record of Tomas, a forty-eight-year-old male around my height and weight. Approximately six months before I supposedly died you will find that he, appears at least, to have moved away for there is no record of him from that time. If you chose to look at police records for south of the river approximately a year ago you will find reference to a female around the age of thirty-six who simply disappeared, for there is no record of her from that time. A similar thing to Tomas took place concerning this woman, to help create the diversion we needed to make Rose, also, disappear as myself."

CHAPTER TWENTY-SEVEN
Decoy

Sonia walked in, she seemed shaken.

"The paparazzi are outside. There are only a few but it's still enough to do us damage!"

"How the hell did they get wind of this place?"

She looked at him, shook her head and then looked directly at Alki and Aaron.

"Had to be!" she said. "It's them; they must have traced her and her boyfriend to her cottage and then followed them here!"

"Surely not. We had them watched, until we made the move here that is." Rose agreed with Reg who now sat down, obviously concerned.

"It looks like they've been sussed since then. Did you two take any precautions against being followed?" Sonia began dialling.

"Er, no." Alki looked a little sheepish. "We didn't see the need. We thought we were the ones doing the following."

"That's it then. They could have blown our cover completely. This place won't stand close scrutiny, not by journalists hungry for a story."

"Can't I just go out and face the music?" Aaron said. "It must be me they've come for. They still think I killed Rose, and so if I go out to them and give them some cock and bull story they'll go away and you can carry on, unnoticed?"

Reg and Rose slowly nodded. Sonia silenced the murmurings of agreement.

"And why would they believe you Aaron?" She said harshly. "They want a story about you murdering a beautiful woman. What can you give them to fulfil that desire? You gonna confess?" She looked at him and almost begged him to answer.

He started to talk but, gave up as quickly.

"We need to get Reg and Rose away from here or the operation cannot continue. Three years of organising will have to be thrown away, but we cannot risk losing the identity swap with you two." Reg and Rose stood back, saying nothing. Aaron spoke.

"I am so sorry. This is my entire fault. If I had not become so engrossed in finding out if you were still alive then your project would have gone on undisturbed."

"It's not your fault Aaron," Rose stepped forward and now took his hand. "I am so sorry to have had to go to such extreme lengths to get the team to the place it is today, but it was necessary I can assure you. I am only flattered that you loved me so much you were willing to do what you did to find out the truth."

He looked at her and had to turn away.

"If your surveillance teams hadn't done such a lousy job we would not be here, in this predicament in the first place!" Alki said.

Sonia was unimpressed. Reg intervened before she spoke.

"They did a good job Alki. It was yours and Aaron's persistence, together with all the twists and turns you employed that bypassed all our safety protocols. Most anti-surveillance measures would have failed against that onslaught."

"It is vital we maintain the mystery of Reg and Roses deaths." Sonia cut through him. "If they glimpse either one of them, giving them just an idea even, with journalists that could be enough for them to investigate and find out sufficient to destroy the project completely."

"Why can't you just leave under cover of night?"

"Because this is the hub of our activity; we cannot just up and leave as we did at The Barn."

"Did you deliberately set fire to The Barn, to try and throw us off the scent?" Sonia nodded. "That was a little extreme wasn't it?"

"It might have seemed it to you Alki. But in the grand scheme of

things, if indeed it had worked and thrown you off the scent it would
have been worth it."

"Why cannot you just move, as you did in Norfolk?"

"As Sonia has already told you this is the hub. This is our jump off
point. Everything revolves around this location which is why it was
picked in the first place. We cannot just abandon it."

"Well, in that case . . ." Alki's voice trailed away.

"What?" Sonia asked as she speed dialled on her phone.

Alki seemed not to hear, looking down and now wrapped in her
own thoughts. Sonia put the phone to her ear as everyone spoke at
once.

"Sanderson. It looks like we have been compromised. Stand by
for opt-out instructions. We need to leave and it seems the operation
might now be a no-go." Sonia held up her hand to stop all chat. "I
shall have to ascertain whether it can be resurrected or not, but in the
meantime we have to go down the abort route. Call me at the normal
time and I'll confirm." She ended the call but speed dialled another,
motioning for them all to be silent. "Just shut up!" she shouted, then
said into the phone. "We have to put things back, Sanderson already
knows." She waited, listening. "I know, but it seems we have no choice
now. Hold the boat and keep the rest on high alert while we prove
this thing one way or another." She quickened her pace. "Gotta go,
got another coming in!" She ended the call and looked at the screen.
Her face registered shock. "Oh hell!"

"What is it?" Rose asked.

"The Boss!" She said.

She answered the call.

"Yes Sir, Sonia here." She looked a little ashen as she nodded,
making her way to the door. She stopped. "They are Sir; they are
standing across from me right now." She looked at Aaron and Alki, a
little bemused it seemed. "Very well Sir, just a moment." She held the
phone down, covering the bottom of it with her hand. She whispered.
"He wants to speak with you!" She offered the handset to Alki.

"What does he want to speak to me for? Does he want to tell me off?" She smiled as she went to take the phone. Reg stepped close to her and spoke in earnest, though soft of voice.

"Alki, it's the Prime Minister!"

She took the phone, then realised what he'd said. She swallowed.

"Hello er Sir, Mr . . ."

"Prime Minister!" Sonia urged. Alki looked at her.

"Do I curtsey as well?"

Sonia threw her arms in the air.

"Hello Mr. Prime . . ." She nodded, and now inclined her head as she listened. "Yes, we are." She said. She now stood up and looked at Aaron. "He is, I'm sure Prime Minister." She nodded once or twice and then listened. It was a few minutes before she spoke again. "Well, I didn't vote for you, but you haven't done too badly so we'll see next time." She listened again while Sonia, Reg and Rose all cringed. Aaron simply smiled. "We will," she said. "Yes, and the same to you Prime Minister. Bysy bye!" She now looked at the phone, then held it at arm's length as she shook her head. "Don't know how this thing switches off!" Sonia grabbed it from her.

"Sonia here Prime . . ." She looked at the screen. "He's gone!"

They all now faced Alki.

"What did he say?" Sonia asked, a little agitated.

"He said you were an idiot! Only joking. He wanted to know if we loved our country, I told him we did. He said that the 'Hildebrand' project?" She looked around for recognition of the term. She got none but carried on. "That it was one of the most important projects during his lifetime, and that if it could be saved it would serve the United Kingdom and the free world more than we might know." She sat down, seemingly concerned.

"Did he say anything else?" Sonia urged. Alki shook her head, looking to the floor.

"They've been vetted," Reg spoke now. "They obviously passed muster; he told her the project name." Sonia's phone rang again. She answered it.

"Yes I know. We have to hold everything for now." She listened for a few moments. Her face fell. "How many?" She shook her head and looked at Reg. "Okay. Thanks, but keep things calm, and wait for my call. Even the PMs on board and so we wait until we have absolutely no other options." She listened again. "The boats alright for now, just keep them all alert. I'll be in touch as soon as we know. Let Sanderson know for me." She terminated the call. "There's more paparazzi turned up."

"How many?"

"About thirty now apparently, so no looking out of the windows. I've got a lot of thinking to do." She began to look through her list of phone contacts.

"It seems to me that we have a fire to put out!"

Sonia turned from her phone, and now they all looked at Alki.

"Just take a rest old lady. Leave it to the professionals." Sonia went to walk away, heading for the door.

"Professionals is it dear?" Sonia stopped and turned, as Alki stood now and faced her. "Your 'professionals' didn't do such a brilliant job, now did they? Following me, then giving up because they thought, the 'professionals' that is, that a little old lady sodden with drink would be no threat! And then when they saw Aaron welcomed into the fold, still they didn't think we were such a threat to your almighty little project! But, it seems, the 'professionals' have not provided you with the goods, because we are here against all the odds, and the 'professionals' of course!"

Sonia came back into the room.

"The point here is, 'Alki'. You have destroyed the work of a highly talented, dedicated team by interfering in your talentless, uneducated, fumbling, imbecilic way!" She stepped up to her and towered over the old lady. "You have meddled where you shouldn't, and because of that we have to back away from a project that would have had serious implications in world affairs. You have taken away, singlehandedly, the pioneering endeavours of two extremely talented and inordinately brave human beings with a single stroke of stupidity. You should feel proud of yourself!" She now turned from the elderly lady, and headed again for the door.

"And there is no-one in this room that is more acutely aware of what our actions have caused than me." Sonia did not falter. "But our bumbling, unintelligent, amateurish attempts at penetrating your little 'project' have proved more than capable of beating your super-intelligent agents!"

Sonia now stopped and turned again, anger swelling in her eyes.

"Oh calm down Sonia! Do you think you are the only one with brains? Well think again."

Alki now turned to her ex-husband and Rose.

"You two have surprised even me, and there are not many can do that these days." She saw Reg smile as he bowed his head to hide it. She smiled also. "And that is why we will make it back to the good for you!"

"Make it what?" Sonia had stepped into the room again.

"Back to the good! Keep up Sonia!" She grabbed Aaron's arm and beckoned for Rose to come to her.

"We run anything by me first!" Sonia took centre ground.

"And so we shall," Alki said. "Have you a wardrobe of clothes here?" She addressed both Rose and Sonia.

"Of course we have," Sonia answered. Rose nodded through a bemused smile.

"Then listen to me and maybe all is not doom and gloom as you are so quick to assume."

CHAPTER TWENTY-EIGHT
Girlfriend

Sonia slunk out of the side door, making her way around the perimeter of the property. She crept away from the house, melding into the shadows and came out about two hundred yards inland from the beleaguered home. Putting her coat on she made her way covertly to halfway up the lane, above where the mass of around thirty paparazzi were grouped around the entranceway to the house.

She started to sidestep in and out of shadows, coming down the lane now and getting closer to the house all the while. Eventually she was spotted and now she hung back in shadow whilst two men and a woman separated themselves from the crowd and approached her.

She was immediately recognised and it was only her urgings that made the three step into shadow beside her, before others from the crowd noticed.

"What the hell are you doing here?" One of the men asked, wide-eyed.

"The same as you," she answered dryly.

"Are you on Aaron's case still?" The woman urged her.

"Isn't that what floats our boat, to get that bastard for what he done?"

"Course it is," the other bloke chipped in. "You got anything to big this up then? Anything at all? It'll be worth your while!"

"Might have! What are we talking about in money terms?"

"Just give, I'll see you right!" The same guy was almost frothing. "How much?!"

"We'll make it five K, if there's anything there."

"There's plenty there. But it's got more in it than five K!"

So give! I'll be there for you; I was before!"

The first guy now turned on him.

"What the . . ."

"I'll tell you about it later!" He turned back to Sonia. "Come on Son. I defo will cough up on this one!"

"You heard him!"

She now turned to the other two. They both nodded.

"You know where he's staying now, in Cornwall?"

"Yeah. We've got it staked out."

"You've seen his landlady?"

"The old bint?" Sonia nodded. "Yeah, what about her?"

"She's not his landlady!"

It was more than twenty minutes later that the front door opened and Aaron stepped through.

He was immediately assailed by more than thirty news reporters who all shouted questions at him and pressed in, stopping him from moving more than a few feet from the door.

"I have nothing to say," he shouted, though nobody heard.

"Why have you come back?"

"What sort of a ghoul are you Mr. Brindley?"

"Couldn't you just have left her to her peace in heaven instead of coming back to Cornwall and desecrating her memory?"

The accusations came from all quarters and he attempted to repel them, but gave up as it soon became clear that nobody wanted to listen.

"We hear that you have a girlfriend now, 'Mr. Brindley'?"

Sonia stood forward from the assembly and the throng parted.

The place fell silent.

"How long will it be until you have this one murdered as well?"

The place erupted and every question imaginable was hurled at him.

"What the hell are you doing here?" he yelled at her. "Haven't you done enough damage to me?"

"You got off scot free, you creepy scumbag!" Sonia bellowed; the whole assemblage yelled their agreement. "We want to know why you came back here, and why you are besmirching my twin sister's name by bringing your whore with you!"

Aaron stepped towards her and raised his arm.

"Go on hit me, just like you hit Rose a thousand times!" He lowered his hand as the crowd jeered. Sonia slapped his face and he stood back, shocked.

A police constable now stepped forward, quieting a lot of the crowd, though many of the questions and accusations were still being hurled.

The officer placed himself in front of Aaron, who thanked him and then turned back to the door, opening it.

A woman stepped through, into full view of the waiting crowd.

"There she is!" Sonia shouted.

Mayhem!

"It's true!"

"He's got a girlfriend!"

The crowd went mad, surging forward whilst taking pictures by the bucket load.

Aaron took her hand and they began to walk through the throng, the police constable taking the lead, shielding them as best he could, despite the countless cameras being placed in their way.

She was almost as tall as Aaron and wore an above the knee dress, off-white in colour with heart-shaped sequins dotted all over. Her hair was almost gold, and in curls that bounced off her shoulder with every step of her four-inch stiletto heels.

"Who is this?"

"Who are you?"

"What's yer name Darlin'?"

Aaron placed his arm around her and attempted to guide her through the crowd, the policeman doing his best to carve out a passage for them.

"You his next slag are yer?" One man shouted, in close proximity

Aaron lashed out and caught him full in the face, squashing his nose with blood gushing.

"No violence now!" The PC grabbed the man and pulled him close. "Watch your mouth!" He said and pushed him away, hard, as he continued to force a way through.

They moved forward, cutting through the crowd and heading to the car park, slowly approaching the hire car. The policeman halted everyone, allowing the couple to get in.

Aaron locked the doors and started the car, inching forward as the policeman now moved to the front and turned, backing away and beckoning Aaron forward. He brought them to the top of the track, onto the road and waved them on. The assemblage went mad at this stage and, seeing their quarry escaping, ran for their cars. The policeman sauntered down the track and faced the convoy of cars as it now began to approach. He stood his ground and halted the mass of vehicles.

"Get out of the way!"

"Come on officer. Move!"

There were many shouts and screams at him as the numerous cars and vans began to line up to get out of the car park.

The policeman continued to hold his hand up, stopping the lead vehicle only inches from his person.

"Ladies and Gentlemen," he raised his voice a little, but not enough to be heard above the engine noises. "You are all guilty of strict parking infringements and so shall be reported to the authorities. You do not have to say anything but if you do then it might be taken down and used in a court of law to the detriment of yourselves and all who sail in her!"

No-one had heard him above the engine noise and shouts and now he smiled as he took out his notepad and seemed to start writing down all of the registration numbers.

It was ten minutes later that Toby stepped to one side, allowing the cavalcade to go on their way.

CHAPTER TWENTY-NINE
Getaway!

"My God! What a plan," Aaron yelled, pulling away from their friendly bobby as he blocked the road. He looked at his companion who was also laughing. "Alki, you look amazing!"

She now turned and smiled at him.

"Thank you Aaron." She dropped the mirror down and checked herself. "All Rose and Sonia's doing though."

"Nonsense. You look stunning!" He laughed out loud, she also. "The dress, the wig, and the body to wear it all! You look eighteen not eighty!" He bit his tongue almost immediately.

"Be amazed dear boy, not insulting! I'm only seventy-three, and don't you ever forget it!"

"Sorry Alki, or should I now call you Ilka?"

"I think the past is what it is. Call me Alki and I shall be pleased."

"A piece of genius Alki, pure genius!"

"The violence helped enormously. Did she hurt you?"

"No."

"The punch was incredible. How did you arrange that?"

"Oh, that was real! I belted him as hard as I could!"

"You did?"

"Of course! Didn't you hear what he said about you?"

"Oh, my hero!" she mock applauded him. He laughed.

"He deserved it!" She now laughed.

"Did you break his nose?"

"I hope so, I nearly broke my hand doing it." She laughed, louder this time. "You were right, I think. This should be a sufficient enough draw to pull the whole lot away from the cottage."

"I do hope so."

She looked a little sad and Aaron saw. He held her hand and spoke softly.

"I had no idea what I would feel like when I eventually came face to face with Rose, and even Reg for that matter. But now, in the full realisation of what they are about to do for our benefit, for the benefit of this country, the people that live in it, indeed for the freedom of the western world, I can only feel a warmth for them."

"I have to admit that, after losing him, my life fell apart and once I realised he was alive I wanted to kill him, but now?"

"I know. It didn't seem possible, at the time of finding them alive that anything they might say would have any impact on the way I felt towards them. And yet, after seeing for myself just what they are attempting to achieve here, I can only feel awe."

Alki nodded in agreement.

They sped along the road, still holding hands.

CHAPTER THIRTY
The Truth

They got back to Alki's home around eleven pm.

They were met with flash after flash as the waiting paparazzi engulfed the car. Aaron slowly manoeuvred it around to the back, eventually managing to park in the garage, and closing the doors behind them.

They made their way through the adjoining doors and corridor, lighting the small cottage up and being greeted with many more flashes through the windows. The curtains were quickly drawn, and sealed with tape to the window frame.

Aaron emerged through the front door and, after refusing to answer the many shouted questions, informed the assemblage that the property was equipped with covert CCTV and if any of them entered the garden or came into the back yard area, then the police would be called and they would be charged with trespassing. He stressed that charges definitely would be enforced and the questions were then thrown at him again, as he backed through the front door and closed it.

"Well, that was fun," Alki said as she handed him a glass.

"I wouldn't quite call it that." He took the glass and raised it. "To us, the decoys, but most especially to the two leading players, Reg and Rose, and all they endeavour to do in our behalf." He went to drink but Alki didn't.

"I think a little music would not be out of place at this time," she said, as she turned the radio on, classical music quickly filling the air. She increased the volume, picked up the bottle of Irish, then turned back and indicated for Aaron to follow her. He went to speak but she stopped him. "I'm only glad we were able to help them," she said, slowly moving toward the kitchen. "It was fortunate we could drag all the stupid media away. I just hope they are not damaged by our actions." She made for him to respond. He stammered a little.

"Er, yes Alki," he said. "I too am pleased." They were now in the kitchen and she went on, through into the garage, closing the door behind them.

"It is too soon to say, but if we make a few errands out together, we might be able to keep them on our tail for a few days at least." She opened the door of the Morris and got in, indicating for him to, also. He did.

They sat in silence for a few seconds.

"I don't think we shall be overheard in here." She reached forward and turned the radio on, quite low. "Just in case," she said.

"What is this all about?" he asked.

"They must have the place bugged Aaron," she said. "That's what they told us and I believe them, partially. They knew things we said, but only things we said in the lounge if you recall."

"I remember, but does it matter now?" She nodded, yes.

"Well, why?" He asked.

"Because, we have just been privy to probably the biggest scam, and given to us by the biggest scammers I have ever seen in my life." She raised her glass. "Now I'll drink; to Rose, Reg, Luke, Sonia, Toby our little policeman and all the others of their gang that we never actually saw. To them all, and to the hope that we may find out just what the hell it is they are up to before our chance is gone!"

Aaron's glass now lowered as Alki drank.

He looked at her and waited. She lowered her glass and now looked back at him, a faint smile playing across her face.

A long moment passed and, eventually, he drank. She just looked at him, and swayed a little from side to side in her seat, in time with the music.

"Well, if you think I'm speaking first after a speech like that you will need to think again."

She smiled a little broader at him now.

"You've just spoken."

"Come on Alki!" He said as they heard the front door knocked.

"Sod off!" He yelled and now turned back to her, indicating an explanation would be appreciated.

She smiled a little and dropped her head. He waited a moment, but could wait no longer.

"What the hell are you talking about?" He said, exasperated.

She dropped the smile.

"Don't forget that I know Reg very well. I know his idiosyncrasies as well as I know his little paunchy body, inside and out."

"Yes, so you know Reg; I am aware of this!"

"And he confirmed that I did hear him on the phone, as he also admitted coming back to our marital home and taking away the pills he thought were killing me."

"Alright, so it proves you know him, and all his little ways."

She sipped at her drink.

"Are you trying to tell me that all the stuff they told us . . .?"

She looked up at him over the rim of her glass, childlike.

"Are you saying all that, at their cottage . . .? That all they said was bogus?"

She nodded and lowered her head.

"What?"

"Every little emotionally laden inflection!"

He lowered his glass, a look of disbelief on his face.

Only the sip she took vaguely covered her broadening smile.

"Do you want to explain, or are you going to continue in this superior, I know it all and you know nothing, attitude all night?" he said, not unkindly.

She fought the desire to guffaw, swallowing the sip of liquor instead.

"Reg," she said, "when he stands, nearly always puts his right hand inside his trouser pocket."

"I put my hands in my pockets when I stand, so do most of the male population."

"I understand what you say, but it's only ever the right hand with Reg; it's a nervous thing and he's always done it, but especially when everyone's attention is on him."

"Oh come on Alki!"

"He does Aaron. When people's attention is on him, he puts his right hand inside his trouser pocket, always has."

"OK, hands in pockets. What are you trying to say?"

"Just the one hand Aaron, his right hand." Aaron shook his head. "I'm a people watcher Aaron. I study the language of the body which always tells the truth, unlike many of the words that emerge from the mouth."

"The body tells the truth," he said. "How can a body tell the truth?"

"Because the body acts independently, it cannot lie." Aaron looked at her, frowning a little. "Oh, of course, if someone points out these idiosyncrasies and the person then works to obliterate them, much like an actor does when creating a character, the body can be trained to lie, like the mouth. But, in the main, the vast percentage of the main, the body will always give away the secrets of the person within."

He looked at her, and took a few moments to take this in.

"Alright Alki, I'm listening," he said.

She allowed herself a slight smile, but continued.

"When he's under scrutiny, when he's the centre of attention, he puts his hand in his pocket, his right hand. It's the nervous thing I told you about. But when he speaks an untruth, he has the habit of tapping the middle finger on his leg and Reg has always done it. I have seen it many times, and it is the most reliable giveaway."

"Like his vocal thing that he does on the telephone?" Alki nodded.

"He only has a few, yet he's always done them."

"But I know Rose very well and I can't tell when she lies, if she ever has."

She looked at him and raised an eyebrow.

"Do you think she lied to you very much Aaron?" He shook his head.

"I don't believe she did."

Alki nodded, and looked away, seemingly thinking.

"You had a full on relationship, right?" He looked at her, questioning. "Physically I mean."

"Of course," he said, almost in defence.

"Did she always orgasm when making love?"

He seemed a little shocked. He looked away from her but nodded after a short while.

"Thought so."

"What do you mean?"

"She's a woman Aaron, and women can always provide men with what they need, what they want to believe, whether in truth or not. They can, nearly always, fool men because men always want to be believed." She picked up the bottle of whiskey.

"Are you trying to tell me she faked her orgasms!"

"No! I don't know. But I do know that we women, sometimes, have to cater for the man's ego. And I also know that women look for the lie, whilst men don't!"

He hung his head, and now laughed.

"I don't give a damn anyway," he said. "She's dead!"

"Oh yes she's dead, but maybe not for the reasons stated."

He looked up, a quizzical frown on his face.

"I think you'd better tell me all you know," he said. She tacitly agreed, whilst pouring.

"I'm not sure why they went to such lengths in the cottage, to furnish us with such an elaborate charade," she said. "But, because of Reg's behaviour, which I have seen many times before and know to be reliable, I have every reason to believe there is something beyond the charade, the huge elaborate manner in which you and I have been dealt with this evening."

"They needed us to lead the media away."

"They did."

"Isn't that it then?"

"I don't know Aaron; I can only see the tapping finger."

"But why did we do that for them, lead the media away, if what you say is right?"

"Because it got us out of the cottage Aaron, under the guise of helping them. But they are still being watched, unbeknownst to them."

"Watched? Who's watching?"

"They think they are so clever, but we shall see who the clever ones are."

"Alki! You're not telling me something."

She looked at him and nodded.

"They knew that you and I were watching them." Aaron slowly nodded. "But they didn't know that I knew they knew."

"What?"

"Yes Aaron, I knew they were on to us ever since we followed the cars."

"How in the hell did you work that one out?"

"The torching of The Barn!" He looked at her, quizzically. "They knew we were close, and that was their attempt to get clean away; and if it wasn't for us finding out about the speeding fine they probably would have."

"But how did them setting The Barn on fire tell you that they knew we were on to them?"

"Think about it. Their lifestyle was low-key, under the radar as you pointed out. The young man, Toby, even took the rap for the speeding violation, keeping Reg completely out of view. They never draw attention to themselves and so should just have moved out of The Barn, which would have kept it low-key. But, because they knew that we knew where they were, they had to torch the place, destroying any clues they might have overlooked and that we might possibly have found."

"So, them gutting The Barn gave it away to you that they were on to us?"

"Of course. Consider what they did in Norfolk, moving the doctor and policeman away, overnight as it were with a minimum of fuss and keeping under the radar because, at that time, they didn't know I was onto them. Oh, I know that Reg said they knew about me, but it was only after Alex and I had carried out our investigations that they found out someone had been looking. If they had known about me before they moved they would have done lots more to cover their tracks, like they did in torching The Barn over here."

"But weren't they two separate, different situations."

"Yes, but they both served the same purpose, to allow their safe getaway. In Norfolk they didn't realise at the time that anyone was on to them and so remained low-key. Here they did know about us, and so they abandoned their low-key stance and torched The Barn, to ensure there were no clues as to where they might have gone."

He shook his head a little.

"It's simply putting two and two together Aaron," she said. "Different situations granted, but they both had the same, ultimate goal."

"And you couldn't tell me all this?"

"I was going to, I just didn't get the chance, us getting caught and all. But it worked out because ignorance makes the best actors in the world, as you proved sitting in the kitchen of their seaside cottage."

Aaron stopped shaking his head.

"The paparazzi turning up was just the icing on the cake, and they had to deal with it which is why I helped them, because it made them believe we had swallowed their story, and it got us away and out of their hair, supposedly?"

Aaron didn't know what to say.

"And so, we follow them from here, as soon as we know just where they are going."

"And how are we going to find that out?"

"Alex."

"Alex?"

She laughed a little.

"Forgive me," she said. "Alex has been on the case for a long time now. He and I have been working together on this since I first began to suspect something was not right. He's been parked up, observing them since we found their location."

"But that was two days ago."

"Yes."

She could see his mind working.

"Hang on!" He said, shocked. "That means that he watched while we got caught!"

Alki said nothing, yet looked him in the eye.

"I don't get it. Why didn't he warn us?" He waited for an answer. Alki didn't speak. "He was watching us at that time, wasn't he?"

"Oh yes," she said. "He's been watching for a long time."

"So why didn't he warn us that they were on the way back, he's got your phone number hasn't he?"

"Yes, he has my number and he did phone by the way, I just didn't get the chance to answer at the time as we were about to be caught. He has your number as well."

"Mine," he said, then smiled and shook his head. "He won't have mine Alki, it's a new one; only a few people have this number . . ." He stopped. "You gave it to him."

"We knew your number long before I even met you." Alki let her head lean to one side, a sheepish look on her face, eyebrows raised. "Sorry," was all she said.

There was a loud hammering on the front door; neither of them stirred at all.

"Are you any good with engines," she asked after a short while, during which the door had been knocked several times.

He now looked up at her, incredulous.

"You've had me checked out?" he said.

"Had to Aaron," she said. "I wouldn't put anything past the people we are dealing with."

He still sat back in the car seat, looking at her. The incredulity had crept away to be replaced with a faint smile tinged with awe.

"You believed I might be in cahoots with them!"

She didn't acknowledge him, but shifted her position a little. It was a short while before she responded.

"Look at the way they 'disappeared'," she said. "To fake a death and use another body as proof of that death is no mean feat. To do it twice is a serious indication of how expert they are in what they do." He seemed to agree. "To then find out about me, that I was hot on their trail, and to fool both of us into thinking we had them sussed; then capture us and give us the story we have just heard, which was not a swift, off the cuff creation but a cleverly rehearsed, albeit improvised, role-play, is not the stuff of amateurs." He nodded slowly, mulling over the argument. She gave him a moment. "If we consider all that and all the other things they have done to eliminate this thorn in their side, me; for them to then throw someone into the mix, someone whom I could possibly learn to believe and confide in becomes more and more a true possibility given their track record. But, more importantly, it was simply not beyond the bounds of possibility and so had to be pursued."

His smile began to broaden as he took this in.

She too smiled and, as Aaron had, now leant back into the car seat.

"Help yourself to Irish sweetheart," she said. "Don't be shy."

"Yes, I am!" This statement broke through the silence that had dominated for a good while.

"I'm sorry," she became fully awake, glass still in hand.

"I always service the Beemer myself," he informed her.

"Er, Beemer?" She enquired.

"The BMW? My car? I service it myself, and do all running repairs."

"Oh," she said. "How nice for you." She didn't seem fully awake after all.

"You asked if I was any good with engines, just before you informed me that I was suspect number one."

"Oh, that," she sat up.

"Yes, that little chestnut."

"That's good, because we are going to have to use it to get away from that lot out there."

"What? Use what!"

"Bertha."

"Who, or possibly what, the hell is Bertha?"

"The engine you need to have a look over."

"OK, so Bertha is an engine, but I'm not talking about a damned engine! Well, I was, but not now. I'm talking about the accusation that I might be the resurrected Mori-bleeding-arty!"

"I know," she said simply, as she got out of the car, and now led him through the garage, opening the far door to another, bigger, garage. "You'll get over it," she said as he followed her, a peevish look on his face.

"Well?" He said, as she stopped by a bundle. He then gasped as she pulled back the tarpaulin to reveal a microlight engine and canopy combined.

"We have to pull Bertha out onto the field just through those double doors, open the canopy, secure it, then fire up the engine and seat ourselves within; all this before the paparazzi know what we are doing. Oh, and we have to do it all in the dark!"

"How can we fly in the dark?"

"We will be able to see street lights when we are in the air. We can navigate from there."

"I thought you weren't allowed to fly anymore?"

"You don't need a licence to fly these Aaron."

"Well, that inspires me with confidence!"

"Don't worry. Baddie and me, Reg and me also, used to use Bertha on regular trips to the coast in Norfolk. You can land these things in a car park you know." He still did not seem impressed.

"But where will we go?"

"We know they will move within three days; they said as much to you and me. If they have been carrying out another scam in this

area, and I think they have, when it's done they will fly the coop.
We'll be ready!"

"I hope you can fly this thing Alki."

"Been flying solo since before I was ten. Piece of cake."

Aaron did not seem to be that impressed.

CHAPTER THIRTY-ONE
Flight

It was dead of night and the two large garage doors began to swing open. Aaron pushed them both slowly, having seriously oiled all the hinges. His diligence seemed to have paid off because they swung almost without any noise at all. He secured one, then the other and came back in to the dark garage where Alki stood by the microlight.

During the evening they had both been busy preparing for this moment. Fuel had been added to the tank and the engine had been serviced as best as Aaron could manage. He had asked Alki to do some washing, and to set the fastest and longest spin speed and, just as the machine began to spin, with music playing in the lounge also, he had fired the engine. It spluttered once or twice but then caught. He had let it tick over for about a minute and a half and then turned it off.

Now they began to pull it, canopy still closed, out on to the dark field. They managed to achieve this with the minimum of noise, but when they reached the desired position they both stopped and stood still to listen, in case their furtive actions had been discovered. After a full thirty seconds Alki smiled at him in the dim moonlight, indicating for the next part of their plan to be put into operation.

The canopy was opened and secured, garage doors closed and Alki sat in the pilot's position. Aaron positioned himself at the rear, propeller in hand and waited. She turned to him and gave the nod. He immediately threw the propeller. The engine spluttered and then died. He grabbed hold again and threw it as hard as he could. It spluttered again but this time burst into life. Alki revved the engine as Aaron quickly came around to the side and sat in the apparatus next to her.

Even above the engine noise they could now hear a commotion from around the front of the house, and quickly heading in their direction.

She needed no prompting and opened the throttle, setting the microlight on its way across the field. It didn't take long before she pushed forward and they were in the air. She heard a loud gasp from her passenger and laughed out loud.

Now she banked the aircraft to the left, away from the approaching mass of paparazzi on the ground. Lights shone out from hand held torches, a couple finding the airborne craft but quickly losing it again as it picked up speed and rapidly left the vicinity, Alki keeping the glorified hang glider close to the ground, avoiding further detection.

"You can fly!" Aaron still held his grip tight on the struts, but had to raise his voice for her to hear. He heard her laugh though.

"Oh ye of little faith," she called back, the laughter still in her voice as she banked to the right, heading for street lights less than a quarter of a mile away.

She followed those sparsely dotted lights for half a mile which brought them to a main carriageway. She banked gently to the right, to follow the well-lit road, keeping the slight craft over a hundred and fifty feet above the ground, Aaron flicking on and off one of two powerful halogen lamps fixed in the rigging whenever Alki asked.

They flew on like this for around twenty-five minutes, by which time they could see they were approaching the coast.

"Look for two red and two green lights, roughly twenty feet from one another," she said.

He acknowledged.

They flew on for a few minutes, Aaron and Alki searching ahead for the promised lights.

"There's something over there," Aaron pointed.

She looked but couldn't see at first. He pointed again and she readjusted. Sure enough, a short distance away to their right there were red and green lights close together, seemingly on the ground. She gently banked the craft to head towards the small runway. She throttled back as they approached in between the two colours. Aaron turned on the lamps to aid in their descent.

Alki brought the craft low to the ground as they approached, throttled back to coast the rest of the way until, with a bump, they were down.

She cut the engine quickly and took off her goggles. Aaron did the same, and both of them got out.

"One day you'll break a spar comin' in like that." The voice of a man approached them behind a now lighted torch.

"Love you too Alex," she said.

A man, medium height, late fifties came into the light. He was shaking his head but with a smile on his face.

"You alright are you Aaron?" he said, shaking the bemused man's hand.

"I doubt very much they'll have the means to have followed us either in the air or on land. However, let's get Bertha and the lights in the trailer a.s.a.p."

Less than half an hour later they were sat in a heavily curtained motorhome in the corner of the field where they had landed, drinking Irish whiskey.

"Whereabouts are we Alex, in relation to the cottage on the beach?" Alki asked.

"About three quarters of a mile, to the east of 'em." He answered, pouring more of the light brown liquid.

"What did you manage to glean?" She asked.

"I watched as they caught you on the sand and then took you in the cottage. It was about twenty minutes after that the paparazzi turned up."

"So nothing else out of the ordinary?"

"Nothing since the paps all charged off after you."

"Here's to us then," she raised her glass as did they.

"They was well chuffed Alks, well chuffed!" He said. "I watched 'em from when you left. When the lad, the one that played the copper, got out of their way all the paps set off like thunder, after you two.

When they knew, or should I say thought they knew they was safe, they all come out and clapped each other on the back. It was 'ilarious. I almost shouted to 'em, I'm 'ere you bozos! Then they went back in the 'ouse and they've been there ever since."

"Was there a boat?" Alki asked.

"No, no boat; nothin'," he told her.

"I thought there would be. No matter."

"How did you see them from here?" Aaron had remained silent, but with a look of surprise on his face.

"Just zoom in pal, see everythin' when they got lights on. But then, when the paps left, the place went dark, except in the 'ouse. But they drew the curtains didn't they. Couldn't see nothin' after that."

"Are we any further forward in knowing their next move?" Alki asked Alex.

"No, but the good thing that's come out of this is that they are all now together."

"Have we heard anything at all in the local area?"

"Nah! The kids have scoured the place but found nothin', yet anyways."

"What is it you're looking for?" Aaron asked.

"Anything that might give us a clue as to just what they are doing in this area," Alki answered him. "They must be here for a reason and I figure it must be something big."

"The kids know to text me if and when they find anythin' unusual."

"Well, it looks like the best thing we can do is bed down for the night." Alki drained her glass.

"Yeah, well, it is a four berth, two doubles so you two can take the forward bunk if you like?"

"We are not a couple!" Alki stood, indignant. Aaron hid the smirk, but not very well.

"Just checkin'," Alex smiled and turned away.

"And you can cease the mirth young man, or should I say child!"

"Sorry Alki, couldn't help it." Aaron tried hard but could not suppress the laughter.

"Yes, Child!" She now turned away, only just in time to hide the smile that forced itself onto her face.

"You can 'ave the rear bunk Aaron, I'm fine in the chair." Alex said, as he poured himself another.

CHAPTER THIRTY-TWO
Harley

"Got a bit of news from the brats," Alex called out from behind the screen of his laptop.

Aaron bolted upright in the rear bunk and now checked the time. It was just 5.30.

"What is it Alex?" Alki emerged, bleary eyed above the driver's position.

"They've gone and spotted somethin'. Quay 'aven I think." He made a few adjustments and looked again. "Yep, Quay 'aven; a geezer got crushed between two ships in the 'arbour."

"I'm getting up," she said. Aaron muttered something similar.

By the time they had clothes on and were looking at the e-mail, Alex had tea brewed. They drank as he opened the attachment.

"Ukrainian by all accounts." He now read: "'A man was discovered by police yesterday evenin' in the 'arbour at Quay 'aven. 'E 'ad, apparently, been workin' aboard the fishin' vessel *Agrippa* on which 'e'd served for just over three months, when 'e is thought to 'ave slipped and fallen overboard. The neighbourin' boat and *Agrippa* had come together in the swell and crushed the forty-four-year-old man to death. 'Is body 'as been taken . . .' It goes on about their investigations and that the police 'ave ruled out foul play and closed the case as it seemed to be simply an accident."

"It fits the bill," Alki said.

"How so?" Aaron asked. "Because it's a crushing?" She nodded.

"Well, there's nothin' else come up in the last twelve months the same." Alex concurred as he now replied to the message.

"So you think this might be of significance?" Alex and Alki both nodded. "Great. But, even with that, shouldn't we be observing the cottage still?"

"Camera's still runnin'," Alex said, looking up to a small monitor above their heads. "Nothin's occurrin' just yet, and all the vehicles are still there."

"What?"

Alex smiled across at the younger man. "Set up above, lookin' 'igh across the dunes. We won't miss a thing cos it's been recordin' all night!"

"All night?"

"Yeah, just in case."

"You have a night vision camera?"

"Nah! Don't need one."

"But, how will you see?"

"Whenever they turn lights on in the 'ouse, or the car's lights, we'll see 'em, night camera or no."

"So you can see silhouette?"

"Not really, but, like you the other mornin'. When I checked the footage, the camera 'ad picked you up as you approached in the car, early, but once you turned the lights out, by the dune where Alki found you, it couldn't see a thing, not till dawn." Aaron frowned, then realised.

"That's why she found me so quickly!"

"Yeah. She called just about daybreak, and so I got up and 'ad a look. In the first light I could just make out the car and realised it was you."

Aaron now shook his head.

"I could have destroyed the whole project."

"You could Aaron, but you didn't."

Alki and Alex rewound the tape and then selectively fast forwarded to see what, if anything, had happened the previous night.

Apart from Luke going out and coming back with, what they all considered to be, a takeaway meal, nothing of consequence emerged.

"Ever driven an 'Arley?" Alex asked Aaron.

"I'm sorry?"

"'Arley Davidson, ever driven one?" Aaron, bemused, simply shook his head. "Come on," Alex said and went outside.

He took the cover off the bike that sat on the back of the motorhome and, with Aaron's help, lowered the ancient motorbike to the ground and gave it the once over.

"The leathers should fit you; maybe just tighten the belt a bit 'ere and there," Alex said.

"You're going to let me drive this?" He seemed shocked.

"Alki told me you could ride."

"Well, yes." He answered, with a slight shake of the head. "But it was only a Bantam."

"Don't 'only' a Bantam sunshine; a beezer's a beezer, and the Bantam was my first ever." Aaron felt duly chastised and coughed to cover his mistake. "Come on then."

He looked at the bike with unmistakable awe.

Alex saw him, a wry smile appearing on his face. He gave him the key.

"She's a beast, but show 'er who's boss and she'll do yer biddin'."

Aaron donned the leathers Alex provided; they fitted where they touched, but he didn't really care as he fired up the machine, revved it a little and finally sat astride her.

"This is fantastic." He was smiling like a child at Christmas. "But I'm not sure why I'm being given this opportunity."

"Just to let you get the feel," Alex replied, putting on a helmet. "In case you need to use 'er, in the future. She takes a bit of tamin'." He got on the back, behind Aaron. "We're just goin' to pop over and get the Bantam. Can't leave the little lady to rust now can we?"

"No, of course not," he said, engaging first gear, a broad smile on his face. "Easy rider was always my favourite film," he said as he set off, tentatively.

He made his way slowly to the main road and turned left. He gingerly speeded up, only missing the odd gear, but, with a little mentoring from Alex, by the time he'd reached the lay-by where the Bantam was parked he considered he'd mastered the 'beast'.

"Yeah, you can ride," Alex said and now sat astride the smaller bike. His phone rang.

Aaron was in the process of turning the Harley around as, seconds later, Alex ran over to him, ending the call.

"Pull 'er over there son, sharpish!" He yelled.

Aaron didn't question, but put the bike into gear and popped the clutch. A spray of dirt shot from the rear wheel as the bike lurched forward, into a small copse of trees, Alex running towards the entrance to the lay-by and quickly bobbing down behind a tree. A few seconds later a sports convertible shot past the entrance. Alex ran back to where Aaron was turning the bike around again.

"Alki saw 'im 'eadin' out. Thought it best if we kept our 'eads down, but 'e's gone straight past anyway."

"Was that one of them?" Aaron asked.

"Yeah, Luke, in the Merc," he said. "'E's probably gone into the town."

"That was lucky then."

"Yeah. Look, I'm gonna get the Bantam back to base; Alki's strugglin' with the camera so I need to 'ave a butchers. You alright on the 'Arley are you?" Aaron nodded. "Why don't you nip down there after 'im and check out what 'e's doing'," he said. "Providin' you keep the leathers on, and the 'elmet and goggles 'e won't recognise you."

"What about the Harley?" He questioned. "She's going to stand out like a sore thumb."

"Double bluff sunshine. Big entrance and everyone looks. But give 'em a minute and you're just part of the scenery." Aaron seemed to take this in.

"What are we expecting to get from this," he asked.

"'E might be meetin' someone," he said. "And 'e might not. We're of a mind they might be waitin' for another member of the gang turnin' up, so it's as well we 'ave a look see, whenever we get the chance."

Aaron nodded, pulled down the visor and set off.

He drove down the high street, passing the restaurant he'd

seen Reg and his gang in the night before. He cruised around the central square and then parked up, not having seen the convertible anywhere.

He got off the bike, trying to look as inconspicuous as possible. He could do nothing about the ape hangers though, and they did attract a little attention.

"You an Orang-utan or a Chimp?"

"Chump more like!"

Two young men had approached Aaron, studying the bike, and were now laughing as they walked by. He ignored them and opened the offside pannier, attempting to appear busy. He reached in and pulled out a polished piece of wood.

The laughter stopped and both young men backed swiftly away at sight of what Aaron now held.

He looked at it, surprised, then quickly pushed it back in and cursed as an elderly couple passed by.

He apologised, which seemed to surprise them.

He looked back into the pannier and cursed again, under his breath this time.

"What the . . . Why have you got a . . .?"

He looked down at the single barrelled shot gun, closed the lid and stepped away.

As quickly he stepped back in and opened it again. He shook his head whilst staring at the weapon in the pannier.

It was then that he saw, out of the corner of his eye, Luke coming out of a shop on the high street. He bent down and pretended to be tinkering with the engine but continued his surveillance through the shaded goggles. Luke, carrying a small paper bag, walked along the main road and turned up a side street. Aaron stood, waited a moment and then quickly crossed the street to peer into the window of the same shop. It was a sports shop, and he could see the shopkeeper through the window tidying items on the counter.

He heard a car engine and, to his right, through peripheral vision, spotted the merc turning onto the high street. He kept his face towards the shop window as it went past, heading through the village, back towards the cottage.

"What was it you think he bought?"

"I don't know Alex," he said. "I saw boxes being put away, but that was when he came past in the car."

"Probably nothing.'"

"We have bigger fish to fry anyway," Alki passed a print off to Alex. "As this man in Quay Haven was killed late last night, we need to check it out so I reckon that's you Alex. If this has anything to do with the gang, then I reckon they will probably make their way there sometime during today. It's worth a try anyway." She turned to Aaron "I need you to watch the camera with me," she said.

He concurred and started to disrobe as Alex gave him a crash course on the camera.

CHAPTER THIRTY-THREE
News

Alex reached Quay Haven in just under half an hour.

The town was alive, what with the police and reporters and sightseers. Alex managed to park the Harley with little fuss on the outskirts.

He took off the overcoat, helmet and goggles, fitting them into the nearside pannier, put on sunglasses and headed for the town, checking a text on his phone as he went.

He walked through the centre and reached the harbour shortly after. He surmised, judging by the crowds who were looking down into the bay, that this was where the supposed accident had occurred. He surveyed the scene for several minutes, took pictures as many people were doing and circled around the harbour wall. He spent some little time there, then went to the nearest cafe and sat outside, observing the quickly changing crowd through the zoom lens of his camera in the guise of taking ever more photographs.

He had been at the harbour just under twenty minutes when a particular couple caught his eye. He moved position around the harbour wall and now focused in on them. Even though they had both donned a disguise, Alex could make out Reg and Sonia, looking over the wall into the harbour, posing as any other would be onlooker.

He watched for some minutes, after which they split up. Sonia seemed to be heading back into the town itself, phone in hand, while Reg strode along the quay in the opposite direction. Alex followed him.

Reg walked only for a short way, along the harbour walls, stopping occasionally to observe a vessel or two out at sea and in the harbour, eventually approaching a small boat tied to the quayside. He stopped, looked casually up and down the quay, then boarded and disappeared into the cabin.

Alex waited for a few minutes, then went and sat in a nearby cafe, in sight of the small boat, all the time making the pretence of photographing the harbour.

He had been there almost half an hour when Reg emerged, folded wheelchair in hand which he now opened up on the quayside. Seconds later another person emerged, dressed in an overcoat, trilby hat and sunglasses. He shambled off the vessel and sat in the wheelchair which Reg now began to push, heading back towards the town, past the seated Alex.

He watched them depart, stood and paid the waiter then set off after them. He'd gone only a few steps when the sound of engines starting caused him to glance back towards the boat. Another man had emerged from the cabin, and was now casting off. Alex began to saunter, photographing the bay area as the vessel eventually pulled away from the quay, heading out of the harbour. He took a few more photos and hurried off.

He soon caught up with Reg and his wheelchair bound companion, Alex now following at a discreet distance as they left the town, heading away from the harbour. Reg eventually entered a car park, approaching the unmistakable Jaguar. Sonia emerged from the car as the man, if indeed it was a man, got out of the wheelchair and now squeezed himself into the back of the Jag. Reg folded the chair and opened the boot. Alex could see him trying to get it in but, clearly, it would not fit. He eventually slammed the boot, in petulance it seemed, and then looked around the car park, his attention coming to a skip which sat in the corner. He pushed the collapsed chair to the skip and threw it in, then made his way back to the car. They exited the car park, heading out of Quay Haven.

Alex took out his phone and sent a short message, then got back to the Harley and fired it up.

CHAPTER THIRTY-FOUR
Cottage

Alex had only been gone for a couple of minutes when Aaron grabbed Alki's attention.

"Reg and Sonia," he said, pointing to the screen. "Looks like they're going somewhere."

They watched as these two came out of the cottage, bags in hand which were packed into the boot of the Jag, with a few being pushed behind the front seats. Aaron zoomed out to see the whole of the track coming up to the main coastal road.

The Jaguar came up the track and turned onto the main road, heading the same way that Alex had gone just minutes before.

"I'd better inform him that they've left and might, possibly, be heading his way."

She began texting as the Jag went beyond the camera's scope.

"Hang on!" Aaron said.

She pressed send, then came back to the screen.

There was fresh activity at the cottage, three people now having come out of the front door. Aaron quickly zoomed in and they could make out Rose, Luke and Toby, all bringing luggage from the cottage to the Merc convertible. Most they put in the boot of the car, but Toby took a single bag to a dinghy that was secured by the water's edge.

The boot was closed and Luke now stood, surveying the horizon inland. They saw him say something to Rose and then point; it seemed like he was pointing at them.

"Could they see the camera in daylight?" Aaron asked. Alki shook her head.

"Alex said not, and he's been here almost two days."

They saw Luke open the boot of the car and reach in.

"I think we should take the mast down, just to be safe," Alki said. Aaron agreed as they both now saw Luke stand up with binoculars in his hands. Aaron rushed to the door.

She heard him scramble up on the roof as she watched Luke begin to survey inland. Seconds later the camera went dead as the mast was lowered.

"I think you got it in time Aaron, well done." She came outside to see him beginning to dismantle the mast.

"Do you think he would have been able to see it?" He asked.

"I'm not sure, but he definitely saw something and so it's best to be safe than sorry." Aaron nodded, continuing to dismantle the mast. "I still think we need to be able to see the cottage though."

"Won't we risk them seeing the camera?"

"Not if we place it only half as high, to just see the cottage not the road; and if we camouflage it as well."

"Yes it was rather high," Aaron said. "So how do we camouflage it?"

Alki smiled as she stepped down from the motorhome.

"You'll see," she said.

Fifteen minutes later saw them both looking at the monitor again, the view just scraping the tops of the trees in the distance, taking in only the cottage and the sea beyond.

"Great idea Alki," Aaron said. "Strapping leaves to it."

"Yes, well. Even if they do look this way they will simply see a little bit more tree than was there before."

"They are definitely leaving though, aren't they?" Alki nodded. "Do you think they'll go the same way as Reg and Sonia?"

"Possibly, but its Toby and the dinghy that interests me," she said. Aaron agreed.

"Shall I make ready to leave?" He asked. "Just in case."

"Yes Aaron. As soon as we know where they are going, all three of them, we shall go too."

It was just over an hour later that they came out of the cottage. The three of them had a few words together, shook hands and then Rose and Luke got into the car and set off up the track and out of their sight. Toby came round the side of the cottage to the dinghy, untied it and dragged it into the water. He got in, beginning to row out to sea.

"Where in hell's name is he going I wonder?" Aaron asked as Alki texted.

Aaron zoomed in to follow the dinghy, then slowly panned out. Now he took a gentle sweep across the horizon and, after a short while, came back to the dinghy that was, by now, about a hundred yards from the shore. He zoomed in on the far horizon again and slowly panned out. Instantly he yelled.

"Got you!"

Alki was watching and now she smiled as she slapped him on the back.

"I knew they had a boat," she said.

In the distance, just down from the horizon, a boat could now be seen on the view screen, heading towards the dinghy.

They watched for a short time, eventually the two vessels approaching one another. The young man threw his luggage up and then got on board, the dinghy being dragged on deck as the boat turned out to sea once more, heading east now. Aaron did his best to follow it but at extreme zoom the movement was too much and so they called it a day.

"At least they haven't torched the cottage as well," Alki said. "But it does seem as if that place has fulfilled its usage. They are moving on Aaron, but where to?"

"Shall I take the mast down?"

She nodded, now in thought.

"I think I might have an idea," she told him as he came back into the vehicle.

"So, where are we going then?"

"I'm not a hundred percent sure but, if memory serves, I think

Harenden on Thames is rather pleasant at this time of year." She said, reading a new text message.

"Harenden on Thames it is." He got into the driver's seat and started the engine. "Are we just going to leave the Bantam here, under the tarpaulin.?"

"Yes, it should be alright. I'll fetch it when we get back. Talking of ancient relics, lets pick up the aging greaser on the way, shall we?" Aaron just smiled and she began to text.

CHAPTER THIRTY-FIVE
Idiosyncrasy

They met Alex in a lay-by and, with the Harley packed onto the back of the motorhome, set off, Aaron driving still.

"So, where are we goin' now?" Alex asked, after explaining all that had gone on in the seaside town.

"We've been doing some research and, with the youngsters help, we think we may have found something." Alki said.

"That's good, because we don't know where they're goin' now, do we?"

"We think we might, especially in light of their new associate coming on board."

"'Ow so?"

Alki pulled up a document on the computer screen. It showed a picture of a man in his early forties, though a little out of focus.

"Your kids are both marvellous Alex. They discovered this info concerning the man who lost his life in the harbour of Quay Haven. He was an asylum seeker from the Ukraine. His name is, or rather was, Ivan Isanov. It seems he was given asylum about three months ago. I've seen this man before and I think I remember where. When I first began surveillance on The Barn, a few months before Aaron and Rose's episode with the tractor, I saw him there with Reg and Luke. I hadn't seen him since then and so I'd forgotten about him until now. I also have footage of him but, sadly, it's back at the house. I'm not sure it would do us any good anyway because it only shows him in the background most of the time; you don't get too good a look at him. But I do think that they must have been waiting for this young man to join them, and as he has been found 'dead', much like Reg and Rose, he can now move around with impunity. It seems to me that their complement is now full, and they'll probably be moving on to the next phase of their mission, whatever that mission is."

"Why do you think they were waiting for him then?"

"I'm not sure, but I do know that everything is now speeding up." Aaron shook his head a little and she noticed. "They've been treading water up until now Aaron." She said.

He still frowned.

"Remember the first time you saw Reg?" Aaron nodded. "For days after that we know they did the same routine, day after day. I had been following them for weeks before you came on the scene and they had been doing the same things all that time as well. Now, all of a sudden, they are no longer doing those same things and everything is beginning to move at a far faster rate."

"That would seem to fit," he said, though still sounding sceptical. "Especially with the torching of The Barn, and also with the mass exodus from the seaside cottage. But why are they going to Harenden on Thames, and how on earth do you know that?"

"It stems from when he and I were a married couple."

Aaron shook his head again.

"When Reg and I were first together he would get phone calls, make an excuse to leave the room as he answered them and then jot down notes on a notepad, but only if I was still outside of the room. For an intelligent man he did some pretty stupid things at times, I must say. I became suspicious, obviously thinking he must have a younger lover, and so I decided to find out for sure. I put a sheet of carbon into the notepad he used, smaller than the paper and four to five pages down so he wouldn't be aware of it. When he received more phone calls, and made more and more notes, I kept all of the carbon copies. There was no sign of a lover, thankfully, but there were various names, places, dates, times and addresses, none of which made any sense at all at the time. Fortunately, I inputted them all into the tablet, thinking there may be a need for them in the future. And I think I was right. The kids and I went through them and we've come up with an address we think might be important in Harenden on Thames. There were about seventeen addresses over the years, all dotted about the countryside, though mostly in the Oxfordshire area. Brit and Ringo have been researching them. They were holiday lets, all apart from four which were made up of airports and train stations. Seven of them are still vacant over this present period and so, obviously, of no significance, which left six that needed checking. Two are occupied by families, all with children and some with pets as well; those have been discounted which left only four possibilities, all in the vicinity of Harenden. All four have been rented out until at least this time next week, one being rented for the entire month."

"Have you checked the names of the people who rented them?"

"Two were booked via agents for celebrities; the kids have checked them out and they are both kosher and so of no significance to us. The other two are just non-descript, one being under the name, Smith; he is an ex professor, apparently writing a thesis on something or other, which leaves just the one we are heading for, which is under the name, Hennigan. The kids have checked it out but can find no info on this person at all."

"Is that significant?"

"Well, yes. We know that the young man, Toby, his surname is Hennigan, it's on the log books for both vehicles. But that is the only information we can find on him, and the same applies to the hirer of the holiday home. That is why its significant, because it means someone's hiding something, just like they did with the doctor and policeman in Norfolk. It seems to be a safe bet that's the place."

"Why Harenden do you think?"

"Don't know. All we do know is, it's a holiday home and it's on the bank of the River Thames."

"So is that where we're going?"

"It is."

Aaron nodded as he drove the motorhome, plus trailer with microlight, up the dual carriageway, all three of them deep in discussion about events over the last days, and debating what new potentialities await them in Harenden on Thames.

CHAPTER THIRTY-SIX
Concerns

Alex took over the driving and their discussions continued long into the journey, mostly about the elaborate story they had been told in the seaside cottage.

"What about the language they were both fluent in, that Rose would have told us about if not for Sonia stopping her?"

"Yes," Alki said. "That was interesting."

"How so?" Aaron asked.

Alki explained that sometimes, whilst asleep, Reg had spoken in a foreign tongue. She said that there had also been times when TV programmes had foreign speakers with subtitles, and that Reg had interpreted without thinking, and then tried to make out it was only a few words he'd picked up here and there.

"I had disregarded these small points until these last few days."

"I have heard Rose speak some words that I couldn't understand, mostly when on the phone. I just accepted that she had a handful of phrases from another language, but I never questioned it."

"I think that is what Sonia must have meant, about them both being able to speak another language. I don't believe it has that much significance."

He looked at her, questioning. "If they can speak Russian Alki, because that is the language we are talking about here, does that not add credence to the story they told us in the cottage?"

She thought for a moment.

"Do you think it does?"

"I think it's a possibility," he said. "It should be considered at least, surely?"

She took a short time to answer.

"I see the doubts you express Aaron," she said slowly. "But 'story' is the right word to use, for it can only be a 'story'!" Aaron waited for her to continue. She seemed to be trying to pick the right words.

"'E needs to 'ave reasons darlin'," Alex chipped in from the driver's seat. "'E gets that you're clever, and that you sussed Reg might be a bit of a fibber, but 'e needs evidence."

"I know Alex; I just don't know how to explain."

There was a moment of silence. Aaron broke it.

"I can only see that . . . Okay. These few things at least. The earnest urgings of my wife together with the probability she might speak Russian; that Reg definitely does speak Russian, and also the PM speaking with you and backing them. It all makes sense." He was clearly incensed. "You seemed so sure back in your cottage about them but, since then, with things calming a little, I've had time to think and I feel that I am nowhere near as sure as you are that what they told us is a scam."

She could see he was genuine, and now sat back in the chair.

Alex, keeping a steady sixty-five mph, spoke.

"All I can say is this. With all I've seen since this thing began with Alks, the stuff in Norfolk, them movin' to Cornwall and the goin's on down there; you and Rose, and all that business with the tractor . . ." He took a breath, eyes firmly on the road ahead. "It stinks is all I can say!"

"Thanks for the scientific approach," Alki smiled and sat forward. "Knew we could rely on Alex." Aaron laughed a little.

"All I'm sayin' is this. In the force when questionin' someone, anyone that is: doctor, lawyer, politician, whore, druggy. If they gives an answer what can't be corroborated, then it stinks! It stinks till such time as it can be proved. So, given that, what did they say to you in that cottage that could be proved then, eh?"

Neither of them seemed able to answer.

"It was routine, and proved over and over in my time in the force, that if someone said somethin' what could not be corroborated with 'ard evidence, then it weren't worth much."

"All I can add to that Aaron is this; prime minister's voices, on the phone, can be mimicked. We can't phone him back to prove it was actually him. The story concerning the dead bodies might be able to be traced, as they pointed out, but what would that prove? They have provided Reg, Rose and this Ivan with anonymity, this we know is true. But, proving what they have said about the bodies, the people they were and what happened to them, has no worth to us now; it has no bearing, except that it gave them new identities."

"That's true Alks. The bodies gave 'em what they wanted, anonymity. If what they told you guys about 'em is right, then great. We can't 'elp 'em! We 'ave to concentrate on the 'ere and now. What's occurrin' now is what matters."

"I think you are right Alex. We think we know where they are going, but we also need to know why."

Aaron listened but did not seem convinced. Alki continued.

"What are the facts? Three dead bodies have been used to take on the persona of three other people. As far as the world is concerned, these three people are now dead and so, because of the success of this replacement body scam it has given all three complete anonymities. Two of those people, we have been informed, are on their way to Russia for reasons of which we are not privy, but a third has also now appeared, who seems to be part of the group but who was not mentioned to us in their little story."

"But they said it was on a 'need to know' basis, and maybe we didn't need to know about this third person."

"Possibly correct," Alki agreed, as did Alex. "And so why are they on their way to a location near London, if they are on their way to Russia?"

"That must be part of the 'need to know' stuff I would imagine."

"Very well Aaron," she said. "The 'need to know' basis was stressed quite strongly and so we shall carry on under that assumption, that anything we uncover is part of their master plan and that we weren't told of it because of their 'need to know' policy, and we don't need to know. But we shall carry on under that assumption, only until such time as one of the six, no seven of them now with the captain of the boat, do anything which *doesn't* fit in with the Russian spy story. Does that seem fair?"

"But what if, in our investigations, we do something that damages their plans, something that might put them in harm's way?"

"That was a serious part of the thrust of their argument, that we had potentially destroyed this project of theirs." She kept her eyes firmly on him. "What did we do apart from observe?" She waited now.

He shook his head and thought. After a time he said.

"We did nothing else. We watched them, that's all."

"We didn't tell anyone else. We didn't communicate our findings in any way at all and we didn't shout it from the rooftops. How could we have jeopardised their project if we didn't communicate, in any way at all, with anyone other than us three?"

"What about the 'brats', as you call them?"

"Britney and Ringo actually know very little. We simply give them a subject or a person we need info on and they use their abilities on the internet to find the info for us."

"They are your children Alex?"

"Certainly are, little darlin's."

"Oh, sorry, I should have explained. Britney and Ringo are Alex's children, from a previous marriage."

"Yeah, and the best thing to come out of it an' all," Alex said with a laugh.

"The info we give them is never linked and they couldn't ever put it all together without the enormous amount of information that we two, three now with you Aaron, have garnered." Alki chuckled a little.

"Well, that makes sense."

"Do you remember, in their kitchen, they told us they heard all that was said back at the cottage, read all our e-mails and heard everything that was said on our mobiles and also the landline?" He nodded. "They didn't seem to know about Brit and Ringo did they? Why was that?" Aaron shook his head. "Because we only ever contact them on Alex's device and my tablet, which they haven't got access to."

"Yeah. They might 'ave been able to 'ear you back there; they probably bugged the place when Alks took up the residency, but they can't get access to all our internet based devices now, or our mobiles."

"Oh, I see. But what about the paparazzi? Couldn't they have blown their operation, turning up like that?"

"Yes, that was an unfortunate accident, or a happy one depending on how you look at it. They obviously hadn't staged that, as we saw when we got back to my little cottage because there were reporters there as well." Aaron agreed. "It did prove one thing though; they are vulnerable."

She saw Aaron wince a little.

"Aaron," she said. "You must understand that I take on board all you have said, and that I, we," she indicated Alex. "We shall never do anything that might put Reg or Rose, or even the new chap in a compromising situation. If their story is true we shall find out soon enough, and we leave them alone from that time. If their story is bogus? I feel sure that we shall also find that out soon enough as well. Whatever happens, as soon as we know for certain who is telling the truth and who is not, we shall act upon that information accordingly. Rest assured Aaron, I shall not stand by and see anyone harmed because of our actions."

"Thanks Alki," he said. "I just want them to have the best chance of success."

"I understand that, but remain neutral Aaron. You didn't know Reg at all, but I did and all I can see is the middle finger of his right hand tapping his leg."

"I shall remain neutral Alki," he said and smiled.

"I hope you will," she smiled back. "Because, to date, Reg's little idiosyncrasies have never failed."

CHAPTER THIRTY-SEVEN
Teddy

The address they had been looking for was advertised on the Internet. It was a holiday home and backed on to the Thames River itself. It was easy to find and once they had physically seen its location, a campsite was found less than half a mile downstream. It was to this site that they made their way and parked up close to the river in a corner of the field.

"We need to get close to make sure it is them."

"The Harley is too conspicuous." Aaron said. Alki agreed.

"I'll get Google Earth up again, so's we can get the lie of the land."

Alex powered up the computer. It was dark now and so he drew all the curtains, taking the bottle from its safe haven on the top shelf. He poured into three glasses.

"We're still going to need to see what's going on." Alki drank. "I think it's just about Teddy time!"

"Oh God!" Alex exclaimed.

"It's the only way."

"It's dark!"

"Oh, is that why you drew the curtains? I did wonder." He just looked at her.

"You've never flown it at night before," he said.

"Hold on. What are you talking about, surely not the microlight again?" Aaron asked.

"Course not," she answered, smiling. "You couldn't fly that in the dark?"

Alex guffawed.

"Yeah. And talkin' about microlights, tell me you've got your licence sorted now?"

"You don't need a licence Alex, not to fly microlights." Aaron told him.

He looked at him with a frown, which quickly lifted.

"She tell you that, did she?" Aaron nodded. "Thought so." He now turned to Alki.

"Cheers," she said.

"Hang on. Does this mean that you do need a licence?"

"You don't need a licence to fly Teddy." Alki sipped her drink, not looking at either of them.

"You've never flown Teddy in the dark before, and it's not just that, you'll be flyin' in 2-D!"

"2-D?" Aaron asked.

"Oh for God's sake it's not all that bad," Alki laughed.

"Do you want to explain the jargon, and about the licence to fly microlights please?"

"You do need a licence Aaron, despite what lady muck 'ere told you! But flyin' the microlight is like drivin', it's in 3 dimensions; you're there! Flyin' Teddy is like flyin' a TV, you miss out the third dimension because you are not bleedin' well there!"

"It's almost the same as flying the micro anyway," she said with a giggle. Alex did not laugh.

"You've never done it before at night, and you crashed it the last time, in daylight as well!"

"Oh, details!" She laughed. "I was a little tipsy at the time."

"Alki, this is not that safe and you know it." He spoke in a soft voice to her.

She looked at him and the laughter faded.

"I know, but what option do we have Alex; we need to know, it's as simple as that."

"Can't we wait till mornin' then?"

"Things are speeding up," she said. "We need to be at their speed if we are to solve this puzzle."

"Would somebody mind telling me just what you are suggesting? And who or what is Teddy, if it is not the microlight which, apparently, you do need a licence to pilot!" He looked squarely at Alki.

Alki and Alex looked at each other and both smiled, Alex shaking his head. It was Alki that spoke.

"Sorry Aaron. I can fly, it's just that I haven't had time to get round to revalidating my microlight licence for a while. Anyway, to answer your second question, Teddy is the teddicopter, or helicopter if you want to be precise." Alex looked at her with a severe stare. "Quadcopter then, if you want to be precise and pedantic." Alex took up the explanation.

"We 'ave a drone what's fitted with a camera," he said, still shaking his head.

"And we could use it to infiltrate their holiday home to find out, first of all, that it is where they are staying, and if that is borne out, then just what they are doing." Alki now looked at Alex and smiled again. "It's just that he's a pessimist, and also doesn't trust me."

Alex looked away, head still shaking but with a smile there now.

"It's the only way we can gain any information at all. We have to work fast now, which is why we must take this chance with the drone."

"All right," Alex said, standing. "I'll set it up."

"Thank you Alex," she said as he left the motorhome.

They both heard him mutter something unintelligible under his breath.

"He's a good man. He just tends to worry overmuch."

"Microlight, drone, Harley Davidson!" Aaron threw his hands in the air. "What the hell is going on around here?" he questioned, then seemed to recall something. "And not just that, what about the shotgun he's got in the bike's pannier?" Alki looked at him with a smile.

"Oh, you found it!"

Aaron mouthed rather than said, 'what?'

"He'd lost it, about ten days ago I think."

"You knew he had a sawn off shotgun?"

"Of course. But it's not all that sawn off." Her smile faded a little as she saw the serious look on his face. "Oh, my dear, he has far worse than that. I'll get him to show you the missile launcher when we've finished with Teddy!" Aaron went to speak but nothing emerged.

"Done!" Alex called from outside.

There was a four engined drone, a quadcopter, with a small camera and mini spotlight attached to it, placed on a metal base on the grass. Alex handed a compact control panel to Alki and then bent down to the drone and turned it on. The four rotors of the small aerial machine sprang to life.

She altered a few settings on her handset and then flicked a switch, pushing a lever at the same time.

Immediately the black machine lifted vertically into the air. She set it down and then made it take off again, flying low over the ground, turning and coming back to them. Alex brought a monitor and placed it before her as Alki brought the drone to a halt only metres away and turned the camera on them.

Aaron could see them all as a group in the monitor as Alki sent the machine skyward once again, keeping them all in view and zooming in as it ascended.

He looked at the monitor and saw the group on screen, and now looked up but could not see the drone, and yet he could hear it, just.

She brought it back down and made it land again as she and Alex went to it. He could see them tinkering with it and then back off, Alki taking the control once again. The machine rose into the air and now headed off across the water, away from them and at speed.

He turned back and now could see in the monitor the progress of the drone at Alki's hands. He watched the relayed images as it skimmed over the river.

They now saw Alki take the aircraft up and could see it flying across the trees, eventually coming back down to the River Thames. She turned it to follow the flow of the river, but with the camera being angled toward the south bank. It flew for some minutes like this, eventually slowing as the grounds of what looked like riverside homes approached. The drone hovered as the camera panned left and then right.

"I'm not absolutely certain which their domicile is from this side," she said.

"See if you can find the car," Alex offered.

"Good idea."

The drone gained height again, camera pulling back to its widest lens position. Alki now sent the aircraft slowly downstream whilst panning across each of the homes on the riverbank. She stopped at one home and checked the laptop.

"I think this is it," she said, looking again at the computer screen. "Yes, this is the one. Still can't see either of the cars though."

She now turned to Alex who was also comparing the two images.

"I reckon you're right lass," he said.

"Good. Now I need you to operate the camera while I take Teddy in close to the windows. We only have about fifteen minutes of battery."

Alex took the second remote as Alki sent the drone high to see the layout of the holiday home. A couple of minutes later, having cursorily circumnavigated the property, she brought the drone back down to hover over the river after checking up stream and down that no vessels were approaching.

"There are no vehicles out front and so I think our friends are out for the night; I hope so anyway," she said. "I just need to gain confirmation that this is their new base."

Aaron watched as these two now worked together.

Alex zoomed in and instructed Alki which way to manoeuvre. She did as he asked with minor adjustments being made to accommodate what he saw in the monitor.

"It's them," she called out, as the camera took its first close up through a downstairs window. "Reg's blazer. I remember wondering where the hell it had gone, only three days after he had 'died'."

The drone was sent all around the house and, almost ten minutes later, and after numerous wide angle and zoomed in shots of the whole of the property, Alki whispered to Alex that they were almost out of time. He acknowledged and she began to take the drone up.

"'Ang on darlin," Alex said. "Take 'im down for a minute, I just need a quick look at water's edge, opposite."

"What for Alex?" she said, but doing as he asked.

"Possibles for Cat."

"Of course." She seemingly understood.

The quadcopter came down to hover just above the river, scanning the opposite bank to the home they had videoed. Alex zoomed in and out as Alki went up and down the river, twice.

"That'll do lass," he said.

Alki took the drone up.

"Post the beacon Alex, I need to see where we are in relation to the drone."

Alex took a mast from the side panel in the motorhome and fixed a lamp to the top. He turned it on and it shone red as he now extended the mast to its maximum length and held it up in the air, the red light shining like a dull beacon almost twenty-five feet above them.

"I think I'll need it higher Alex, the trees are huge in this area."

"No worries darlin'," he said. He stepped across to the motorhome and climbed the ladder fixed at the rear end. Once on the roof he extended the beacon to his full reach.

"Keep it there dear," she said. "I'm looking now."

Aaron saw her flicking the switches on her control panel.

"There you are! Well done Alex, I'm bringing him home."

Aaron could see on the monitor a dim red light in the distance and watched as it came closer and closer. Shortly he could hear the light hum of the drone's motor. He looked into the sky but could see nothing.

"Bring the beacon down Alex, and to me." Alki said.

He did just as she asked, shortening the rod in stages and bringing the beacon down to the ground, to where she stood, the drone now descending to approach the motorhome, slowly coming back to the landing place with only the slightest of bumps.

"Well done Alco!" Alex laughed.

"And I've had a drink!" She laughed too, with only a slight coyness.

"Alex?" Aaron came up to him as he dismantled the mast. He mumbled something, Aaron couldn't make it out. "I found a shotgun in the pannier of the Harley," he said.

"That's where it is. Thanks."

"I just wondered why you would have such a lethal instrument."

He now looked up at Aaron, nodded and stood up.

"Did Alki tell you that I used to be a policeman?" Aaron nodded. "Did she tell you I got in a bit of a scrape?" Aaron winced, but then nodded. "It's alright fella," he said. "I'm not ashamed, I was screwed over."

"I see," Aaron said.

"But about the shotgun; it was took from a dodgy geezer and, at that time, it just didn't seem right to 'and it in so I kept it. Good job too, because it's come in 'andy a time or two I can tell you."

"Okay, I see," he said. "It's none of my business anyway but," he hesitated. Alex looked at him and raised his eyebrows. Aaron went on. "Alki said, and I'm sure she was joking." He seemed to be hoping more than anything. "That you had a missile launcher?" Alex held his gaze, and nodded. "You have?" That was when Alex laughed.

"No missile launcher Aaron," he said. "But I do 'ave a couple more guns, a few grenades as well as a Tazer." Aaron's eyes grew wide and he gave a questioning look.

Alex went past, beckoning for him to follow. They went to the side of the motorhome and Alex unlocked a compartment, opening the drawer inside. Sure enough, there was a Tazer gun and a box of eight hand grenades! Aaron's eyes nearly popped out of his skull. Alex laughed, but then explained.

"Once I started up as a PI, after the police thing, I thought these might come in 'andy, and I was right, although not to actually use any of 'em 'cos I 'aven't, but the effect they 'ave on people when they see 'em? Well."

Aaron was speechless.

"And with all that little lot, comes this little frightener."

He went back into the motorhome, Aaron following. He pulled out a gun from beneath the front bunk mattress, and pointed it straight at Aaron.

Aaron backed away, fearful. Alex laughed.

"Replica," he said, putting it back. "But it looks real enough. It's all run o' the mill stuff Aaron," he said. "Apart from the sawn off, and the tazer. Oh yeah, and the stunners, they're a bit illegal an' all."

"Stunners?"

"Yeah, the grenades, they're stunners," he said.

"Where did you get all this from?"

"Amazin' what yer gets given durin' a few years in the force, don't you think?"

"Given?"

"Well, somethin' like that." He winked, stood and switched the kettle on. "Tea?"

CHAPTER THIRTY-EIGHT
Footage

With the drone down and secured away, they began to study the footage.

The riverside cottage seemed bereft of life, but some lights were still on and the curtains left open. Once the drone had dropped to window level they could see evidence of new occupancy, Reg's blazer being one certain item to be identified, Alki explaining it was from Reg's RAF days and one piece of his past that he was obviously loathe to let go. As the drone skirted around the dwelling they could see bags dropped on beds in the upper level, plus provisions and assorted accoutrements left dotted around the ground floor, but no sign of actual life at all.

It was a cottage and almost square; it had two levels with a lounge, dining room, kitchen and utility room on the ground floor, a front door that opened out onto the street, and a 'back door' which opened onto the gardens that extended down to mooring blocks on the river. On the first floor there were three bedrooms and a bathroom, all with their curtains drawn back.

"That's typical of the man Reg is," Alki said. Alex and Aaron both looked to her for explanation. "He only takes precautions if he considers it necessary." They still looked. "He hasn't closed the curtains because he believes he has given us the slip with his story of spies and dangerous missions. He is confident we took the bait and believes they are not under scrutiny anymore, and so conducts his affairs with relative abandon."

"Surely if he knows you, which he does, it would occur to him that you might still be on his tail?" Aaron asked. "And then add your ability to use things like the microlight, and even the quadcopter, he would know, or at least consider that you might still be following him."

"He wouldn't know about the quadcopter Aaron. He might just pick up on the microlight though, but I've set things in motion to lead them away from us on that one." Aaron would have questioned that, but she continued. "As to the model flying, I'd given it up thirty years earlier and never got around to mentioning it to him. Oh no! He thinks the story that they spun us has done the trick, and that it was sufficient to deter us from further forays. He always was a fairly arrogant man."

They watched on the monitor, the drone approaching the lounge of the holiday home once it had finished its cursory examination.

They could see evidence of occupancy here also as the camera panned left to right, stopping occasionally to zoom in on various objects.

The drone banked left and approached the dining room.

The table and chairs were laden with bags and coats, but the drone's camera immediately began to zoom in on the table itself. As the image became clearer they could see a bunch of laid out papers, the top one looking like a ground plan.

The camera now pulled back and began to look into different corners of the room, much to the disgust of Alki and Aaron.

"I know, I know, I know!" Alex halted all verbal attacks. "If you keep watchin' you'll soon be apologisin' as well."

They did as he said and, sure enough, the camera came back to the ground plans on the table.

"Sorry," Was all Alki could say as they all now scrutinised the footage, Alex smiling smugly.

There were two, three or even more plans on the table but only the top one was visible, the others lying beneath.

It was obviously difficult for the drone to reach an optimum position to view the document from outside, but it rose to the top of the window frame as the camera zoomed in and the aircraft now hovered.

It was a groundplan of a house, with three distinct storeys which were outlined in stages to the left of the main plan. It was difficult to make out certain features but the main aspects were unmistakable.

Many notes and drawings were made as the video footage was played, paused, rewound and then played over and over again, eventually allowing it to play on, covering its survey of the rest of the house.

Nothing more of interest emerged and so scrutiny of the notes of the groundplan began.

"It looks pretty grand." Aaron commented.

"It does, but where is it, and why are they concerned with it," Alki said.

"It must be in 'Arenden or they wouldn't be 'ere. I know. I'll send the footage to the brats and they can research it whilst we put plans into gear to keep 'em under surveillance." Alki agreed as did Aaron. "The first thing though, is to deploy Cat."

"Cat?" Aaron said.

"Yeah, the Catamaran," Alex answered.

"A catamaran? I don't understand."

"Yeah. She's equipped with a camera, same as the drone."

"Why not just use the quadcopter?"

"Teddy 'as limited battery and is also conspicuous, bein' in the air. We use Cat for longer term surveillance, cos she 'as an 'ydraulic arm which pulls 'er out of the water makin' 'er stable, and 'er batteries can last far in excess of forty-eight hours."

"This I've got to see," Aaron said, smiling.

"I've seen a few possibles where to put 'er on the footage, and if they're secluded enough with a good view of the place, we'll check to see if there's anythin' there we can use to 'oist 'er up, out the water."

He lifted the mattress off the rear bunk, took the wooden bed base off and began to take out a large tray.

"This is Cat," he said, as he opened it up revealing a matt black

Catamaran, almost four feet long by three feet wide with a camera at the front in the middle, a tri-sectioned hydraulic arm to the back and LED lights on each of the pontoons. He pointed to the hydraulic arm. "This little beauty can reach up to eight feet, latch onto a bough or an RSJ under a jetty, or whatever there is around, 'oist 'er up out of the water which makes 'er stable and then she can monitor whatever. A right little darlin' she is."

Almost an hour later saw her on her way, being shadowed by Teddy in the air.

A suitable position was quickly found opposite the holiday home and, using a blue light from one of the LED lamps, Alex neatly positioned her and lifted the vessel out of the water with the hydraulic arm. He tested the camera, zooming in to provide a tight shot of the whole property, but with the edges of properties either side in frame as well. He left her recording.

It was around a couple of hours later that they saw, on Cat's monitor, two cars pull up. Alex quickly zoomed in and, sure enough, even at the distance Cat was from the riverside home, they could make out the Jaguar and Merc convertible. They watched as the gang disembarked from the cars and went into the house, all five of them, the newest member still in overcoat with trilby and sunglasses.

Alex and Aaron smiled at each other, Alki just seemed relieved.

They decided to set a watch all night, taking it in turns. But now, in celebration, the Irish was once again brought out.

CHAPTER THIRTY-NINE
Plans?

They were up early, showered and breakfasted and the overnight footage from Cat was now perused, but the night's vigilance revealed nothing out of the ordinary.

They could see that the gang had brought wine and beer and seemed to be in high spirits, but the curtains had been quickly drawn and a few hours later the lights went out.

There had been no other movement throughout the night and now, a few hours after dawn, they could see lots of bustle in the house, but nobody yet venturing forth. Most of the activity seemed to be in the dining area, and especially around the dining table itself. Cat could make out five individuals but, due to the distance between the vessel and the building on the opposite bank, could not discern much more, even with Aaron zooming tight in.

They watched throughout the day but it was early evening when they saw Reg and Rose coming downstairs, accoutred in the finest, what appeared to be, formal evening dress. Sure enough, shortly after, a chauffeur-driven limousine arrived and minutes later saw them seated in the back of the vehicle and driven off.

Teddy was sent up straightaway, Alki quickly heading after them with Alex operating the drone's camera and swiftly finding the limousine as it headed towards the town.

Aaron, monitoring Cat's screen, informed them he'd caught glimpses of two of the remaining gang members inside the house, going from room to room. And it was only minutes later that Sonia and Luke, both dressed casually plus the mysterious fifth member, still in the overcoat with hat and sunglasses, left also in the convertible.

"You go Alex," Alki said. "I can take care of the camera." He needed no prompting, quickly donning leathers.

The limousine had gone just over a mile and now, with Teddy monitoring high in the sky above, was seen entering the main gates of a park, heading down the drive leading to the mansion at its core. Alki kept the quadcopter in hover, the camera in wide angle as she surveyed the scene for a short time.

"About eight more limousines have gone in since they got there," she said. "It looks like it's a ball or a dinner. I think they'll be there for some time."

"Their place seems totally deserted now." Aaron was still studying Cat's monitor.

"I'll bring Teddy back then, and we can take him for a trip around their house whilst they're out."

The images from Cat showed only a few lights left on in the home. Aaron now pulled the camera back to its widest angle, raising it to watch for the drone.

It approached with little fuss, dropping in from above, and as soon as it came into sight on Cat's view finder Aaron brought the suspended spy's camera back down to water level, leaving it in wide angle to watch for any approaching danger.

Alki took the drone straight to the dining room window. The lights were off in this room and so Alki switched Teddy's spotlight on, immediately revealing several ground plans on and around the table. Many seemed to be discarded though one plan was left, with numerous pencil marks on it. They could make out the word 'Spa'.

Aaron called out.

"A light's gone on upstairs!"

"What?"

"A light," he whispered as he zoomed Cat in. He could see movement in the upstairs room but couldn't make out who it was. "Kill the light Alki," he said, pulling the lens back in order to view the whole building. She did as he asked.

"Damn! There's a boat coming as well," he called.

"How far?"

"It's close."

"Zoom Cat in on the porch of the back door."

"What the hell for?"

"I can't take Teddy up Aaron, whoever is in that room might see."

"They might have seen him already!"

"We have to take that chance," she said. "I'm going to land Teddy on the porch roof."

"Isn't that a bit dangerous Alki?"

"Only if I can't see what I'm doing," she said. "And if you zoom Cat in I'll be able to see what I'm doing."

"So what will we do then, even if you manage to land him successfully?" She gave him a look.

He tutted but did what she said.

"I land Teddy on the porch roof where no-one, either in the house or on the river can see him. When the boat passes we use Cat's camera and wait and see just who is in the house, where they are in the house and then, when it's safe, bring Teddy back without being detected."

He didn't comment, but watched as the black drone, spotlight switched off now, settle on the flat roof. He quickly zoomed out again to watch the approaching vessel.

"Hang on. Isn't that their boat?" He asked.

"Their boat?"

He nodded, flicking open various folders on the laptop whilst manoeuvring the levers on Cat and zooming in on the now slowing craft.

"That's the one at Quay Haven," Aaron confirmed, cross referencing the photo's that had been downloaded from Alex's phone.

"And the same one that picked Toby up at the cottage on the coast?" Alki asked.

Aaron concurred and they both watched as the boat approached the mooring station of the home, beginning to turn now and eventually facing downstream as it pulled into the bank.

"Zoom in on the stern," she said. "Can you see its name?"

He adjusted the camera to its maximum zoom.

"There it is," Aaron said. "*The Pearl Dulang.*"

"*The Pearl Dulang*? Does that mean anything to you Aaron?"

He shook his head.

"What about Teddy?" He asked. "Isn't he in a precarious position where he is?"

"He is," she said. "But I can't risk taking off now. They would see him."

He agreed as he looked at the drones monitor, its position showing only the upper walls of the building.

"That's Toby," Alki said as Cat's camera remained on the vessel.

They watched the young man clamber off the boat and begin to moor it to the posts. Another man appeared.

"The one with the cap was driving." Aaron said, intent on the screen.

"I think the driver of a boat is termed 'captain', Aaron." He didn't seem to hear.

The back door of the cottage opened, throwing light onto the path leading down to where the boat was now moored. A middle aged man appeared and called to them both.

"Who the hell is that?" Alki said. "Is he the one they picked up in Quay Haven? I thought he'd gone out with the others. He seems a bit . . ." She shook her head, and watched as the man approached the boat, shaking hands with each of the new arrivals.

"He must be the Ukrainian."

"But we saw him go out, with Luke and Sonia."

"He's roughly the same height," Aaron said.

"He must have come back as Alex set off to follow them. "She checked her phone and discovered a missed call, and it was from Alex. She tried to call him back but got no answer.

They now watched as bags were brought up from below and carried ashore. The lights on the boat were switched off and all three went into the cottage.

"I should think now is as good a time as any to bring Teddy back?"

Aaron agreed and they both watched Cat's monitor as the drone went up.

It was shortly after Teddy was decommissioned and put away that Alex appeared.

He confirmed that Sonia, Luke and their accomplice had set off, but stopped a hundred or so yards down the road. The man in the overcoat had got out, talking on the phone, and headed back up the road towards the cottage as the Merc had set off again. He had tried to phone but got no answer and so decided to follow Sonia and Luke. They had driven just a few hundred yards down the road and parked up at a pub.

"I swanned in and 'ad a swift 'alf at the bar, just next to where they was sat. I starts to chat to the barman and makes out I was moored up on the river and asks 'im what all the fuss was about, what with all the limo's, the Bentleys and Rollers that was flyin' about?"

He took a sip of Irish that Alki had poured for him.

"'E tells me it's to do with this Russian geezer what owns a place the other side of the river and that it's somethin' like a state do. I says to 'im that the only good Russian is a dead Russian and 'e laughs, but the gal and geezer what's sat be'ind me, you could almost feel the seethin'."

"Wasn't that a bit risky Alex?" Aaron asked.

"Nah; they don't know me from Adam," he laughed.

"I meant insulting Russia!"

"It's what you do Aaron," he said, turning to him. "Always slag off the others, whoever they are, always gets a laugh! Besides, she and 'im was more interested in 'er tablet than me, it kept pingin' all the time."

"Did you hear anything?" Alki asked.

"Nah, not a lot," he said. "But I took a few piccys while I was there!"

What?" They both looked at him now. He laughed out loud.

"Not too clever these would-be spies are they?" He said, taking his phone out. "There they are in the corner, peerin' into 'er tablet and thinkin' they're as safe as a turd in a toilet, but they've got a mirror be'ind 'em!"

"You took pictures Alex?" Alki could not help the smile that appeared.

"How on earth did you manage that without them seeing?" Aaron was not smiling.

"Big un an' all it was, the mirror. I just reverses the camera on the Sammy and sets it to record vid. I've got my back to 'em, me Sammy's tucked in just above me chest and zoom is at max. Got about five minutes!"

"Sammy?"

"He has a Samsung phone and camera Aaron; his Sammy," Alki explained.

Alex laughed, and got a refill as he quickly downloaded the pictures onto the laptop.

His video was a little blurred but they could make out the tablet clear enough and when they blew up the images being shown, could make out numerous stills shots of the interior of a stately home, though mostly being of male clothing, it seemed, from the contents of a large walk-in wardrobe.

They continued to view the video content until the footage ended.

"By this time I thought it might be pushin' it a bit if I stayed any longer, so I slung me 'ook!"

"And you didn't hear anything?"

No, too noisy." He said. "Only a bit about a leisure spa, that's all."

"Spa?" Both Aaron and Alki spoke together, and now looked at him.

"What?" He said.

CHAPTER FORTY
The Plan?

"It's the kids," Alex said, picking up the phone. He put it on speaker. "Alright guys, any news?"

"The ground plan you sent us seemed to be from a seventeenth century building and, as there is only one seventeenth century building in or near Harenden, it led us straight there. It's a mansion house all right Alex," Ringo said. "We checked it in the archives and it's called Harenden Reside. It's a big mansion type house on the estate of the same name, and it was bought by a Russian banker whose name is Nicholaus Klevchenky, almost five years ago."

"Good lad." He turned the volume up. "Alki 'as a couple of questions."

"Hi Ringer well done, and you Brit. Did you get the video we sent with the floor plan of the spa?"

"Yes we did Alki."

"Great. And would you, in your estimation, say this could be part of the mansion in Harenden Reside?"

"The spa's a modern layout Alki," they heard Britney say. "It doesn't look like it would be part of this building, it's really old."

"What do you think Ringer?"

There was a pause, during which they could hear animated discussion.

"No, it definitely isn't part of the mansion."

"Thanks kids, well done." Alki said. "Seeing as you two are still on the line, and because you are so slick with this Internet thing, could you see if there is an upmarket spa in the vicinity?"

"Ahead of you Alki," Britney's voice rang out. "There are a few but

I'd imagined you'd be looking for one of elite status, given that you've been looking at a stately home, in which case we found it, just outside of Harenden on Thames but on your side of the river."

"Well done Brit. Can you . . ."

"Hang on a sec," Britney called. "Just looking to see . . . Yes, there is one!"

"One what?"

"A ground plan. And, yes, the plan of the spa that you sent us matches with this one."

"It seems you kids are ahead of us on the mind-reading stakes as well."

"Obvious when you think about it," she said. "We're sending you all the details now, both for the mansion and its owner, as well as the location and details of the spa in Harenden."

"Thanks Brit."

Alki ended the call and turned to Alex.

"So, it seems that their focus now is the spa, but why?"

The info arrived from the kids straightaway and was quickly opened.

"It looks like this must be it." Alki was looking at the information the kids had sent them. "So, what do we know about this 'Harenden Reside' then?"

"They've sent us a link." Alex clicked on it.

It was an article from a local newspaper and he read it out.

"Mr. Nicholaus Klevchenky was a very successful banker in Russia, but 'e 'ad left the country under a cloud and been given asylum in England. The political powers in Russia 'ad wanted 'im back from that time on, to answer certain questions concernin' substantial amounts of money which 'ad disappeared from the numerous banks where Mr. Klevchenky 'ad worked."

"So, there does seem to be a link with Russia after all," Alki smiled. "It has to have something to do with this banker?"

"It's feasible. They're 'ere for a reason and this 'Nicholaus Klevchenky' would seem to be as good a bet as any, especially as Reg and Rose seem to be in 'is circle of friends, what with bein' invited to the ball an' all."

It was then that the phone rang again.

"Hello Brit," Alki said. "What have you got for us now?"

"We did some research Alki, and you're gonna love it!" Britney sounded bright. "We looked through magazines and papers that circulate within a ten-mile radius of Harenden and found a few references to Nicholaus Klevchenky, but there was one that was of particular interest. It showed two people, from Russia, who had come over specially to see this Mr. Klevchenky. And this is the really, really good bit; it's Reg and Rose!"

"What?"

"Yes Alki, it's them, it's definitely them!"

"How can this be?" Aaron asked.

"Oh, it gets better," Ringo now chipped in. "After I found it in the newspapers, Brit decided to check the news over the past week. She found nothing, but then looked further back, over the last month. That was when we began to find out stuff; we even found the date when these two had come in to the country."

"You are joking of course?" Alki said. "I have been on the tale of Reg and Rose, seen Reg almost face-to-face as it were, over the last five, six months. How can they possibly have flown in to this country without me knowing they'd even left it in the first place?"

"This is where it gets really interesting," Britney now took up the baton. "We even found footage of them coming off the plane and going through customs."

"Britney? Are you going to explain all this or are we simply going to continue tearing our hair out?"

The youngsters could be heard laughing over the phone.

"I really do think I could become guilty of child murder!"

"Get in line," Alex chipped in.

The laughter was heard to increase.

"Well!"

It decreased enough for Ringo to speak.

"Our theory so far is this. When you look at the footage of them coming off the plane it is obvious, to us at least, that they were not allowing anyone a good look at their faces. They both wore loose fitting coats which were quite long, and each of them had large sunglasses with hats to complete the camouflage. Both of them walked slowly and so it was also difficult to recognise any particular sort of gait. They didn't stay long in the public eye and were whisked away in a blacked out limousine, the destination of which, it seems, no one knew. And get this; they arrived in this country on the first of October this year!"

"That can't be Reg and Rose. If they'd left the country their new identities would have been scrutinized, both leaving and coming back. They wouldn't risk that, not after all the trouble they went to get them in the first place."

"They were both the same height and, roughly, the same weight also of Rose and Reg. And so we think they are, possibly, two lookalikes who have come into this country from Russia for the sole purpose of their identities being taken on by Reg and Rose."

"We think so anyway aunt . . . Sorry, Alki," Britney said.

"Well, it could make sense I suppose."

"Do you have their names?" Aaron asked

"Of course," Ringo said. "Its Rostislav and Larisa Ivanov and they come from St. Petersburg."

"Do we know anything else about them?" Alki asked.

"Not a thing. We managed to get the number plate from the limo, but when we tried to trace it, it proved to be fake."

"And so how do you know that Reg and Rose have assumed the identities of these two people?"

"This is the great bit! There is footage of them Alki, three weeks ago, coming out of a hotel in London and getting into a limousine which took them to a theatre in the West End and brought them back later on. We have a picture which we'll send to you. It has a caption which reads, 'Mr. Rostislav and Larisa Ivanov leave a top hotel in London to visit a West End theatre'."

Ringo now took up the story.

"We checked the license plate of that limo as well and this one checked out. They seem to be maintaining a high profile now," he said. "There are even photographs of them, from a distance, meeting and greeting Nicholaus Klevchenky at a restaurant in Windsor."

"When was that Ringer?" Alki asked.

"It was last Thursday."

"Last Thursday? That was . . . Yes it was; it was the day they torched The Barn!"

"By God, it was!" Aaron said.

"Well done Ringo, Britney. You have done us proud." Alki now turned to Alex and Aaron, keeping the phone on loudspeaker. "It would seem, based on the information garnered by our young accomplices here that torching The Barn seems also to have been a diversionary tactic, and that Reg and Rose are now in the position they wanted to be in right from the start. Nicholaus Klevchenky must be their goal."

"Hang on Alki." Aaron now stood. "Why would they do that; become high profile I mean? Surely, if their faces are going to be spread all across the news, they would be recognised?"

"They don't really look like they used to," Britney answered him. "It's only coz Ringer and me know Reg so well that we knew it was him; his hair is lighter, he's put on weight and wears spectacles now as well as looking a bit taller. We don't know Rose at all, apart from the pictures you sent us, but she looks completely different as well."

"Don't forget Aaron, after each of their supposed deaths their pictures were only in the public eye for a short while, it was me and you that dominated media scrutiny," Alki said. "And that fact, together with the disguises they have adopted should give them almost solid credence in the roles they are now playing. They would not be recognised as who they used to be by anyone, apart from you and me that is because we know them so well, and Ringo and Brit but only because they were looking at these people with an overview of Reg and Rose in mind." Aaron now agreed.

"And also," he said. "Torching The Barn that day certainly did hold our attention, and it diverted us away from any form of news where we might have seen their faces."

"Thanks guys," Alki said. "Keep doing the good work, and keep us informed of anything else you find out."

"Will do Alki," Britney said, and the line went dead.

"Let's take a look at this 'Nicholaus Klevchenky' then, shall we?" Alki said.

Alex inputted the name and his picture came up within seconds. Alki started, shook her head and laughed out loud.

"That's where I knew him from!"

"Yes, he does look familiar," Aaron agreed.

"What are you two goin' on about?"

"I think I might have seen him on the news a while back." Aaron said.

"You might well have, but I don't mean Nicholaus Klevchenky. I'm talking about the doppelganger."

"Doppelganger?" They both looked at her, bemused.

"Yes, doppelganger. The new man, the Ukrainian. He looks the image of Nicholaus Klevchenky!"

"Hell, he does!" Aaron agreed. "How can that be?"

Alki now pulled up the few recent photographs they had of the Ukrainian man and, sure enough, even at a distance, he did have a similar look to the man on the screen.

"But why would he look like Nicholaus Klevchenky? How could he, why would he?"

"It weren't no accident, I'll bet."

"What do you mean?" Alki asked him.

"I reckon they've been waitin' for this new geezer all along, especially since he turns out to be a looker for the fella what Reg and Rose have befriended. That can't be a coincidence can it?"

"I get that Alex, but what is the reason for him looking like this Nicholaus?"

"It's obvious isn't it; they're goin' to swap the doppelganger for 'im!"

A moment passed, and then she nodded. She now scrutinised the photographs.

"He wouldn't pass muster for very long. Admitted, he does look like the real Nicholaus from a distance but he would not pass close scrutiny; he couldn't last for more than a single day."

"Maybe 'e doesn't 'ave to."

"Explain," Alki said.

"Coz they would 'ave got the real Nicholaus out of the country by that time?"

"It figures I suppose."

"I've worked on kidnap cases before Alks, and they always move the victim straightaway, either locally or some distance, whichever is best to throw whoever's followin' off the scent." She was listening. "'E's a Ruskie; my bet is, they're gonna take 'im back 'ome."

"I think you might be right Alex."

"As soon as they complete the swap, they'll set in motion their escape plan. From where they are, 'ere in 'Arenden, it wouldn't take anythin' like a full day for them to get their man out of the country."

"If that is their plan," Aaron offered.

"'Ow do you mean?" Alex asked.

"We don't know for certain that the plan is to kidnap Nicholaus Klevchenky do we?"

"Well, if it's not the plan, what is?" Alex countered.

"I'm just saying . . . Maybe that is the plan, maybe it's not. We don't know either . . ."

"Well, whatever it is," Alki interjected. "We know the Ukrainian is a dead ringer for Nicholaus, that has to mean something." Aaron now nodded in agreement.

"We also know that 'Arenden Reside 'as an equal significance insomuch as it was on one of the maps in the cottage, and it belongs to this Nicholaus geezer, and Reg and Rose 'ave gone there tonight for the ball."

"Correct." Alki agreed. "And further on from that, the spa must come into play in some manner."

"Yeah."

Alki stood.

"So, based on what we know, let me offer a précis of the situation, see what you think. Teddy showed us a floor plan of, what turned out to be, Harenden Reside, a mansion house here in Harenden on Thames. It is owned by a former Russian dignitary, Mr. Nicholaus Klevchenky, and the floor plan of this mansion was also being scrutinised somewhat by Reg and his gang. We then saw, later on, that it had been discarded in favour of yet another floor plan, but of a spa this time. We are as sure as we can be, because of Brit and Ringo's research, that the spa is not a section of Harenden Reside, but it turns out to be an elite spa here in Harenden itself. We know this as the floor plans match. The Ukrainian who was supposedly crushed to death in Quay Haven has turned out to be a lookalike for Mr. Klevchenky. Reg and Rose have taken on the identities of the couple that arrived from Saint Petersburg more than four weeks ago, and who have close links with Mr. Klevchenky it seems. Their identity adoption has been proven by TV footage of them in society and even greeting Mr. Klevchenky himself, and so corroborates that they do indeed have a close friendship with him. All this, together with the fact that Russia would probably want to see this man back home, seeing as he left under a cloud with a shedload of money if the cost of buying Harenden Reside is anything to go by, should lead us to draw some serious conclusions concerning Mr. Klevchenky, don't you think?"

Silence reigned for a while. Aaron was the first to speak.

"If abduction is their game, it would seem that the location of their enterprise was initially to be Harenden Reside itself. Now, however, with that floor plan seemingly discarded and the plan of a spa being perused instead, it would seem the location of the proposed abduction has been altered."

"Yeah," Alex agreed. "Security in a mansion would be significantly 'arder to penetrate than that of an outside spa, even an elite spa."

Aaron and Alki concurred.

"With a man in the gang whose features closely resemble Klevchenky, facially and in body size and shape, and also with two people from St. Petersburg posing as friends of his, putting them, therefore, in a close position to him, it might seem fair to assume that they do intend to swap the real Nicholaus. It might then also be fair to assume that they shall attempt this at the spa."

Alex and Aaron nodded, looking at Alki. A moment passed and she spoke again.

"I don't think I have anything to add to that."

"I 'ave! The clothes they was lookin' at, on the tablet in the pub?" Alki and Aaron both shook their heads. "They was all for a male, about the size of old Mr. Ruskie man Nicholaus." Alki stopped him.

"And so, if they were to swap these two men, they would need identical clothes."

"Yeah. The doppelganger would 'ave to wear the same gear so's 'e could jump into 'is place in an instant."

"And Reg, being in his entourage which it seems he and Rose are, could easily tip off the rest of the gang exactly what he was wearing before they even set off to the spa!"

"Got to be, 'asn't it?"

Alex looked at them both and grinned.

"I reckon we 'ave a plan," he said.

CHAPTER FORTY-ONE
Spa

"We need membership!" Alki turned to Alex. "But Aaron and I can't go to a spa using our real names as they might be recognised, and we need us all to be there, it won't be sufficient with just you Alex. Is there anything you can do?"

"Take about an 'our darlin'," he said, turning to his small laptop. "Annette Starlin' do you Alks?" She nodded, laughing a little.

"What? Will you make up forgeries?" Aaron asked.

"Already got 'em, just need to swap photos and make a few alterations." Aaron seemed at a loss for words. "They don't need to be top dollar. After all, it's just a bleedin' leisure centre, a spa. Robert 'emmin's be alright for you Aaron?"

"Robert Hemmings?"

"I could give you Percival Strangelove if you wanted." Aaron, once more, seemed lost.

"Mr. Hemmings will do thank you Alex. And stop making fun of our friend here."

"Sometimes," Aaron said, shaking his head. "I get a little lost as to just who the baddies and goodies actually are."

Alex turned away, laughing.

"We need you to be able to go anywhere in the complex Alex," she said. "So, if you give Aaron and me status, and make you something like a . . . What, a PA?"

"Course," was all he said as he began to work.

"It gives credence that way, so that you can inspect the place on our behalf."

"Yeah." Alex said. "And as a personal secretary I can vid the joint, so that my 'bosses' can 'ave a preview of their new leisure facilities."

Three hours later Alex returned with three new spa memberships and copious footage of the leisure centre.

The spa facilities were first class as his video footage gave testimony. Alex had also insisted on looking at all of the back areas too, including laundry, kitchen and maintenance. He'd met and introduced himself to lots of different members of staff, and it was this particular section of video that they now looked at.

"What sort of accent is that Alex?" Aaron asked with a smile.

"Yes, I have to admit I can't quite place the area. It sounds slightly Mexican but with a hint of Ecuador? I could be wrong." Alki was stifling laughter.

"I'm thinking more Cuban?"

Alex did not seem to be amused.

"Well, they just thought I was unique and besides, I got the job done, that's all that was needed." He now quickly pointed to the screen. "That's the one, the geezer in the tails," he said. "'Is name is Montague and 'e does days from ten am until ten pm all week. I slipped 'im a score and 'e agreed to phone me the next time Mr. Nicholaus whatsisface turned up at the spa."

"Score?" Aaron asked.

"Score," Alex reiterated.

"So, what the hell is that then?"

"Oh, come on Aaron," Alki said. "Twenty quid. Everyone knows that."

"Well I didn't," he said. "Anyway, did he just accept this, without question?"

"I gave 'im the cock and bull story of me 'avin' an interest in Russian dissidents, and wantin' a photo of 'im. 'E seemed to understand that and said I wasn't the only one, and was even more pleased when I slipped him the sco . . . the twenty. I did the same with one of the kitchen staff and a receptionist."

"So what will we do when Nicholaus eventually does go to the spa?" Aaron asked.

"We shall simply observe and follow."

"'Follow'?" Aaron continued. "What do we do then Alki?"

"If they do go ahead with the kidnap, because he is such a high profile person I would assume that they intend to take him out of the country, and back to Russia is my guess." Alex and Aaron both concurred. "That would seem to be the logical move anyway. And if it goes that far, and we are lucky inasmuch as we can follow them, we might be able to thwart them somewhere down the line."

"Do you really think we would get such a chance?" Aaron asked.

She looked at him for a moment.

"I'm not sure Aaron."

No one spoke for a short while.

"Because of the situation we find ourselves in," she said, slowly and deliberately. "We are constantly playing catch up. We don't really know if kidnap is their proposed course of action but, to all intents and purposes, the abduction of Nicholaus Klevchenky does seem to be the focus." Both Alex and Aaron agreed. She went on. "I have, several times now, tried to alert the authorities as to what we believe is going on. I have repeatedly been told that without evidence they can do nothing. This last time, in the event of a potential kidnapping, I thought they would listen a little more attentively. I was wrong. And so, with the authorities paying us no heed at all, we are most definitely on our own. But we know, due to all the shenanigans these guys are playing, all the twists and turns they have employed to wriggle their way into obscurity, that this is of singular importance to them, to the powers they are working for. With that in mind, and also the fact that we are the only ones privy to their actions and intentions, we have little option but to follow them and to keep on winging this until such time as we find ourselves in a position to place in their way an obstacle of sufficient mass that it disrupts their plans and knocks them so far off course they have to abandon this venture."

Aaron and Alex said nothing.

"Did you manage to find out when they were likely to attend the spa again?" Alki asked.

"My mate Monty told me that Nicholaus was there with his entourage just yesterday mornin'. Apparently 'e only comes in about twice a week, so I reckon it might be in a few days' time."

The following morning Alex got a call.

"Hi," he said into the phone as he waved earnestly. Getting their attention, he mouthed the name, 'Monty' as he listened. "Thank you," was all he said as he ended the call and looked up. "They're all there."

"All?"

"Reg, Rose, Nicky-boy, 'is wife plus two 'eavies Monty says."

They were ready in ten minutes and on the way to the spa.

"Alex, you must go in and monitor things from inside; you're the only one they don't know. Aaron, you stay in the car, sunglasses on and stay low. You can text us with reports, but call only if you really need to. We all must keep our phones on vibrate so as not to attract any undue attention."

"Where are you going Alki?" Aaron said, turning into the main gate.

"I have to keep out of sight as I am too recognisable and so I'm going round to the back of the spa. Hopefully, if they try it here, I can be in a position to see what goes on."

She too put sunglasses on and covered herself with a large, dark shawl.

"What's the plan if they do fulfil the swap? And 'ow will we know for certain they've done it?" Alex asked.

"Look for anything out of the ordinary. I would have thought they will create some sort of diversion, but if we keep Nicholaus firmly in view then we should know if the swap has been made. Don't forget, the Ukrainian looks like him but he is not a perfect match. Even in the flurry that such a diversion would probably create they will have to cover the doppelganger so those close to Nicholaus, those that know him well, like his wife, don't get the chance to question."

Both men agreed as the car approached the front of the purpose-built spa.

They could see the dignitary's limousine in a dedicated parking bay close to the entrance, but there were no other free spaces close by.

"I'll park in the disabled bay," Aaron said.

"Don't draw attention to yourself."

"I shan't Alki, but I need to be in a position to see." He put sunglasses on.

Alex sat in the rest area, positioned so that he could see into the gymnasium and also reception. He had informed the receptionist that his bosses were due this afternoon and that he was simply going to await their arrival. He had his tablet placed on the table and now, to all who surveyed him, he was working.

The gym was busy and it took a few minutes for him to locate Nicholaus and his entourage across the other side. He spotted Reg and Rose immediately, also Nicholaus' wife together with two bodyguards. Nicholaus and Reg were mid work-out and seeming to be enjoying each other's company as they worked.

Alex texted this info to Alki and Aaron, and waited.

It was half an hour later that Nicholaus and his group vacated the gym and took up seats in the rest area across the way from Alex. They were in a jolly mood.

Refreshments were ordered and they continued in their affable manner, chatting and laughing between themselves as the bodyguards looked on. Alex simply watched discreetly from his table, seemingly deep into his work but covertly taking snapshots of Nicholaus and the others and sending them to Alki and Aaron.

Ten minutes later Nicholaus spoke to one of the bodyguards who now stood and made his way across the rest area, past the seated Alex and on to the gents' toilet. He disappeared inside and, shortly after, came out and stood by the door, nodding discreetly to his boss when he, eventually, looked his way. Nicholaus got up and headed towards the men's amenities, but then Reg took to his feet calling to Nicholaus. He caught him up and obviously made a joke as they stopped, looked back at the seated bodyguard, laughed again and then carried on their way, going past the bodyguard into the gents'.

Nicholaus' wife seemed to be enjoying Rose's company, and also that of the bodyguard as all three were laughing out loud. Alex switched to video and repositioned.

It was over a minute later that banging and crashing was heard from the amenities. The bodyguard shot to his feet as his partner by the entrance turned and ran into the gents', just missing colliding with Nicholaus who almost fell through the door, followed by a very dishevelled Reg who quickly bent down and began to pick him up. The second bodyguard was by his side in a moment, followed quickly by Nicholaus' wife and Rose.

Reg helped him to his feet as Alex zoomed in to see blood all over Nicholaus' face and shirt. He was mouthing words but little was heard. His speech seemed unintelligible and it was Reg who spoke.

"A madman!" Reg pointed back to the gents', seemingly out of breath. "He went for Nicholaus. I tried to stop him."

The second bodyguard now headed for the door, smashed it open and ran inside. They could both be heard banging doors and shouting to one another in Russian.

"Stay back," Reg said to Nicholaus' wife as the man leaned on him, blood dripping. Rose took her arm and pulled her back. "Pointless getting blood on you as well," he said as members of staff rushed to them. Reg motioned them away as he helped Nicholaus towards the door.

"Can I help?"

A man stepped forward from the back of the cafe, bag in hand. Nicholaus waved him away as he tried to remain standing with Reg's help.

"I am a doctor and I think I might have something that could aid in stemming the blood flow."

Reg held Nicholaus up and, despite further inaudible protestations from the dazed man, beckoned for the doctor to come forward. He did so and began ministering to the bloodied man, attempting to stem the flow of blood it seemed.

"We'll be all right," Rose said to the approaching spa staff as she and Nicholaus' wife followed Reg, the doctor and Nicholaus to the door.

The bodyguards came out and looked around, one heading back into the gym the other following Reg, Nicholaus and the doctor past reception, heading for the car park.

"Stay with us Doctor, please. We shall see you get back again for your vehicle."

"There is no problem," Alex heard him reply as they exited.

They crossed to the limousine and Reg helped the injured man into the back seat with the doctor and Rose, ushering Nicholaus' wife into the front passenger seat. He got into the driver's side as the second bodyguard came out into the car park. He started the motor and indicated for them to follow. They both got into the car that was parked behind as Reg drove off at speed, the bodyguards swiftly following.

Alki came from around the corner as soon as the limousine had disappeared from sight. She stopped, double checked back around the corner and then headed straight for the car, Alex coming out of reception, tablet under his arm and heading for them at a jog.

"'Ad to be didn't it?" Alex said, getting into the front seat. "Pretty slick, nothin' anyone could do because it went so quick; bodyguards kept at arm's length, and 'is wife as well, Rose saw to that." Aaron started the car.

"Wait a minute," Alki said getting into the back.

"What for?"

"We wait and watch!"

"Aren't we goin' to get after 'em?" Alex asked. Aaron also turned to look at her, car ticking over.

"Watch for the hire car," she said.

"The convertible, the Merc?" She nodded, intent on watching.

"Round the back."

"What about the doppelganger?" Aaron said.

"They have to be going back to the mansion," she replied. "So we leave them to it. It's the real Nicholaus we need to be following, not the bogus."

Just then, three vehicles came from the delivery area: a van, a small saloon and the third being the Mercedes.

"They've put the top up," she said. "Slowly pull out Aaron; follow them, but at a reasonable distance."

"What's goin' on?" Alex asked.

"Luke is driving but he's wearing a wig and sunglasses," she said. "Sonia is in the back with the real Nicholaus."

"How do you know?" Aaron said reversing out of the parking space.

"I was at the back when I saw them bundle him out of the spa, blood all over his face and Luke and Sonia keeping him upright till they got him to the car and threw him in."

They were now heading down the lane towards the main road, the Merc in their sights less than two hundred yards distant.

"So, if they really 'ave done the swap, and it seems they 'ave, they'll be movin' at speed from now on to get 'im out of the country, quick."

"Okay," Aaron said. "As you say, it does look like they have done the swap, but so what?" He said. "The authorities don't want to know, so what do we do, what can we do?"

"We follow them," Alki said. She seemed a little uncertain.

They pulled out onto the main road, two cars now in between them and their quarry.

"It looks to me as if they are heading back to the holiday home," she said. "In which case we tag along and prepare our next move."

"And just what will that move be?" Aaron asked.

"I'm not sure at this moment Aaron," she said. "Cat is still in position isn't she?"

"Yes." Alex answered.

"Good," she said. "At least we'll be able to see their movements at the house. Tell the kids what has happened, maybe they've seen something that might have a bearing."

Aaron felt she seemed more hopeful than anything else.

CHAPTER FORTY-TWO
Action?

They watched the holiday home from the moored position of the Catamaran as Alex panned the camera across.

"Reg hasn't done his checks."

"Checks?"

"He always checked the perimeter, anywhere we went and regular as clockwork."

"What are you saying?"

"He does his checks religiously, and he should have done here." She looked across at them both. "He hasn't and I'm not sure why."

"But they had gone out by the time we got here, Teddy showed us that. Couldn't he have done his checks then, before we arrived?"

"Probably, but he hasn't done them since," she said, frowning. "We should have seen him do them. We haven't and that concerns me."

Alex smiled.

"Well it shouldn't do."

"What do you mean?"

"Don't forget Alki, if they knew to bug your place, they'll also 'ave known about the micro, defo. So they'll 'ave checked it out, and where it went. Reg 'as probably settled for the fact you'd buggered off."

"What are you both talking about?" Aaron seemed lost.

"Do you member when you guys was captured? They let you go, even 'elpin' you to escape and then carried on like everythin' was fine, like the wart 'ad been removed." He smiled at her. "They reckon they're safe girl, cos they think they've scotched the snake and it's tumbled off the cliff, i.e. gone to see your sister. What they don't realise is that the wart has got nine lives and you ain't used 'em all up yet!"

Alki shook her head, eyes widening.

"Not sure if that's a mixed metaphor Alex or just appalling prose, but point taken, they could have taken the bait."

"Well, they still seem to be unaware that we can see 'em, and so it looks like we still 'ave a chance," Alex pointed out, then shook his head. "To do what, though, I don't really know."

"I still don't understand," Aaron said.

"Alki sent a red 'errin' down to Brighton, to 'er sisters down there. We think they fell for it and so they should reckon that's where she and you 'ave gone, to get away from the paps." He quickly called them over to the monitor before Aaron could comment. "Things is 'appenin'," he said.

The back door of the holiday home had been opened and, as they watched, Sonia emerged and looked right then left. She stepped out, turned and beckoned.

Luke and Toby came out together, another man in overcoat and trilby hat between them with his arms around their necks. He was obviously being supported and they made their way to the boat, the captain of the vessel following. Sonia had gone on board and now aided them as the seemingly unconscious man was lifted aboard and taken down below.

Minutes later saw Toby and the captain re-emerge, the young man casting off and quickly getting back on board as the motor was fired up. The vessel pulled onto the river, heading downstream.

"So, what do we do now?"

Both men looked at Alki, as the phone rang.

"It's the brats!" Alex put it on loudspeaker.

"Have you seen the news?" They heard Britney's voice. Alex turned to Alki and Aaron; both shook their heads.

"No, we've been busy."

"It's the Russians!" Ringo said. "They're claiming that the British have been spying on them, and they also reckon they've got proof."

Alex turned to Alki and Aaron, arms spread wide.

"So?" He said.

"Well, it's a smokescreen for what's going on up your end, don't you see?"

"No, I don't see. What the 'ell are you goin' on about?"

"If they've swapped Nicholaus for the fake, they won't want it to be made known will they? duuuh!" Britney said.

"All right Britney, no need to be rude darlin'," Alex smiled and shook his head.

"It's classic fogging Dad." Ringo said. "Remember them torching The Barn? It put you right off the scent and no mistake. Well, it's just the same here only bigger. The Russians make a big statement so it hides the smaller stuff. The authorities won't know that Nicholaus' kidnapping is big; they probably don't even know that he has been kidnapped yet. But when it gets out, the spying story will seriously overshadow it."

"Yeah, and so, if you don't do something about it soon, they'll get away with it, obvious!" Britney chipped in.

"Thank you Britney, we shall consider your words." Alki had stood by now.

"It needs movement now aunt Alki or else they'll get away with it!"

"I know that darling, and drop the aunt else I'll drop you!"

"Okay Alki." She heard her niece laugh.

"Dears?" She said in a serious tone. "Would you stay by the phone for me; I am thinking that we shall need your help this day. Bye now."

She turned to the men.

"We have to do something, whatever that 'something' might be, but we have to do it now."

CHAPTER FORTY-THREE
Cat

"We follow the boat."

They both looked at her.

"Nicholaus must be the reason for this whole operation."

Aaron and Alex said nothing.

"They need to get him back to the homeland! When you think of the embarrassment the Russian government suffered, you can see why they have gone to these lengths to get him. It's one thing stealing money from them, claiming asylum in this country and buying one of the most expensive houses in the country, but then living the high life with all their money for all to see? No wonder they're cheesed off with him."

"It would seem to make sense, what with Reg and Rose in the position they're in now, and the new boy lookin' too much like Nicholaus to be a coincidence."

"So, are we thinking they mean to leave by boat?" Aaron asked.

"We are."

"But, surely, that would take upwards of a day, possibly more from here." She agreed. "But why take such a long protracted route? Surely there are quicker, easier ways to take him out of the country?"

"There are, of course," she said. "But this is low-key and private. No-one can see him, no security to pass through, no chance of people accidentally recognising him; and they can keep him tied up and silenced throughout the entire journey."

"I suppose so," Aaron still seemed sceptical.

"Add to those facts that they also think nobody knows anything about it, and so can just take their time, thus arousing no suspicion."

"Yeah. All that does make sense," Alex said. "But the other geezer, the one they swapped 'im for, 'as to fool 'em, 'is family, for at least a day. That's a tall order."

"I agree Alex," she said. "But that has to be the reason they have put Reg and Rose there, to aid in that deception." Alex nodded. "And don't forget the injury he is supposed to have received? They even have their own doctor to minister to him. I only saw him on the footage you took Alex, and he does look different, but I would swear he is the same doctor they used in Norfolk."

"'E's 'ad some work done, but I'd swear 'e was too."

"I'm sure, with that entire infrastructure in place, they will have little trouble in fooling his family for the single day they need to get Nicholaus out of the country."

"But what about Reg and Rose, and the doppelganger afterwards; what will 'appen to them then? They, surely, can only keep up this charade for a small amount of time. People close to Nicholaus will realise fairly quickly that somethin' isn't right, even with a doctor tellin' 'em 'e's unwell."

"You are right, they will eventually discover the swap, but not yet. They only need the time it takes to get Nicholaus out of the country. The best way would be by air, a far quicker way as you point out, but they would have to take him through a rigorous identification process at any airport and that would be difficult with a semi-comatose passenger who resembles a well-known dignitary. And an unscheduled flight would simply alert the authorities. The second quickest would be by boat, and that would alert no-one. So Reg, Rose and the doppelganger would only need to keep up the charade for the length of time it takes a boat to cover the distance from here to the open sea. Once that has been accomplished they can discard the false identities and disappear."

"Wouldn't it be rather difficult for them to just 'disappear?'"

"They are already dead don't forget, those three Aaron. They can easily slink off somewhere and take on new identities that have probably been created already anyway. Even the doppelganger can alter his appearance again, to become unrecognisable. But Sonia, Luke, Toby and the other guy, the captain, with their captive will be at the mouth of the estuary well within a day, and who knows what has been prepared for them from that point."

She looked at each of them in turn. Nobody argued.

"All right Alex," Alki said. "I think we've seen all we need to see. Bring Cat back and let's set off."

"If you're sure girl?" he said.

"I am."

The image on Cat's monitor swivelled round to see the hydraulic arm clasped to an overhanging root. Alex lowered the Catamaran onto the water and the arm released its hold, the vessel now bobbing about on the swell of the river. The camera was turned to look up stream and then down, there were no craft in sight and Alex eased the Catamaran away from the riverbank, heading upstream.

"How can we follow them?" Aaron asked. "They're on water, we're on land."

"There are numerous locks from here to the estuary." She took out a map from inside the driver's door and opened it. "There are many places from which to observe the river along the route."

"So, you believe they are heading for the estuary?" She nodded. "And then open sea?"

She looked at him, now with a frown on her face and shook her head slightly.

"I don't know what else to believe at this moment," she said. "Have you any ideas?"

"I wish I had."

"In that case let's prepare to depart," she said. "As soon as Cat is on board, we get underway."

They set off, heading east. Alex had printed out a list of locks from Harenden to the sea and they reached the first within minutes. There was no sign of their quarry and so they continued on to the second. They spotted the boat within a minute of approaching the lock. It was downstream and continuing on its way at a sedate pace, easily melding in with all other river traffic as night began to close in.

Two hours and eight locks later the boat pulled in to the side and moored.

They quickly found a place to park, not too near the river but still within sight of the vessel. Curtains were drawn and tea was made as they, all three, took it in turns to keep watch. Alex set up a camera on top of the motorhome in order to record, but in the meantime he decided to view the recent footage from the Catamaran.

Twenty minutes later he called Alki, urgently.

"What is it?"

"I'm not sure girl," he said. "But there's somethin' not quite right, I think anyway."

Alki stepped down from the passenger seat, leaving Aaron with the binoculars observing the moored vessel and came to look at the monitor. Alex set it going again and pointed.

"Just there," he said. "Watch and see."

She did as he asked but saw nothing.

"Try again."

She got closer to the monitor and he pressed play. She saw something this time.

"A fish?"

"Bloody big fish," he said. "Look again."

She got even closer to the monitor, as did Alex. They both watched again.

"Too big to be a fish, you're right," she said. "Have you noticed any other splashes as big as that?"

"No, and that's what makes me wonder." He got up. "You try and work it out while I keep an eye on the dodgy geezers. I'll take over Aaron."

She began the process again as Aaron came to sit with her. Alex sat in the passenger seat and took up the binoculars.

Ten minutes later she called him back.

"You were right Alex," she said. "It was a body, possibly two."

"A body?"

"Yes, but not a dead one!"

"Well, that's a relief."

"No, it's not Nicholaus."

"'Ow do you know?"

"Look."

She showed him the splash at the bow, and now pointed out further discrepancies. She played them over and over and they all scrutinised each section. Half an hour later and they were in agreement.

"Two splashes. They've gone and snuck off the boat!"

"It certainly would seem that way, but why?"

"You think it's two of them then?" Aaron asked.

"Looks like it," she said. "Luke and Sonia at a guess."

"'Ave to be, wouldn't it," Alex said. "And left the young lad to guard Nicholaus, with the other geezer, the driver!"

They shared a look, and an agreement was tacitly made.

"Aaron," she said. "We might be too late, but I think it's imperative we find out just what's been going on back at the house."

"You really think it's that important?"

"I do, based on what we've just seen," she said. "If you take the Harley you could be there within the hour."

"What would I be looking for?"

"Check out the house for one, and also see if the cars are still there."

"Okay," he said. "What do I do then?"

"We'll have to play it by ear," she said. "Just get back there as quickly as you can and report back."

"What are you going to do?"

"We'll keep watch here until we know what you come up with." She looked down, deep in thought. "They are playing games, the likes of which I'm not that familiar with."

Aaron began putting on the leathers.

CHAPTER FORTY-FOUR
Move

"The Merc is gone, and the Jag?"

She now held the phone down, looking at Alex. She nodded, seemingly to herself. "The time for subtlety is over. We need answers and we need them now." She lifted the phone again. "Get a torch Aaron, there should be one in the panniers." She looked across at Alex. He nodded. "Go and look inside the windows of their holiday home."

"That's a bit rash isn't it Alks?" Alex said, binoculars still trained on the moored vessel.

"We need to know what is going on Alex, and we need to know it now." She spoke into the phone again. "I don't believe you will find any evidence of occupancy any more Aaron. I firmly believe that at least two of them left the boat, but I need to know for certain. If the house has been emptied that proves it." She ended the call and looked at Alex. "If you hadn't seen those splashes at the bow of their vessel, we would still be of a mind that we have the upper hand. Thank you Alex, for everything."

"Shut up," was all he said.

It was five minutes later when the phone rang.

"I knew it," she said after listening for a few seconds. "This changes everything Aaron. You must get into a position to see the mansion. I know it's a long shot but it's all we have at present. Get back to us as soon as you're at the vantage point." She hung up.

"What's 'appenin' Alki?" Alex now turned to face her.

"Aaron says everything in the house has gone. So they did leave the boat, and they've moved out."

"They've 'ad us!"

"Looks like it," she said, a faint smile appearing on her face.

"They've probably gone to pick up Rose and Reg and the Ukrainian. That was why they both snuck off the boat, with two cars to drive."

"Have you got your tablet handy?" She asked. He nodded, eyes squinting a little as he opened a pocket on his trousers. He took out a small tablet which he now switched on. "Whose tracker is up at the moment?"

"Just the bike, as we agreed, and the motor'ome of course." He pointed as the screen came to life. "There's Aaron, back at 'Arenden, and 'ere we are, in the van."

"Can you turn mine on?"

"Course, but you won't see it coz it'll blend in." He made a few adjustments.

"With the motorhome do you mean?" He now tapped the screen a couple of times.

"Yeah. The two trackers'll appear as one." She nodded as he tapped the screen again. Alex began to frown.

"That's odd," he said. "Yours is way down there. Did you drop it Alks?" She shook her head, intent on the screen. "Mind, when the 'ell did you get yourself that far south in the last few days?"

Alki came close to the screen and almost yelped. He looked at her, shook his head and now scrutinized the tablet.

"Bloody 'ell," he exclaimed. "It's movin'!"

"Yes it is," she agreed, and wrung her hands in glee. He checked a few things on the tablet and shook his head again.

"Well, do you want to tell me what the 'ell's goin' on or not?"

She looked at the screen and smiled.

"These are the slipperiest eels I have ever come across," she said. "And yet, we might just have one more chance to cook their goose!"

"Eels? Cook their goose? Jeez! You talk about me and mixed . . . wassernames!"

Alki's eyes were ablaze with excitement.

"And, do you want to tell me what the 'ell your personal tracker is doin' down there?" He pointed to the tablet screen as the phone rang again.

She answered it, putting it on speaker.

"The lights are on at the mansion but I can't see much at all," Aaron said. "There is movement inside but I can't see who it is, I'm too far away."

"Can you see if the Merc is parked outside?" Alki asked.

"Hang on a sec," he said.

"What we gonna do if the Merc is there?" Alex asked.

"I don't think it will be," she said, looking at the tablet screen. "I think something else is going on."

"There are only five cars there," Aaron said. "I can't see the Merc or the Jag."

"Alright Aaron. Stay there for the moment and keep observing." She ended the call and turned to Alex. "Something definitely feels not right," she said, dialling again.

"Yeah. What with people sneakin' off boats, together with this little saunter of theirs down the Thames, it makes me wonder an' all. As well as trackers bein' miles from where they ought to . . ."

"Britney? Ringo?" She spoke into the phone and put it on speaker as she picked up the binoculars to view the moored vessel. "Have you still got access to your auntie's microlight?"

"Yes we have, but it's busted!"

"No it isn't."

"She trashed it!" Britney almost shouted. "And then she tried to make out that it had been you!"

"Do you mean two days ago when she was dressed in my old clothes?"

"Yes. Virtually the whole village saw her trash it 'cos she landed in the high street and, afterwards, when she came back to dismantle it after changing back into her own clothes, told everyone it had been you flying it."

"Did they believe her?"

"Course! She even made me and Ringer think twice, and we were there and knew it wasn't you, she's that good. And she had a blow up doll by the side of her wearing a man's suit, which she made out she was helping into her house as if it were a real person."

"Did anyone question that?"

"Well, no. They all reckoned she'd got a new boyfriend. She loved it."

"Go and see her, get it out and fire it up."

"But it was trashed."

"No. It might have looked that way but it's not the reality."

"Aunt Alki, we saw it happen."

"You might have sweetheart, and what have I told you about calling me auntie? But anyway, she crashed it on purpose Britney, it was part of the plan so that anyone witnessing the event would believe it really had been me and Aaron and thrown them off the scent as to where I actually was." There was an audible, 'oh' on the other end of the line. "Exactly. Now, Alex and me are following the boat with Nicholaus in, but I want you two to go and see your Auntie and get the micro, it will have been repaired, trust me. Test the engine in the garage and cover the noise with the radio or whatever, then set it up at the back of her house. Once you've done all that, phone us again."

She heard a hurried and muffled discussion on the other end.

"What's all the secrecy for Alki?"

"Brit, Ringo?" she said urgently. "There just might be someone watching your Auntie's house, kids. I don't want them to know the micros up and running, but, more importantly, I don't want anyone to know you two are going to be flying it!"

"Okay Au . . . OK!" was all that was said and the phone went dead.

CHAPTER FORTY-FIVE
Ruse

Alki looked out at the moored vessel, Alex did too.

"Could we send Teddy out?"

"There's no light out there on the river, and we can't use 'is spotlight 'cos it'll give 'im away."

"We need to board them then."

"You reckon?"

"If Sonia and Luke are not on board now, and it does seem logical that it was those two who slunk off the boat, then that says a lot to me, doesn't it you?"

She was still looking out of the window, through the drawn curtains. Alex thought briefly and nodded.

"So, there's only the captain, Toby and a, probably tied up, captive left on board? That makes me wonder too. I would 'ave thought Nicholaus whatsisface would've been more important than that."

"My thoughts exactly Alex."

"You want to board 'er then?"

"I think we have to," she said, resigned.

"All right girl," he said. "Get the gun out of the bunk, we might need it." He started the motor.

"The shotgun is in the Harley, surely?"

"Course it is. But we'll use the replica!"

"Replica?"

"Yeah." He pointed to the forward bunk. "The Magnum forty-four darlin', the most powerful 'andgun in the world!"

"The what?" She said, searching.

"Magnum. Didn't you see the film? loved Dirty 'Arry I did!"

Her hand found something and she pulled out the weapon from under the mattress.

"Oh my god!" She exclaimed. "This is not real, is it?" She seemed hopeful.

"Nah!"

"It certainly looks like it is!"

"Well let's 'ope they think so too," he said.

"They won't make out that it's not the real thing will they, I certainly can't?"

"Not in this light, not if I keep it pointin' down."

He took it from her, laid it in his lap and set off towards the moored vessel.

They parked up by the moorings and hurried over to the boat, Alex holding the gun under a carried jacket. There were only two other boats moored up on this stretch of water, both more than a hundred yards away. Alki called as she went on board, Alex following.

The cabin door opened and a man emerged, the captain.

"What the . . ." He stopped as he saw Alki on board, then came up the last two steps. "What are you doing?" he asked, then saw Alex step aboard. The gun was revealed and the man stepped back, shocked.

"Where is Nicholaus?" Alki asked. The man looked a little bemused.

"An answer would be a good idea." Alex waved the gun a little. "And the right answer would be the best one, unless you want to make my day!"

Just then they heard a noise below, in the cabin.

"Is that him?" Alki said. "Make him come out, or is he tied up?" The man didn't answer.

Alki called out.

"Is that you Nicholaus?" The movement stopped and they heard an answer, or so it seemed. Footsteps on the stairs and a man emerged.

Alki gasped.

He came up the steps and stood before them. He was the image of the man, Nicholaus Klevchenky, but with significant flaws in his make-up that would not fool anyone for long. He was followed by the young man they knew as Toby.

All three stood side by side facing Alki and Alex.

"My god, it's not him, it's not the real Nicholaus!"

Alex Stood forward, gun held on the two men who now stood with the captain.

"What 'ave you done with 'im," he asked. "What the 'ell 'ave you done with Nicholaus?" No-one spoke.

Alki stepped forward to look at the doppelganger closely. He didn't shy away.

"Who are you and what have you done with the real Nicholaus Klevchenky?" The man simply looked at her and shook his head. The captain of the boat had a faint smile on his face.

Alki stepped back. A moment passed as she looked at them each in turn. She gave a brief nod of the head, turned, looked at Alex and cursed.

"They've had us as fools! He never was in the boat. They've kept him back at the mansion, probably drugged."

"But we saw 'im belted, dragged out of the spa and into the limo." Alex was not convinced. "We followed 'em back to their 'oliday 'ome and saw him put on this boat. It 'ad to be 'im, all the trouble they went to, to get 'im."

"We didn't see him get hit Alex," she said. "We only saw a bloodied person being helped by Reg, and a doctor who just happened to be there. At the back of the spa I saw a bloodied man I assumed to be Nicholaus being bundled into the merc." She thought just for a moment. "Why would he be bloodied?"

"To 'ide 'is face, so as to fool anyone what was lookin'."

"Yes, obviously at the front of the spa, to fool his wife, his bodyguards and any staff which were present. But they didn't know I was looking around the back, did they."

Alex went to speak but stopped.

"They knew!" Alki swore. "They damn well knew I was there! They bloodied the doppelganger's face to hide it, to fool me!"

"So they didn't swap the geezers around?"

"He's stood here isn't he? Clearly they didn't!" She looked at the three men being held at gunpoint. "It seems we were duped. Nicholaus must be back at the mansion still!"

Alex looked at them, then at Alki.

"It seems that you're right sweet'eart." He beckoned with the gun for the three men to move towards the stern of the vessel. They obeyed. "So, where do we go from 'ere then darlin'; but first off, what we gonna do with these three geezers?"

CHAPTER FORTY-SIX
The Chase

A short time later and both Alex and Alki were back in the motorhome.

"They were here on the boat just to lead us away," she said, taking out her phone. "Start the vehicle Alex; we need to get to a quiet stretch of the river."

"What for lass?" He started the motor.

"We need the micro."

"Oh, right," he said. "Flyin' in the dark again. And am I right in thinkin' you're plannin' on takin' off on the river as well?" She nodded. "That makes sense!"

"What choice have we got; the motorhome is too heavy and encumbered to drive at speed, and so it's next to useless now. We need to get to . . . wherever we need to get to, quick, and the micro is the only option we have left."

"Takin' off on the river?"

"There is nowhere else Alex, unless we use one of the main roads, and that's hardly viable. The river is the only place open to us."

"It's still dodgy Alks; and what about landin' then eh? 'Ave you thought about that?"

"I'll discard the pontoons before I get there."

"Alright then. There! Where is 'there' exactly?"

"I'm not too sure yet," she said, dialling.

"And I'm not too sure either, about all of this girl?"

She didn't look up.

"Hello Aaron," she said. "Any news?" Alex watched her. She nodded, then shook her head. "You're certain the Merc is not there?" She nodded, and a faint smile appeared. "Hold on then and I'll get back to you in a minute or so." She seemed to get an answer and hung up.

"Tell me what yer thinkin'," Alex said. "You're gettin' me worried 'ere."

She lowered the phone, studying the three trackers on the tablet screen.

"Can you really follow them with that Alex?"

"The trackers? Yes sweet'eart, I can. Just one little thing though." He turned to face her and his voice increased in volume as he pointed to the southern-most flashing marker. "That little dot should be in your bleedin' pocket!"

"I know. Sorry." He waited a while, but nothing seemed forthcoming.

"What the 'ell is it doin' down there Alks?" He now virtually stabbed the tablet screen.

She faced him, eyes ablaze.

"I put my tracker on their car!"

He nodded irately, then realised what she had just said. He shook his head and began to frown.

"You did what?"

"I put my tracker under the left rear wheel arch of their Merc." She fidgeted nervously as she watched his mind beginning to make sense of her words.

"What!" He yelled.

"I put my tracker un . . ."

"I 'eard you!" He yelled again.

"I should have told you."

"Their car, the Merc?" She nodded.

He looked at the screen and shook his head. He turned back to face her.

"And you're bettin' that they've scarpered, in the Merc with the real Nicholaus and that they're 'eadin' south, probably to the coast, to make their escape?" She could hardly contain herself, but she managed to nod.

He grabbed her and kissed her cheek.

"So we can follow 'em," he said, staring at the tablet screen. She nodded again. "'Old up!"

He turned back to her.

"'Ow did you manage that? When did you . . ."

"At the spa," she said.

"At the spa?"

"Yes. When I went around the back and . . . Well, before I saw what they were doing with Nicholaus, what we then thought was Nicholaus, I just . . . well, I just did it. Gut instinct I suppose."

"You placed your tracker on their car, a bloody 'ire car?"

"Yes," she said a little shamefaced. "I know it was a gamble." He shook his head.

"Gamble! They could just 'ave 'anded the car back!"

"I know," she said. "Sorry."

"That could be some new pillock that's 'ired the same car!"

"It couldn't!"

"'Ow the 'ell do you know that!"

"The car was there before we left. It was on a long lease to Toby, remember? And even if it had been given back straightaway, the hire company couldn't have turned it round and re-hired it out, not so soon. It is them!"

Alex looked at her and drew breath.

"Well," he said, smiling now. "It's worked out, what you did, reckless or no." He turned back to the tablet screen. "There it is, well south of 'Arenden, 'alfway to the coast."

"Is that me Alex?" She pointed. "Or them I should say."

"It is darlin', travellin' sedately down a little 'B' road. Keepin' a low profile by the looks, but defo 'eadin' south."

"Alex, this is important. Can you show me Harenden and the coast together?"

"Course I can," he said tapping the screen a few times. "There you go."

She peered at the screen, flicking from Harenden to the south coast.

"What are you thinkin' girl?" He asked.

"Hang on a sec."

She measured, with her fingers, the distance between Harenden and the dot and then from the dot to the coast. She now studied points west to east and back again.

"I'm not sure. Alex, can you hazard a guess, an educated guess as to where they might be headed?" He shook his head a little.

"Not sure Alks. It must be the coast though."

"There's lots of scope for a plane to put down en route."

"If it was to be by air, they would 'ave gone by now," he said. "There's lots of places for a plane or chopper to land just south of 'Arenden itself, let alone as far south as they are already." She agreed.

"It must be the coast then, but where?"

"Their 'eading would suggest west of Southampton."

"About there?" She pointed on the tablet screen.

"Yeah," he said, leaning in as he now enlarged the section she had pointed to. "The cliffs?" She nodded. "I think I know what you're thinkin'."

"I think you do."

"And I think you're right! The route they're takin' 'as seriously slowed 'em down though. They obviously think they're in the clear, but still playin' it safe, stayin' off the main roads. It gives us a chance to get down there before 'em."

"You are right of course Alex. But we need help with this one." She scrutinised the map on the laptop once again. She began dialling on her mobile. "Can you get Britney and Ringo please Alex? We're going to need them too if we're to stand any chance of success."

Alex picked up the phone and made the call. Within a minute the two youngsters were on the line.

"Hi Alex, what's happening there?"

"Just listen Kids. We've been and boarded 'em. This guy isn't Nicholaus, 'e's the doppelganger. It seems the real Nicholaus is still back at the mansion."

"What?"

"At least 'e was back at the mansion. I'll let Alki explain. It's on speaker darlin'."

"Alright," Alki said, ending her call. "What Alex says is true. We have been duped and, it seems, they are on their way to the south coast. Britney, Ringo, please tell me you have the micro up and running?"

"Yes we do Aunty," Britney answered.

"It was just as you said Aunt Alki. There was only a spar broken, but it's fixed now and we've tested the engine."

"Good job, well done; remind me to punch both of you. Now listen in. We know they are going to the coast, and we think we know where. This is where Alex comes in." She now turned to him. "You must keep us aware of the direction they are going, and guide us all to converge on that destination." She pointed to a cliff section on the south coast. "Britney, Ringo, you two both head across to west of Portsmouth. I shall fly from here toward the same destination whilst Alex will remain in the motorhome, keeping us supplied with up to the minute intellect."

"Intel Auntie. Sorry, Alki!"

"Thank you Ringo. You're still getting punched, twice! If we all use our satnavs, and I'm sending you the location as we speak, then Alex can keep us informed as to our quarries progress and we can alter our headings accordingly."

There was a cacophony of noise as both began to talk at once.

"Shut up!"

Silence.

"Britney, you go first."

"Is it legal Auntie, to fly in the dark?" Alki went to answer but Ringo spoke.

"It's okay Brit. Don't worry Alki, I've flown in the dark many times before."

"I know dear, my sister told me!"

"Sorry?"

"She keeps me well informed dear, have no fear."

They could now hear a heated argument going on between the two youngsters. Alki stopped them.

"I wouldn't ask you to do something I felt you couldn't. I have ultimate faith in your abilities, both of you. Now, do you remember the game we used to play, when you had just learned to fly, both of you?"

They replied vigorously.

"Good. Do you remember the protocol you were taught to observe?" Once again they both did. "Reverse protocol to be observed tonight dears. Are you both at speed with that?" Both began to speak at once. Alex quietened them again. "Alex will explain all darlings, don't worry."

"No problems Auntie. We're all set up and ready to go. See you there." Their signal closed and Alex switched off the phone.

"Can you get Aaron for me now?" He looked at her, questioning. "Trust me just one more time Alex, please," she said.

He smiled at her, nodded and dialled.

"It seems they might be going south and so I'm making my way down there in the microlight. Do you think you could get down there also?"

"Of course I can. There's nothing happening here anyway."

"Thanks Aaron."

"I'll see you down there then."

"How long will it take you?"

"Not sure."

"Just turn on the satnav and it'll tell you."

"I haven't got a satnav."

"Course you 'ave, it's in the 'elmet," Alex chipped in. "Just turn it on and pull the mike in front of your mouth. The password's 'eavy metal'."

"Thanks Alex."

"No problems. Just keep 'er under the ton, there's a pal."

"Keep to the speed limit Aaron, ignore Alex." Alki said, as Aaron's signal blinked out. "

Alki turned to him but he spoke first.

"I suppose you want me to get the micro ready, is that it?" She now smiled.

"Please. And after I've left could you call the kids and explain reverse protocol to them, and why they need to employ it tonight?"

He nodded and they looked at one another for a moment.

"What do you think?" she asked.

He held her gaze.

"I think you're very clever Alks; maybe a bit too clever for your own good sometimes."

She smiled at him, a little sadness creeping into the eyes.

"'Ere," he said, opening the drawer beneath the sink. "Take this, just in case."

She glanced at what he held, then looked up at him.

"Is that the real one?"

"It's the real one," he said, and she took the hand gun he offered. "You know 'ow to use it!" She nodded, still looking at the weapon. She now looked up at him.

"Microlight?" She said.

He smiled, then laughed a little.

"Mad as a March 'are," he said. "Always 'ave been!"

CHAPTER FORTY-SEVEN
Air, Land and Sea

They reached a quiet stretch of water and it took only minutes for Alex to prepare the microlight for take-off. He gently slid it from the land and now stood on the pontoons as he erected the canopy while Alki watched, donning helmet and goggles.

He now cranked the engine and it fired into life. He helped her down, strapped her in and two minutes later she was in the sky.

Aaron was parked in a lay-by on the dual carriageway shouting 'heavy metal' into the microphone. After numerous tries he gave up and took out his phone.

"It doesn't matter that I'm younger. Alki taught me to fly when you were playing with lipstick and dollies!"

Britney's argument didn't seem to be going anywhere. She still argued though.

"But I have the knowledge!" she yelled back, over the engine noise.

"What's the first rule then, for flying in the dark that is?" He sat with arms folded, and looked at her through goggles. She looked back and knew she'd lost. She turned away, put her helmet on, made a noise through her teeth and turned on the satnav. Ringo said nothing yet smiled as he took off, mouthing 'keep higher than a hundred feet so's you miss the telegraph poles, little miss Brit-nee!'

"You don't shout at ladies Aaron, you talk nice to 'em else they won't play ball."

"I've said it every which way Alex, but it won't turn on."

"All right, all right. Just put the phone to the mike and I'll do it."
Aaron did so.

"'Eavy metal."

"Please state your destination." The satnav spoke in Aaron's ear.

"How the hell did you do that?" he said, still annoyed.

"Please state your destination," the satnav answered. Alex
laughed.

"Like I said Aaron, treat 'er nice, she'll treat you nice."

With Alki and the youngsters both in flight, together with Aaron on
the road, Alex had his hands full. He looked at the tablet with five
dots on the screen, four of them beginning to converge on a point
along the south coast.

The merc had not stopped as far as he could make out, but was
still travelling at around the twenty-five to thirty-five mph range.
He could now see the other three dots beginning to focus on a point
south of the sports car. He decided to call all three.

"They're still 'eadin' due south, still drivin' relatively slowly.
Aaron, you're almost level with 'em, they're about five miles west of
you. Alki, you need to 'ead due west for a while to cross their path
at the rear of 'em, else they might 'ear your engine. Come back?"

"Do you still want me to carry on to the same point on the
coast?" Aaron had to raise his voice above the engine noise of the
Harley.

"Whereabouts are we Alex?" Britney asked.

"Just be quiet a second," Alex raised his voice. "I don't seem to
be in contact with Alki."

He made some little alterations on his phone and checked it
again.

"'Ello Alki, can you 'ear me?" He looked at the phone again
and made more alterations. "Alki its Alex, can you 'ear me girl?"
He cursed silently. "Guys, there must be somethin' wrong with 'er
phone. Aaron, she's not far from your position now. You need to
stop 'er or she might overrun 'em."

"How do I stop her?" Aaron asked.

"The torch in the pannier. Turn the lens to red and when you 'ear 'er approach, flash the SOS at 'er. If that fails, take the shotgun and fire in the air.

"Won't they hear the shotgun, even five miles away?"

"They'll certainly 'ear the microlight if she passes anywhere near 'em. That'll definitely give us away. They'll ditch the car, change their plans, fade into the countryside and we'll 'ave lost our only chance to stop 'em."

"I've parked up Alex, but I don't know if I'll hear the micro above the traffic noise."

"She's about 6 miles away from you now, and she'll approach from the north east. Move away from the street lights, at least ten yards, and start signallin' when she's about 'alf a mile away. 'Ang on."

He turned back to the tablet and made a few quick calculations. He cursed.

"She's altered course; she'll pass about a mile further down from you now!"

"Are we anywhere near Alex?" Britney called.

"No you're not sweet'eart, but change of plan for you. 'Ead out to sea and make for a more westerly point, I'll send it to you in a minute. Aaron, can you get on the bike and move south at speed?"

"Ahead of you Alex, moving now."

"You'll have to gun it, or else she'll have passed!"

"Tell me when I'm in position!"

He watched the screen and could see Aaron's marker now moving at more than twice the speed of the microlights. He smiled.

"Well, you're on the motor to do it at least." He said to himself, crossing his fingers whilst staring at the screen. Thirty seconds later he was on the phone again.

"Pull over Aaron, she's almost on top of you!" He could hear the engine noise drastically reducing, and a tyre squeal. The phone went dead. He picked it up and dialled again. The phone rang out, but no one answered. He tried again, with no success. He was about to dial one more time when it rang.

"Alex, I think we've been spotted by a fishing boat. Will they report us do you think?"

"Let's 'ope so. Just call me when you're at the coordinates. Reverse protocol, don't forget." He rang off and dialled Aaron again. No answer. He went back to the screen and could see Aaron and Alki's markers together. He watched as one detached itself, heading south-west. He cursed again as he dialled Aaron once more. No reply. There was distance now between the two markers. "Well, that's it," he said in resignation.

The phone rang. He picked it up and could see it was Aaron.

"Don't worry Aaron," he said. "You did your best."

"She's turning," he shouted. "I was about to use the shotgun but she must have seen the sign. She's turning, coming back over the road." Alex was virtually jumping up and down but managed to contain himself.

"Is there anywhere she can put down without being seen?"

"The field I was in is fallow, I'll bring her down in there."

"Good lad Aaron, I knew you weren't no dick'ead!"

Aaron was running but still managed to answer.

"We'll discuss who the dick-head is at a later date."

The phone went dead.

"Hi Alex."

"What 'appened Girl?"

"Dropped the blasted phone didn't I!" she said. "And then I saw some dick-head flashing OSO at me! It was only because I recognised the Harley parked on the grass verge that I decided to turn around and see if he was all right." Alex could hear a disgruntled Aaron in the background. "Good job I did if what he's told me is correct."

"It is, but the main thing is you're all right. You are all right, aren't you Alki?"

"Yes I'm fine, but what do we do now?"

"We're doin' ok; it looks like they're still in the dark. Alki, you take the phone off Aaron, and don't lose it this time. Aaron, look in the right pannier and you'll find a small tablet. You'd be better off 'avin' that instead of Alki, she'll never be able to manage it and fly at the same time. Open it up mate, the code is ''eavy metal', and my email should be displayed straightaway. Make sure the volumes up full and I'll mail you to keep you in the loop. If you put it in your inside top pocket you should 'ear it even on the bike."

Aaron gave her the phone and Alex brought Alki up to speed as Aaron took the tablet out of the pannier and fired it up.

Within a few minutes, they were both off again.

Alki took to the skies and looked down to see Aaron set off at speed on the Harley. She opened the phone and dialled.

"Got it," she said.

CHAPTER FORTY-EIGHT
Convergence

Alex could only watch now as four of the five dots on his screen slowly began to converge on a section of the south coast of England.

Alki flew on.

Things were coming to a head and she knew she had to rely on many uncertain factors. She cast that thought from her mind as she took out her phone and dialled.

Ringo altered his heading at Brit's direction, following the new course on the sat nav, and heading out to sea now after employing reverse protocol in the village on the coast.

Aaron drove at high speed down the dual carriageway, having to stop odd times to check messages sent from Alex on the tablet.

He headed off once again and came off the carriageway at the next junction, heading more west than south, along a deserted B road, but still at a good speed.

The Merc climbed steadily onto the downs approaching the south coast, and turned off the road into the barren parkland. The Jaguar followed and now drew level as both cars turned their lights off, the only aid in the virtually pitch black, almost moonless night, being the faint blue beam from a flash light held out of the Merc passenger window.

She saw two cars ahead. The distance between her and them was decreasing at a rapid rate. She looked across, forward of her and to left and right, hoping to see more lights. There were none, and it was then that the lights of both cars up ahead went out.

She suddenly felt all alone, but quickly shrugged off that feeling as she began to drop her altitude, still gaining on the darkened vehicles. She turned on the spotlight to her right, widened the beam and eventually picked them up, both vehicles, only about three hundred yards ahead of her now.

"Hi boys," she said in an undertone. "Here I am."

She had a wry smile on her face, but it quickly faded.

"Here we go then."

She overshot the cars, only feet above, lifting her aircraft higher into the sky as she turned off the spotlight and opened the throttle, heading straight for the coast.

Aaron saw a light appear up ahead, in the sky and about three miles distant. He saw it go off again as, now, he flicked on his main beam and gunned the engine.

They had flown a distance out to sea, after repeated dive bombings of the small village nearest the cliffs, especially the small police station, and now turned to face inland, having reached the coordinates that Alex had sent. They saw a light inland, and then it went off.

The throttle was pulled back as they headed into the breeze which came off the cliffs of the coast they were now facing, and which they now slowly approached.

She reached the coastline and banked hard to her left, throttling back as she climbed and headed back to shore, reaching it in seconds and reducing altitude to less than twenty feet. Now she switched the spotlight back on.

She throttled back even more, bringing the aircraft close to the ground, eventually killing the engine as she touched down, the Merc and Jag ahead of her in the spotlight now, less than a hundred feet away.

She could see a single headlight approaching, far in the distance, as she stepped out of the microlight, taking off her helmet, gauntlets and goggles.

The cars approached her, stopped and the doors opened.

"Hello Reg," she called, turning on the left spotlight. "How are you darling?"

He was doing almost eighty on grassland but now began to slow as he approached the cars, giving them a wide berth and coming to a halt in front of them, his headlight full on. He took off the helmet and goggles, whilst opening the right pannier. Alki waved to him.

"Just in time Aaron," she said.

"For the love of God Alki," Reg emerged from the Jag. "What have we got to do?"

CHAPTER FORTY-NINE
Standoff

Alki stepped forward as Aaron, to her right by the Harley, took out the shotgun.

"Did you forget to say goodbye Reg?"

Rose emerged from the Jag, Sonia from the Merc and both came to stand by Reg's side. Luke remained in the Merc, seemingly tending to a figure that was slumped over in the back.

"Luke and Nicholaus not going to step out and stretch their legs then?" She smiled at them all.

Aaron now stepped forward; he stepped forward again towards the two cars and pivoted, aiming the shotgun now straight at Alki. She looked at him, eyebrows raised.

"Aaron?" she said, though seemingly not surprised.

"I would love to have kept up the charade, but there doesn't seem to be a reason anymore; and besides, you'd find things out soon enough, and with your fertile mind you'd quickly put it all together."

She just stood and looked at him, then a slight smile spread across her face.

"I knew I should have trusted my gut instinct."

Now he smiled.

"I'm glad you didn't. But I must admit, you had me worried a time or two, though I did have a plan if you managed to suss me. But you fancied me Alki, that covers over a lot of doubt, it does it every time."

She now looked at him quizzically, then down at the gun.

"And just what are you going to do with that?"

"Nothing, if you behave."

"What can I do? I am the age I am, and a woman. What could I possibly do against two younger, stronger men?"

"It's just insurance, in case you come up with something we haven't thought of; you usually do." He smiled, but now she laughed.

"Blanks Aaron! It only ever has blanks in it. You don't think Alex would leave a live round in a shotgun do you?" Aaron's face fell.

"Blanks?" He questioned. She nodded.

He pointed the gun slightly to the left and fired.

The microlight exploded in a ball of flame.

She flinched and stepped back, but quickly regained her composure to face this man again.

"I took the liberty of changing it for live. Hope you don't mind." He smiled.

Alki shied away from the fireball as she fumbled in her pocket. Aaron turned back to her, barrel lowered as he snapped open the weapon and the spent shell ejected.

She drew the revolver Alex had given her and pointed. Aaron looked up.

"You wouldn't shoot me would you?" he laughed at her as he began to re-load the weapon.

"Don't Aaron," she said. "Or else I will shoot; I am trained in these things and I will shoot to kill!"

He snapped the barrel shut.

"Stop!" She shouted, aimed and fired, the revolver kicking back in recoil.

Aaron stood there, smiling, shotgun now aimed straight at her. She fired again. He laughed and lowered the barrel.

"Too much Irish Alki," he said. "It makes you comatose at night, or else you might have seen me check the kitchen drawer and change the revolver rounds for blanks. Hey," he shouted with laughter still in his voice. "Shotgun blanks changed for live rounds, handgun live rounds swapped for blanks. A bit poetic, don't you think." The smile quickly faded. "We drink tea in Russia comrade, far better for you than Irish.

Reg stood forward, alongside Aaron now.

"Just what in hell's name do you think you're doing Alki? What do you hope to achieve?"

"Anything that stops you bastards from achieving your goal!" She let the revolver fall to the ground.

"Look around Alki, there's only you," he said.

Sonia came to his side, a hand gun trained on her.

"Ah, the bitch from hell!" Alki stepped forward. "And how do you propose to extricate yourselves from this little problem then?"

"We have what we came for. It is simply a matter of time now for you have shot all of your bolts and there is nothing more you have to offer." She now half-turned to Aaron. "Have things changed Drãgan? Are you coming with us?"

"I have to, for she will discover many things in time."

"Very well. Any news?"

Reg checked a handset.

"They are on their way. We can go down soon," he said.

"And what 'things' will I discover Aaron?" Alki folded her arms, looking directly at him. "What dirty little secrets shall emerge when I begin to rummage about, eh?"

"Who said you will live that long," he replied sombrely.

"Oh, not going to break your non-aggression pact are you? You are such nice people I can't believe you would kill in cold blood; more like, creeping up behind and stabbing them in the back, isn't that more your style?" Aaron now stepped towards her, with a look on his face she had never seen before.

"Just be thankful we do have a directive similar to which you refer, or else you'd be first!"

"Drãgan!" Reg's voice had raised. Aaron turned to face him. There was a quiet moment between the two.

"Keeping you happy in the pocket and in the bed seems to have paid off dear husband, don't you think Aaron?"

He met her gaze, lingered and then turned to walk back towards the cars.

"So, what is it you are going down to then eh? Submarine is it?"

Sonia smiled, but simply held the gun on her.

"So, you thought I fancied you did you Aaron?" Alki called after him. "How do you say arrogant in Russian?"

"The directive is to avoid aggression, it does not rule it out Alki and so I would be careful how far you push Drãgan, or Aaron to you. He has a shorter fuse than you might think."

"Thank you Sonia, I shall bear that in mind."

"I think it better if you sat." She gestured with the gun.

"I think not. catch my death on this damp grass."

"Sit Alki!" She shouted.

"No Sonia!" Alki replied as robustly.

The younger woman hesitated, shook her head and went to speak but thought better of it.

"You've won, what does it aid you to harm an old woman just because she won't sit at your command?"

"Whatever."

Alki continued to look at her and smiled.

"So, Aaron is Drãgan it seems. And what is your name Sonia, your Russian name I mean?"

She looked back at her. She did not smile.

"Oh Come on Sonia. It helps to pass the time, while you wait for your . . . lift?"

Sonia looked straight at her, derision in her smile. She laughed.

"It's Sonietta, after my mother." She said.

"Of course, and Rose?" She looked past Sonia, to look at her sister. Rose shrugged her shoulders.

"Mother was known as Sonia Rose," she said.

"Very English names for a Russian mother, Sonia, and Rose?"

"Rosanska. Sonietta Rosanska was her name, but she loved the English very much and so adopted their version of our Russian names instead."

"Your father, was he English?" Both of them nodded. "And so, why did you both opt for Russia then. What was it that weighed the balance in favour of communism?"

"Their father was an English spy." Reg volunteered. "But once he knew the goodness of a true Russian his allegiance altered. He became a communist instead of the self-centred capitalist he had been turned into. As soon as he saw the honesty of humanitarian values that is communism, he turned his life around and became a comrade."

"And was it like that with you Reg?"

He smiled.

"I had been a socialist from the age I could first see injustice Alki. I joined the party and helped them with naive eyes until I realised that this country would never see things the way I did. That was when I became a true party member, a sleeper from that time on."

"I see. And it was only true communist values that spurred you to live the high life with all my money I suppose?"

He laughed out loud.

"I had to play the role Alki, and what good was it doing just sitting in your bank. I think I played it pretty well, don't you?"

"Oh, you played a blinder Reg." She said with a slight laugh. "You did so well you might even have earned yourself a Victoria Cross, or whatever it is you give yourselves in Russia as a pat on the back."

"You mustn't be upset Alki. You were up against the best my country has got. You didn't really have much of a chance against us."

The smile left and now she just looked at him.

"Yes, I think you must be right," she said. "What was it that gave me away then? And when did you think to put Aaron into the . . . or rather, Drăgan, into the game?"

"Aaron will do, for the time being at least. He walked forward from the cars. "He is beginning to come round."

"I'll see to him," Sonia said, handed the pistol to Reg and walked back to the car, Rose going with her.

"So, you drugged him then, back at the spa?"

"A quick shot kept him dazed, till we got him back to the mansion."

"Drugged, but still conscious? Very clever." Aaron allowed himself a faint smile. "So why didn't you just do that with me Reg, it would have saved sending Aaron in."

"You were doing it yourself with the drink and drugs. We only got an idea just how much of a problem you'd become when we discovered you'd disappeared from Norfolk."

"Up till then it was going fine." Aaron continued. "But then you decided to follow us, and that proved to be a problem we couldn't overlook."

"Father always said I could be a nuisance."

"He understated it." Aaron said, but didn't smile; Reg did.

"You should've stuck with the pills and alcohol love, and saved us a lot of trouble."

"Sometimes I wish I had Reg." She said with a laugh. "Thanks for looking after me after you, er, left." He looked at her and a faint smile appeared on his face.

"They went mad at me, Sonia anyway. But I couldn't let you destroy yourself."

She smiled back.

"So, sleeper or not, you still retained good old English values."

"Humanitarian values Ilka. We have them in Russia as here, the difference is in applying them in life, which we do. Sadly, the bulk of Brits do not!"

"I still thank you Reg, for caring." He looked at her and there was a moment between the two. Alki broke it. "Forgive me, is that when Aaron was thrown into the mix, when you discovered I had left Norfolk?"

Reg looked at Aaron and there seemed to be an exchange of sorts. Aaron turned to face her.

"We decided that, due to your inquisitive nature and the fact that you have a very active mind, together with Reg's endorsement that you are an extremely pursuant character and would not normally just let things go, that we would infiltrate your campaign at source. In simple terms Alki, I was the Trojan horse which you welcomed in."

She now nodded.

"You were very convincing Aaron, sorry, Drágan."

"It matters not which name you afford me."

"How did you know I would contact you?"

"You are a very diligent and passionate lady, Alki. Once you had checked Reg's dentist, and then gone to the lengths you did to find the doctor and police officer, it was obvious you would not settle. When you moved to the cottage in Cornwall and began enquiries again, we knew we had to act. That was when I was brought in. Rose was always going on this mission, we knew that many years ago but when you came on to the scene it was considered sensible and appropriate that we play the 'badly done by husband', and you took it in; 'hook, line and sinker' I think is the term you use in this country." He now smiled at her.

"All this for him?" She gestured toward the occupant in the car.

"He has questions to answer back home."

"Why couldn't you just ask him here?"

"He's coming back, to pay for his crimes against the state. That's the mission."

"Nicholaus?" She asked. He nodded. "So, you were just waiting until you had Reg, Rose and, finally, the doppelganger in place?"

"Of course Alki. Quite simple really."

Alki thought, only for seconds.

"And all the couples you followed in Cornwall. That was just to keep me guessing?"

He smiled.

"We knew you would be watching."

"Elaborate!"

"It kept you busy, and we needed you off our backs."

"I saw the stunt, with Rose and the tractor."

"Yes, we know. Great staging, don't you think?"

There was a moment.

"It was all an act!"

"I think Rose and I might just go into films when we get back."

His smile broadened.

"All the stuff in the seaside cottage, the elaborate story you gave us. That was all pre-arranged, to put me off further investigation?"

"Should be a writer shouldn't I."

"Sanderson? Where's he then?"

"Fabrication. Just a name."

"Thought so. The PM?" He laughed.

"Young Toby. Great with voices isn't he."

"It didn't fool me."

"It furnished you with doubts, and that was enough to keep you guessing, until the trade-off. We had to alter a few things. We were initially to swap our stooge for Nicholaus, but that had to be changed because you sussed it. We had to make you think we had actually done the switch though. It should have been plain sailing from then, but you had to go and board the boat didn't you."

"Sorry." She smiled a little. "You see, you're not quite as clever as you think you are."

"Clever enough to fool you. Look around Alki. Here we are, at projects end."

Alki's face hardened.

"We saw you Aaron," she said. "When you took off from my place early morning and I found you on the dune by the seaside cottage? We saw you!"

He just looked at her. There was a muffled noise, and Alki took her phone out of her pocket.

"Sorry Alex," she said. "Did you want to say something to our friend here?"

She put it on speaker and held the phone up. Aaron heard Alex's voice.

"Yeah, we saw you on the dune, and before!" He said. Aaron faltered, then smiled a little.

"You can't have!"

"We have a night vision camera Aaron, don't we Alex?"

"Course we do Alks. I lied Aaron! A bit like you've been doin'

from the beginnin'." Alex shouted. "I watched you go into the
cottage, and stay for a good 'alf 'our, then come out and take your
place on the dune, waitin' for Alki to arrive. I saw it all pal!"

"We have known since that time Aaron."

He now looked at her, face morose. He shrugged his shoulders.

"Why did you suspect him Alki," Reg looked at him sideways.
"In the beginning I mean. What did he do to give himself away?"
There was restrained anger in his voice.

"You know, when you have a phone and you don't get phone
calls, I mean any phone calls, it makes you wonder."

"I told you at my place, only people that I want to know will
have this number."

She nodded, seemingly understanding.

"Funny though. Because PPI don't know that; or the 'have you
had an accident and it wasn't your fault' dicks. We always get those,
new phone or not! You didn't get any!"

He went to answer but stopped. He looked at Reg.

"It's alright. It's all worked out in the end."

"Has it," she said, staring hard at the man. She brought her
phone up. "Make the call Alex!"

He heard a harshness in her voice. She put the phone back into
her pocket.

"What do you mean?" He asked. "What call?" Reg stood
forward.

"What the hell Alki," he said. She ignored him.

"You know you gave me your phone Aaron?" He didn't speak.
"You know, the phone that nobody knew the number for, which you
gave to me almost an hour ago?"

Reg turned back to him.

"You gave her your phone, the contact phone?"

"I had to," he said; "or arouse suspicion."

"It's the bloody contact phone!"

"She said she'd dropped hers." Reg seemed seriously annoyed.
Aaron responded with anger. "She needed a phone. She had to

fly the damned microlight, I had to give it her! It's the end of the mission anyway."

"If she has access to it . . ." Reg now looked at Alki. "You haven't got access, have you Alki?"

"Access? Me? No, of course not."

She saw Reg relax.

"But MI6 have!"

Her ex-husband seemed to cave in. He looked at Aaron who was silent and tight lipped, then came back at her.

"What have you done Alki?"

"Oh, don't worry Reg, nothing bad, well, nothing too bad," she said. "Well, it is a bit bad but not really, really, really bad.

"What!"

She smiled.

"I just phoned them, MI6 that is, and asked if they knew this number and they said yes they did. Fancy that? I then explained who I was, what I was doing and where it was going on; you know, whatever it is you lot are doing right now, and where it was actually going on. They said they'd see me there, or here whichever is correct grammar."

Reg turned on Aaron.

"I told you not to underestimate her!"

"Me? You can talk! If not for your finger twitching, and writing things down we wouldn't be in this mess in the first place." Reg Just looked at him. A moment passed.

"Finger twitching?" he said, quietly.

"It gave you away, back at the cottage during the interrogation; your finger, twitching. She saw it you idiot."

"What are you talking about Drâgan?" he asked quietly, shaking his head.

"And writing instructions down. She placed carbon beneath the paper, on the pad you used. She found the address in Harenden, that you had damn well written down!"

"I never wrote things down. I always committed instructions to memory, as we were taught. And what the hell did I give away at the cottage Drâgan?" His voice had risen.

"She told me about your finger . . ."

"What bloody finger?"

"She said you twitched your finger when you lied and . . ."

"I twitched my . . ."

"That's what she said."

"She's had you over you mu'dak!"

Aaron turned on him, gun trained.

"I did nothing with my finger, hand, leg or any other part of my anatomy! What did you tell him Alki?" Reg shouted, whilst looking down the barrel of the shotgun, anger flaring in his eyes.

"Oh, just a white lie, well two really. Sorry."

"I told you about her!" Reg yelled. "You had him over, didn't you Alki?"

"Yes, well, it was fairly easy; he fancied me Reg, it does it every time!"

Aaron now turned back to Alki, face like thunder.

"How did you know the address?" His voice was low and carried a threat. Alki lost the smile instantly. "He didn't write it down, did he?" She shook her head. "How?"

She went to answer but nothing emerged.

"How Alki?"

She seemed a little frightened but managed to answer.

"The Harley has a scanner."

"What?"

"And it listened to every phone conversation you had Aaron. Sorry again." She lowered her head but could still see the rising anger.

"And what the hell did she say about my damned finger?" Reg pursued.

"It doesn't matter. We're here, at project's end."

"But what about the contact phone?"

"She'd never be able to access any info, not without the code."

Reg turned to face his ex-wife. She had a finger raised.

"Have you accessed it Alki?" He said, quietly. Her head now rose a little as well. She spoke softly.

"Er, the scanner records codes as well?" she said.

"Oh, shit!" Reg turned to Aaron, fuming.

"She's bluffing." Aaron walked forward, gun raised. "You are bluffing aren't you Alki?"

"Am I Aaron, sorry, I mean Drágan. Very confusing for an older woman you know, all these names."

"Stop playing games."

"Oh, don't they play games in Russia?"

He pointed the gun at her, inches from her face.

"You do not have the code, and you have not given that number to MI6 now have you Alki?"

She looked past the gun barrel, straight at him, defiant.

A sound now escaped his lips. He dropped the barrel, looked her in the eye then brought it up again.

"Did you call MI6?"

She could see a change in his countenance. It alarmed her, though she did not allow it to show.

"Of course I didn't," she said. "Where would I get the number for MI6 whilst flying a microlight in the dead of night?"

"Because if you did, the non-aggression pact we have adopted, by choice, could be countermanded."

"I didn't phone MI6 Aaron; I haven't even got their number."

"How can I trust what you say, old lady?"

"I have not contacted MI6; I give you my word." She took a single step back. "The authorities haven't listened to anything I've said, you know that. And, as you say, I am just an old lady."

He looked at her for several seconds.

"I don't know whether to believe you or not," he said and backed away. "But I shall give you the benefit of the doubt, this time."

"Anyway, your submarine is here is it not? Isn't that what you have to go down to the beach for?" Her voice raised a little. "What could possibly go wrong now?"

"What indeed Alki." Reg said, eying Aaron as he turned to go back to the cars. "For it has just surfaced, and so we shall now take our leave and wish you a long and prosperous life."

Alki could see Luke, Rose and Sonia aiding their victim out of the car. He seemed heavily drugged and fell as soon as he was clear of the vehicle. Aaron came to their aid and he and Luke took the man's arm around their necks, pulling him to his feet once again.

"And you can have whatever information you might find in that phone. By the time we leave it will have little value."

"You activated the fail-safe?" Reg asked.

"As soon as I knew she was on her way down here." He now smiled a little. "All contacts change as soon as that code is received Alki. The phone holds nothing for you."

A sound could now be heard, increasing in volume from beyond the coast, coming from far out to sea it seemed. They all turned and as they did two spotlights shone out, straight at them. The sounds of a helicopter approaching drowned out the shouts of alarm.

Lights now also lit up the scene on the land, to the east, by an entrance to the cliff top park. A loudspeaker rang out.

"THIS IS MI6 THIS IS THE MI6. WE HAVE THE PLACE SURROUNDED. PLEASE STEP AWAY FROM THE VEHICLE AND PLACE YOUR HANDS ON THE BONNET. DO THIS NOW AND WE SHALL NOT OPEN FIRE. I REPEAT, DO THIS NOW AND WE SHALL NOT OPEN FIRE."

Reg, Luke, Rose and Sonia dropped to the floor, dragging their victim with them. Aaron stood by the Merc and aimed the gun at Alki.

"No need for aggression Aaron. You've come this far, why spoil it now. They only want Nicholaus."

As if by prompt the loudspeaker rang out:

"WE HAVE NO DESIRE FOR BLOODSHED. WE SIMPLY WANT NICHOLAUS AND YOU ARE FREE TO GO. PLEASE BE ASSURED, WE ARE NOT HERE FOR YOU. WE SIMPLY WANT NICHOLAUS AND YOU ARE FREE TO GO."

"How the hell did they find us?"

"I'm afraid I lied," Alki said. "Again."

Aaron still held the gun on her.

"What are we gonna do?" Reg's voice came over in a loud whisper.

"Have you any weapons in the cars?" Aaron asked.

"Nothing."

"Damn!" He slowly lowered the gun.

Now there could be seen at least three vehicles approaching the entrance to the cliff-top park, blue lights flashing.

Aaron now backed away, keeping low. Sirens also could now be heard.

"We can't leave him, not now."

"What else can we do?"

The voice rang out once more.

"WE ONLY REQUIRE NICHOLAUS. JUST LEAVE HIM AND THE REST OF YOU ARE FREE TO GO!"

"We have to," Reg said. "We have no option."

"What will they say, if we come back without Nicholaus?"

"What can they say; at least we get back and that has to be good enough."

"WE ONLY WANT NICHOLAUS. THE REST OF YOU CAN ALL GO FREE!"

"Alki!" Reg called to her. "If I didn't love you so much I would seriously want to do you harm!"

"Harm?" she said. "He could still see her smile, even in the dark. "Do you mean the kind of 'harm' you used to enjoy doing to me in the bedroom?"

"God, I hope they broke the mould."

"Oh, come on Reg. Sex was always good, I made sure of that!"

"We need to leave" Aaron now dropped the shotgun and sprinted to the car. He grabbed the pistol from Reg and dragged Nicholaus to his feet, bringing the gun to his head.

"Stop Aaron," Alki cried. "They have destroyers in the channel, as well as the helicopter! If you shoot him they hunt down the sub and you will not be allowed to escape." She could see Aaron pause. "Let him go and escape yourself. They will allow it!"

"The authorities took no notice of you. There are no destroyers!" He yelled.

"I lied about that too," she said. "Sorry!"

"I don't believe you!"

"Tell the men in the chopper then, not me."

Aaron turned to look out to sea, at the helicopter lights hovering beyond the cliff edge, then turned back. He was seething with anger and eyeballed Alki.

"WE ONLY WANT NICHOLAUS. THE REST OF YOU ARE FREE TO GO!"

There was a moment, a long moment

He hesitated for only a second longer, and then pushed him towards her.

"Don't shoot," she yelled. "I'm just getting the kidnapee." She ran forward, grabbed Nicholaus and pulled him to the ground.

Luke, Sonia and Aaron got into the Merc, the top now being lowered. Reg had also lowered the top of the Jag and he and Rose now got in and started it up.

"Go down to the beach," Alki yelled. "They're not going to let you drive out of here."

Reg called back to her.

"They have operatives up here, they'll have them down there too. Bye love!"

Both Reg and Aaron now gunned the vehicles, drowning Alki's response as they shot back, increasing speed until the engines virtually sang.

They slammed the brakes on and, with a look from driver to driver followed by a nod, engaged drive and floored both throttles.

"No," Alki yelled as they careered forward, both vehicles picking up speed rapidly. "You'll all be killed!"

She could only watch as they hurtled past her and her ward,

heading for the cliff top. She screamed something that, later, she would not be able to recall.

The vehicles accelerated at an alarming rate, hurtling across the barren ground of the cliff top park and heading for the edge, eventually bursting through the wire fence and launching into the void beyond.

Alki ran after as both vehicles dropped out of sight. Just before they disappeared she thought she saw five shapes throw themselves from the cars, and now fall to the sea below.

She reached the edge of the cliff top but could see nothing more as she peered into the blackness beyond. She called a few times but the wind whipped her words away and so she stood silent, watching with hope.

Someone ran up to her and she half turned.

"A bit dramatic, don't you think?" The man said as he reached her.

She turned back, once more to peer into the darkness below.

"How could they do that?" She said. "They had to perish. No-one could survive that fall."

Oh, I don't know. Just like off the top board in a pool that's all."

"What?" She turned to face him.

"Not much higher, and the speed those two got up to they would be pretty far out, well past any rocks below. Do they have rocks in Dorset?"

"Do you really think so?" She turned back.

"Come on Sis. Suicide plans are one thing, but they could die an easier way than that. This had to be their fall back. It figures it was actually, because they had two convertibles; you couldn't do that in a saloon now could you. And if the sub is out there they must have a boat ready to pick them up, probably doing so right now if you ask me."

"Oh god, I hope so."

The man laughed.

"Scuse me. Whose side are you on?"

She now turned back to him, watery eyed.

"The MI6?" She asked with disdain. "Since when has it been known as 'The MI6?' And just how do they 'step away from the car and put their hands on the bonnet'? They either step away from the car *or* put their hands on the bonnet! One or the other Baddie."

"Hey, if it was good enough for Michael Douglas, it's good enough for me."

She shook her head, laughed with one final look out to sea and then turned back, inland.

"Let's go and see if Nicholaus is alright. Did you manage to phone the authorities?"

"Yep; they told me to get back to the asylum."

"Great. Well done with the lights though. It looked like there were dozens of you." She took her phone out from her pocket. "Brit, Ringo? Did you see if they survived?" A chopper noise suddenly blared from the handset, drowning Britney's voice. "Turn the chopper off kids, please," she yelled, holding the phone away from her. The noise suddenly abated.

"There's two little inflatables with outboards. Shall we buzz 'em like we did the cops?"

"No. Let them go Brit. Come in to land. You both did great by the way." She heard the two youngsters laugh as their link went dead. "Did you get all that Alex?"

"Yeah. Every bit. But what was the 'call' you wanted me to make darlin'? We didn't re'earse that one!"

"Oh, just a bit of theatricals Alex, to add to the tension, nothing to worry about."

"Okay. Well done Alks."

"And you Alex." She could see the blue flashing lights coming into the park. "We shall have to go and explain all this now. Will you make your way down?"

"Been on the way since you left girl. See you shortly."

Just then a microlight with two very bright spotlights, plus two extremely excited youngsters, flew past them.

"Hi Alki!"

"Hi Auntie, did we do good!"

"Of course you did good, you know you did. And if you call me auntie once more Britney I really will punch you!" Ringo laughed out loud with his sister, as they landed softly on the grass beyond.

Alki and Baddie walked back towards the approaching police cars.

CHAPTER FIFTY
Aftermath

The police stood looking, bemused, by a semi-awake Russian dignitary and the blazing wreck of a one-time microlight aircraft. They had made straight for the youngsters as soon as they landed, and it was only Alki's intervention that had stopped the extremely annoyed officers from immediately arresting them.

She explained that Britney and Ringo's remit had been to gain the attention of the police in the village, and lead them to the cliff top. She then pointed out the half-dazed, barely awake, Russian gentleman and his part in this scenario, explaining that she had tried numerous times to gain the attention of the powers that be, to point out the danger Mr. Klevchenky was in.

It was only after several calls to headquarters, most of which were to ascertain this man's identity, that the police began to see there was more to this series of events than met the eye.

The coastguard had been alerted, the police having seen the two cars fly off the cliff edge. And when Alex arrived shortly after, being immediately interviewed by the police, he was able to show them the remaining tracking signals on the tablet, particularly the one that had been on the Merc. Minutes later the coastguard vessel was heard out at sea and, by use of the police walkie talkie, Alex was able to direct them to the exact spot where the Merc had entered the water, the last known position of the tracking device. Divers were sent down to investigate.

As this was taking place a real helicopter landed on the cliff top and two official looking people alighted. Within a minute they had herded Alki, Alex, Baddie and the two youngsters into Alex's motorhome.

"Thank you Mr. Cox, for allowing us to use your mobile home as our HQ."

"Motor'ome darlin'," he said. "A mobile 'ome is a static, and usually found on 'oliday camps."

"Quite." The two officials now stood by the door, the others scrunched together on the seat at the back of the motorhome. The female spoke again. "This is now officially an MI6 enquiry and, therefore, vital you now give us all information you have regarding this incident. So, who is going to tell me what has gone on here?"

"Well, that's rich I must say! We've been trying to get your attention for months now dear but nobody has wanted to know, until now that is."

"It has been noted, Miss . . .?"

"Mrs. Actually, but please call me Alki. His name is Alex by the way, and I'd call him that if I were you because I feel sure he'll puke if you insist on this Mr. Cox business. This is Baddie, my brother, and these two are Alex's progeny, Britney and Ringo. Ringo is the male, despite the long hair and multiple ear rings!"

"So," the female agent began again as she now sat, facing them. "What exactly has gone on here? Shall we start with you Alki?"

"You're up sis. Give 'em hell!" Baddie leant back, hands behind his head.

Everyone now looked at her.

She began with the 'death' of her husband and her investigations into the whys and wherefores of that case, which had led her to Cornwall and her many surveillances there, leading up to the 'death' of Rose. That, in turn, had led to her approach of Aaron, gaining his assistance and their attempts at fathoming just what was going on, right up to the appearance of the doppelganger in Quay Haven. She informed them again of the many attempts at alerting the authorities, and the negative responses they had always received. She told them about her and Aaron's many investigations, but that it was when Alex had seen Aaron approach the seaside cottage before dawn, alone, and then saw him welcomed into the dwelling, staying inside for around thirty minutes, that she and him then knew for certain that Aaron was part of the very gang they pursued. Because of this they had decided to play on the fact that the authorities would not listen, hoping that it would destabilise the gang if she bluffed that the authorities *had* listened, *were* aware, and so MI6 were waiting in ambush.

"It was only down to the brilliance of my troops, and their ability to aid in deceiving the gang this was true, that our plan succeeded."

She handed Aaron's contact phone over.

"We didn't know what to do with it," Alki continued. "But we thought it might make them nervous if we had it, and it seems we were right. We just added it to the bluff, as indeed we've bluffed our way through virtually the whole of this caper."

It was handed to the male agent who scrutinized it, eventually making a call on his own phone as he stepped out of the motorhome.

"What about you two?" The female agent now turned to the kids. "What was your role in this?"

"We knew we had to reverse protocol to get people's attention and get the cops up here, and that's what we did."

"Reverse protocol?"

Alex explained. The kids then continued.

"Alex told to us to cause a commotion in the village below, to get the cops attention which should, hopefully, lead them up to the cliff top. So we buzzed them and generally made a nuisance of ourselves in the village, and it looks like it worked."

"What about the helicopter charade?" She asked. "How did that little trick come about?"

"Alki taught us." The agent now turned to her.

She smiled at them and began to explain.

"My father used to play a game, jets and choppers he called it. He'd made it up for Baddie and me, to help him teach us to fly when we were kids. The sounds were put on cassette for us, and Baddie flew one micro with the jet sound whilst I flew the other with the chopper sound. It was just Father's way of teaching. It worked for us and so we did it for Ringo and Brit as well which was why it was easy for the kids to employ their abilities here tonight to replicate the appearance of a helicopter, and to great effect if I may say so Ringo, Britney, you have the ability to soar off to a fine art."

"Thanks Alki," they said in unison.

"Impressive," the female agent said. "What about the lights at the park entrance, and the tannoy. Where did they come from?"

Baddie sat up.

"Me," he said. She turned to him. "That was me." He smiled at her, and everyone else. The male agent came back in to the motorhome.

"She wants to know how it came about Baddie," his big sister urged.

"Oh. Right. Well, I drive an off-roader, which has eight spots and four fogs on the front. Oh, and I've got a megaphone as well. Mega it is!" He laughed. No-one else did. "So, when Ilka called I just popped up here quick as you like. Worked alright didn't it?"

He was beaming at her, and winking.

"Eight spotlights?"

"Yep," he said. "Well, got four on the front bar and two each on the fold-out bars."

She just looked at him, unsure.

"You know. The two bars that face the rear, until you fold them out each side to face front."

She now nodded, and thanked him.

"By the way, is it MI6 or *The* MI6?

She simply smiled, and turned back to Alki.

"And how was the timing of all this managed?"

"We could 'ear everything 'cos we was all on a party line." Alex said. "Alki left her phone on, in 'er pocket."

"We could hear everything that was happening on the cliff edge," Britney said. "And so when we heard the cue line we just gave the sound system full belt, together with the spotlights, gained some height then powered our engine back and turned into the breeze coming off the cliff so we could soar."

"Cue line?"

"'What could possibly go wrong now!'" The kids and Baddie said in unison.

"As soon as she said that, then we knew it was time," Britney explained.

Both agents looked at one another, with only the faintest raising of eyes.

"By the way, you'll find three more of the gang tied up in a boat called *The Pearl Dulang*, moored somewhere east of 'Arenden; the captain, a young lad, Toby, and the doppelganger fella."

The female agent got immediately on to the phone.

"Reg, and the others? They all got away safe then, did they?" Alki asked, hopefully. Baddie laughed.

The male agent answered her.

"They are all believed to have survived the fall. The divers reported no bodies found in either car or the immediate area. The submarine is considered to have picked them up and so, yes, they got away it seems. Now, let's go through it one more time."

EPILOGUE

They were questioned into the night and on until the dawn. Numerous aspects of the attempted abduction were highlighted and gone over and over again. Positions of cars and of people were marked out on the ground, and the dialogue between Alki and the gang picked over with a fine tooth comb, Alex and the kids and Baddie chipping in as and when they could.

Just an hour into the cool morning saw breakfast arrive in the form of bacon, and bacon and egg, sandwiches, being brought from the village below, together with numerous teas and coffees. The investigation then continued on.

The agents seemed oblivious to the fatigue being clearly displayed on everyone's face, but continued with their questions and proposed theories until just gone mid-day.

They thanked all of them and said their goodbyes, but with the caution that they might be in touch at a later date to corroborate certain aspects of the night's events. The helicopter then took off with both of the MI6 agents aboard.

The police also then departed, after ensuring that the cliff top fence, where the two cars had launched themselves into the sea, had been repaired.

They watched as these representatives of authority departed, leaving them alone on the cliff top park. They all looked around, surprised, it seemed, at the now pervading quiet.

It was over.

With smiles they hugged and congratulated each other,

swearing to have a get together quite soon for a 'thwarted abduction reunion'.

Alex packed the kid's micro onto Alki's old trailer, the destroyed micro remains having been taken away on a low-loader earlier that morning at the insistence of the MI6 agents. He took Britney and Ringo in the motorhome and Baddie took Alki to her home in his off-roader.

Alki was exhausted, yet feeling good in the knowledge she had been instrumental in saving a man, a stranger from being kidnapped, yet quite sad that her, supposed, new friend had turned out to be less than the man she thought him to be.

Even though she had known the truth since Alex had observed Aaron colluding with the gang prior to her finding him on the dune, it still impacted heavily on her, particularly having seen the real man she had faced on the cliff edge, and knowing he had played false with her all the time she had known him.

She went to her rest with mixed emotions, images of her day causing a fitful restlessness until the exhaustion dragged her into a dream-filled sleep.

Nicholaus Klevchenky had been whisked away by the authorities as soon as MI6 had been alerted, and his whereabouts kept secret from that time.

The police in Harenden had followed Alex's description of where the boat was moored with the three captives bound and gagged in the cabin. But the report came back that no boat of that description had been found.

The two travellers from Russia, whose identities had been taken on by Rose and Reg, were also investigated, but nothing emerged as to their whereabouts or even if they were still in the country.

The bodies that had replaced Reg and Rose, as well as the doppelganger, were exhumed but their identities were never ascertained.

The phone had been accessed but the authorities quickly found that the information it held had been rendered useless.

It was just under a month later that Alki received a letter from Nicholaus Klevchenky's secretary, but that contained a hand written note from the man himself and a second, smaller envelope entitled 'Alki'.

In his note he outlined his admiration and gratitude for what she had done. He asked if she would pass on his thanks also to Alex, Baddie, Britney and Ringo, and to any others that had assisted her in their valiant rescuing of him from his abductors. He pointed out that his life would have become a living hell had she not been successful and he had been taken back to his homeland. He thanked her again.

He apologised for the vulgar usage of money to aid him in his thanks, but explained that it was the only way for him to express fully his gratitude. He asked for her forgiveness in this, and pointed her attention to the accompanying envelope. Finally, he informed her that she would be receiving two packages in the next few days as part of his recognition of what she had done for him. He thanked her once again, stating that he was in her debt, and signed it personally.

She found ten cheques in the second envelope, all signed and each for the same amount, with five of them made out individually to the single names: Alki, Alex, Baddie, Britney and Ringo, with the other five being the same, but with the payee section having been left blank. They were accompanied with a note from the secretary which explained that Alki was to use the five blank cheques for any others of her band that Mr. Klevchenky might be unaware of.

Two days later she opened the door to find a courier standing there, with two heavy rectangular cases before him. She opened them to discover twelve bottles of the finest Irish whiskey.

Later that day a wagon arrived and dropped off a brand new microlight aircraft of the very latest design, and top of the range, complete with trailer and all available accessories.

It was about a year later that Alki received a postcard. It was from Russia and its message was written in Russian, though short.

She smiled when she eventually managed to translate it.

"That's good to know," she said, as a happy tear fell.

The End

Writings by Geg

The Altruis Duad.
A two-volume fantasy novel.

The Heffle-Fiffle-Foffle-Faffle-Foff.
A children's story.

Princess of Birds.
A story for youngsters.

Fleam
The fantasy sequel to *The Altruis Duad.*
This is also the conclusion of The Altruis Saga.

Our Lion Young (working title).
A young adult's story.

Website: www.altruis.co.uk
Email: nellymcgriff@aol.co.uk